SUCCUBI ARE FOREVER

JILL MYLES

Part I

WITH

JILL MYLES

CHAPTER ONE

"Once upon a time there was a beautiful woman with great big knockers and shitty taste in men."—*The True Story of a Porn Star*, by Remy Summore

~*~

If there was one thing I struggled with, it was being deliberately sexy. Unfortunately for a succubus, if there was one rule of our so-called afterlife, it was that I could get a lot more by using my boobs than my brain. Sad but true.

Even with this in mind, I grasped the front of my low-cut black gown and hauled it up a little higher. The bodice of the darn thing was super tight and angled so that my breasts jutted forward and jiggled like they were trying to make a run for their freedom. If I wasn't careful, I was going to put someone's eye out.

"Quit fidgeting." My best friend Remy slapped my hand as I tugged on the straining spaghetti straps. "You look fine."

"I look ridiculously busty. Like, tavern wench busty."

"You're supposed to, remember?"

Well, sure. As a porn star, Remy was used to all her girly bits hanging out. It still unnerved me—I was far more comfortable in a sweatshirt and jeans. And besides, she was missing the point of this conversation. "Yeah, but I also thought we were supposed to blend. How can I blend if I look more like a pair of torpedoes primed for the launch sequence? That's not blending."

She rolled her eyes at me and gave a little bounce in her own tight red dress, like a boxer heading in to a fight. It was a move, I realized, that was designed to make the dress slide down and reveal even more of her ample cleavage. As it was, her dress was barely clinging to her top. The thin straps were held together by a knot at the base of her neck that looked ready to give at any moment. "Like anyone's going to care if you blend or not. They'll be too busy staring at your tits and ass to think about anything else. Come on. Do you want to get this crappy old book of yours or not?"

"Why are you so excited about it?"

"I'm not. I just came up with the perfect title for my memoir."

I stared at her. "Memoir?"

"Hell yeah," she said with a brilliant smile. "All porn stars quit the business and write a memoir. Gotta do something to increase the cash flow again." With that, Remy put her hands on her hips and sashayed into the crowd. I caught a brief glimpse of her head as she introduced herself to a silver-haired man in a tuxedo, flipped her hair, and gave him a charming smile.

And that was that. A memoir. Good God.

I adjusted my boobs again, smiled at a few people who were nearby, and headed to the back of the room, pretending to head for the bathroom. With Remy taking her place to be the center of attention, I could move on to my goal. I heard a bright peal of her laughter as I moved to the outskirts of the crowd, watched heads turn in her direction. All part of the plan. I gave my uncomfortable dress one last tug and slipped into the crowd, trying to blend in with the dark formalwear of the partygoers as I stepped past. The ballroom was crowded, but I wasn't interested in the party itself.

Men paused to smile at me, gazes raking over my figure in the revealing floor-length gown. Occasionally a bolder one would step in my direction, but I'd gotten adept at avoiding eye contact and looking busy. As I walked, a woman in a champagne-colored sequined dress scowled at my fire-engine red hair, my sleek black gown with the high slit, and my too-jiggly breasts. That was the sort of reaction a succubus always received. Nothing to be done but ignore it and focus on my goal.

At the far end of the massive ballroom, there was a short hallway cordoned off with a velvet rope, leading to a pair of gilt double doors. The hall was lit with flickering candles in ornate sconces on the wall.

Why *hello*, goal.

4

I moved toward that velvet rope with single-minded purpose, murmuring excuses to the people I moved past. I smiled and nodded and even cast a flirty look at one man, since I needed to shove past him and he wasn't moving. I brushed my breasts up against him and slid by with a smile. He looked as if he wanted to speak to me, but I quickly stepped around a waiter, losing eye contact and disappearing into the crowd. He'd follow me if he saw me again, but I didn't stop. Eventually, I made it to the other side of the room and stood at the rope.

This end of the packed ballroom was quieter than the other end, though in about fifteen minutes, it was going to be the spotlight of the party. I needed to move fast. With a quick glance around to ensure that no one was looking in my direction, I unhooked the rope and stepped on the other side. If anyone asked, I was just looking for the ladies' room. Or something.

"Can I help you find something, miss?" A waiter paused near me, frowning as I re-buckled the rope to the pillar.

Oh. Oops. Where was Remy with that distraction? "I'm just running to the ladies' room," I said to him with a bright smile.

He raised an eyebrow and then his gaze dipped to my generous cleavage. "That's not the restroom."

I put a stupid look on my face. "It's not?"

"That's the unveiling room. It's off-limits for party guests. No one should be back there until Mr. Melledin gives the word."

"So it is," I agreed, thinking fast. He was staring at me expectantly and I had frozen like a deer in headlights. "Thank you."

His gaze dipped to my breasts again.

An idea occurred to me, and I stepped forward, reaching for a glass of champagne. I smiled at him and gave him a very blunt, appraising look. "Is it a private room?"

The waiter stared at me. My chest. My face. "Private?"

"You know." I winked at him and then glanced back at the room I was dying to enter. *'Private.'* When he hesitated, I added, "I'll meet you in the room at the end of the hall in three minutes?"

And to make sure he caught my suggestion, I licked my lips and trailed a finger down my exposed cleavage. If that didn't do the trick, I was going to have to start drawing him pictures. Maybe a crude hand gesture or two.

He swallowed, hard. "The unveiling is in fifteen minutes."

I bit my lower lip, and gave him a hungry look. "We won't take long."

He gave me the dazed, dopey smile of a man who had just been wrapped around my finger. His hands clenched the edge of the tray eagerly. "Three minutes."

I wiggled my fingers at him and moved toward the shadows. "See you soon," I purred. *Creep.*

The waiter stumbled backward, grinning at me, and then disappeared into the crowd—presumably to dump his drink tray. I continued to smile in his direction until he disappeared from sight and then bolted down the hallway.

Now to find a good hiding spot to ensure that he wouldn't be able to find me for the rendezvous I had just promised and had zero intention of following through with.

"Nightingale to Robin Red Breast," buzzed a voice in my ear. "Nightingale to Robin Red Breast, do you read me?"

I rolled my eyes as I moved farther down the hall and touched my finger to the earbud headset hidden by my long, thick red hair. So far, despite the crush of the party, no one had noticed me heading for the room other than the waiter. That was good. "Hello, Remy," I replied. "I can hear you."

"Nightingale to Robin Red Breast," she repeated cheerfully, ignoring the fact that I was not using our code names. "The Vulture is heading in your direction. I repeat, Vulture is heading your way."

Who the heck was the Vulture? No one was supposed to be heading in my direction. I tested the double door and found it unlocked and slipped inside. "Who's heading my way? Remy? We don't have to use code names. We're the only ones on this frequency—"

"I have a bogey on my radar," she said, interrupting. Her voice dropped to a stage whisper. "Gotta go." The headset clicked off.

"Isn't a bogey golf?" I asked, but she was no longer listening.

I sighed, then glanced around the room I'd just entered. A massive sitting area, furnished with what looked like Louis XIV chairs and crystal dishes that probably cost more than I had made at the university last year as an archaeologist. Paintings in gilt frames lined the tall walls, and there was a fresco of fat, naked cherubs on the ceiling. It was all very old money and all very rich.

Well then, they wouldn't mind if I stole a little something, right? I told myself that, anyhow, and moved farther into the room, eyeing the heavy red velvet drapes next to each incredibly tall window. It was night, so they were pulled shut. I stepped forward and examined the first window carefully. Wires ran along the sill and a light flashed in the top corner. Alarm system. I peeked out the windowpane, wincing at the sight of the security guards walking the grounds outside. Sheesh. It was like our wealthy billionaire host didn't trust his guests or something.

The handle on the door clicked.

I froze as the door opened, then flattened myself along the wall behind the curtain. That damn waiter. Ugh. Hopefully he'd assume the room was empty and that I'd bailed on our rendezvous, then quickly leave again. And if not, I'd have to take more drastic action.

The door shut and revealed the person who had just entered. His back was turned to me. I stared at a broad pair of shoulders covered with a long, floor-dusting black leather coat. It might not have been that unusual except for the fact that it was summer, and his beat-up coat was squarely out of place at the party.

But my heart gave a happy little flip at the sight of it anyhow, and my internal tuning fork thrummed with pleasure. It always stirred when an immortal was around, but the sight of this particular immortal never failed to make me quiver.

He didn't turn around. As I watched his broad shoulders flex, he reached into a pocket and pulled out a cigarette, placed it between his lips, lit it. My body gave a tingle as he glanced over his shoulder, and I saw the beautiful mouth, which was keeping the cigarette held firmly in place edge into a smile.

"You playing hide-and-seek, Princess?"

I stepped out of the curtains and moved forward, drawn toward him. When I reached his side, I ran a hand along the back of Zane's long leather coat, feeling the twitch of his wings underneath. "I thought you were waiting in the car in case we had to make a quick getaway?"

"Thought I might come in and make sure everything was okay. You know I don't trust Remy to have your back." He shrugged, and the faint scent of tobacco touched my nostrils as I stepped into the smoke of his cigarette.

A momentary twinge of annoyance swept over me. I'd spent the last three months blissfully happy with Zane at my side... that is, blissfully happy unless he and Remy were in the same room. Then it was more like I was stuck between two bickering siblings. I thought we'd gotten past that, though, ever since Zane had helped me free Remy from her master. "Remy has my back just fine—"

"Really? Because I saw her in the main room," he said, gesturing back in the direction he'd just come from, "with a leg wrapped around some guy and her tongue down his throat."

She worked fast. "She's providing a distraction for me."

"I'll say she's a distraction. I'm not sure Ethan would approve if he saw that." He frowned at me and more specifically at my low-cut dress. "You know that you can do other things than just manipulate people with your bodies."

I leaned up and kissed him. "Who are you and what have you done with my Zane?"

He gave me a chagrined look and tossed his cigarette down on the Aubusson carpet, then ground it under his boot. "I'm the guy who just had to bite the oversexed waiter in the hallway who was looking for you."

Aw, that was sweet. "You're so sexy when you're jealous."

"I'm not jealous," he said in a tone that indicated that he was, in fact, very jealous. "I just worry about you."

"I'm a succubus," I said, poking him in the chest. "We don't have super strength, super speed, can't fly, and can't charm people or influence them like the fallen. So shoving our boobs under everyone's noses to distract them? That's what we do." It wasn't like this was a revelation to him—the first time we'd met, I'd been doing something very similar, and he hadn't disapproved of my tactics then.

"I'm Ethan's friend. You know if he could see Remy right now, he wouldn't be pleased."

Zane did have a point. It was odd to think that Zane and Ethan had been at each other's throats a few months ago and somewhere along the line had turned into friends. Now they were buddies like Remy and I were BFF, and they looked out for each other. And apparently the friendship extended to watching out for the other guy's girlfriend. This was the reason behind Zane's grumpiness, then.

Ethan was normally the fourth member of our little troupe. As an Enforcer, his job was to handle tasks given to him by the Serim. No one seemed to think that an Enforcer could have—or possibly want—a life of his own, so Ethan's superiors were mystified by his relationship with Remy. He was visiting his monastery at the moment, requesting permission to remain out in "the wild" a bit longer. I didn't know what Remy would do if his permission was turned down.

But I knew what straight-laced Ethan would think of Remy's flirty diversions. He would *not* be happy.

Good thing he wasn't here.

I glanced at my watch, frowning. Much as I loved seeing Zane here, we only had a few minutes before the unveiling of the manuscript would draw the crowd into the formal antechamber that we currently occupied, and I needed to get to it before that happened. I grabbed Zane's arm and turned him toward the door. "I'm going to steal the page. You go find Remy and pry her off her latest conquest."

He gave me a mock salute. "Your wish is my command."

"Tease," I said to him, and turned away.

Zane grabbed my hand, spinning me around and pulling me back toward him again. My body pressed up against his, and I could feel the heat of him even through the layers of clothing. The Itch spiraled through my body, pulsing with need. "Kiss before you go?" he said, leaning in to me with a smile. "And then I promise I'll behave."

"Maybe just a small one." I slid my hand to the back of his neck and twined my fingers in the short black hair at his nape. Who was I to resist a vampire? Especially such a delicious one.

His eyes flickered red down at my own, and his mouth slanted over mine. I felt his fangs brush against my lower lip before he slid his tongue against mine, giving my mouth a slow, tantalizing graze that made me weak in the knees. Over and over he licked into my mouth, each thrust a suggestion that I was more than receptive to. I clung to him as the kiss grew more intense, heat coursing through my body.

Even if we were together a thousand years, I'd never get used to the way Zane kissed me. It was as if he wanted to devour me whole, and every touch was barely leashed, every stroke of his tongue speaking of need and desire and lust.

Just as quickly as he'd begun to kiss me, Zane released me with a grin. His eyes had flared bright red, and he stared down at my dazed face with a hungry gaze. "Hurry up and get your page," he said in a low growl. "Because you have exactly five minutes before I rip that dress from your body."

Hot damn. I quivered at that and melted in his arms. "Five minutes," I echoed dreamily. "Got it."

Zane pressed a kiss to my forehead, made sure I could stand on my own two feet again, and then left the room, shutting the door behind him with a soft click.

In a haze, the Itch pounding through my body, I stared after him until he was out of sight. Then, my senses snapped back into place, and I straightened my dress. Right. The page. Get the page and then we could be done with this little adventure and go back to our hotel for a few hours of frisky bed-play. I was always game for that.

I touched my finger to the headset. "Remy, Zane's coming to get you. I'm going to grab the page and then join you two out front. Understand?"

No answer. Well, it might have been difficult to reply if her tongue was stuck down someone else's throat like Zane had said. I clicked the headset off, fluffed my hair to hide it again, and set off on my mission.

I'd first heard about the Melledin Manuscript in a magazine. I'd been reading in bed while waiting for Zane to awaken from his daily hibernation. For months, I'd been studying haloes, looking for clues in historical data, searching for mentions of miracles and unexplained phenomena that might lead me to one of the missing archangels. I followed up on every single name that Zane could give me, looking for immortals who had affected the course of history in oblique fashion.

And when that failed, I just buried myself in research. I loved research, after all. I'd been reading an article that compared a newly-found mysterious manuscript to the Voynich Manuscript. They thought the author of it was John Dee—a famous Elizabethan mystic—except for the fact that it seemed to be hundreds of years older than anyone had thought. Scientists viewed the manuscript as a mystery.

Then, Zane had woken up and distracted me, and I'd forgotten all about the manuscript...

Until I found him reading the same magazine a few days later, a funny expression on his face. It turned out that not only could he read the ancient angelic script that the Melledin Manuscript was lettered in, but it provided the first real clues we'd had toward finding the two missing haloes. The Melledin Manuscript had recently been on a tour in the US, visiting several prominent museums along the way. Now it was back home in Switzerland, and that was why we suddenly found ourselves in Europe.

One page of the manuscript in particular held the key to the information we sought. Unfortunately, the picture in the magazine spread had been an extreme close-up and Zane needed to see the entire thing. Thus we were resorting to... less ethical methods of getting our hands on the page.

And now here I was, crashing a charity function so I could get inside and rip apart a thousand-year-old manuscript that was lauded as one of the most fascinating finds of the last century.

Sure, we could just take a picture of the page instead of ripping it out of the book... but that also meant that the information would be out there for other immortals to discover. I needed that halo to win a boon from the Archangel Gabriel. Something told me that he'd be just as happy giving that boon to someone else. And given that the Serim and vampires did not play well together...

Well, it was just best if I confiscated the information, even if it hurt my soul to deface a priceless book.

The book wasn't in the room, though. There was another set of double doors at the far end of the room, and I headed toward those. I tested the brass handle of the door—not locked, and no alarm. Well, that made things easier. I entered the room and shut the door behind me.

"This room is off-limits." A man in a security guard uniform stood by the lit case where the massive book rested.

"Oh, I'm sorry." I gave him a bright smile and closed the door behind me.

He frowned in my direction, gesturing that I should leave the room. And when I didn't move, he continued to approach me. "I said, you need to leave—"

I reached out and brushed his cheek with my hand, shutting down his mind and sending him to sleep. Okay, so succubi weren't completely helpless, as I'd intimated to Zane. But the powers we had weren't exactly subtle ones, either. With my fingers pressed against the guard's forehead, I rummaged through the dream I'd forced on him, looking for pass-codes or security keys. Nothing, luckily for me. With a pat to his cheek, I stood and approached the dais.

The book lay spread before me on a pedestal, a lit glass case protecting the valuable object inside from onlookers. It was beautiful, I thought as I stared down through the glass. The pages were thick and yellowed with age, the ink crisp and vivid with color. Scrollwork decorated the edges of the paper with a story that archaeologists hadn't been able to figure out, but Zane had told me involved the fall of the angels. Not just any angels, but specific ones.

The ones I was looking for.

Biting my lip, I grasped the glass case and pulled it off the book. My entire body was tense, ready for an alarm to go off, but nothing happened. With relief, I placed the case on the ground at my feet and leaned over the book. I'd normally wear latex gloves to handle a book like this, since the oils on my fingertips were sure to destroy it... but I was just about to rip out a page and stuff it into my bra. Did it even matter if I left fingerprints on the damn thing?

We'd discussed taking the entire book with us. After all, if one page had the info we needed, the others might have useful information as well. But our plan meant slipping in and out unnoticed, since the place was crawling with security. And my dress was tight enough that only one page was fitting down the front.

I laid tentative fingers on the thick vellum of the manuscript. It felt sacrilegious and amazing all at once. I was touching something a thousand years old. With gentle fingers, I turned the page, wincing. The lambskin sheets of parchment felt thin and weak under my fingertips. After a few cautious flips, I found the page I was looking for—seven rings of different colors seemed to be interconnected by golden chains on the page and surrounded by small, cribbed text in strange, looping handwriting. This was the page I needed. This one, Zane insisted, would lead us toward a missing halo, maybe both if we were lucky.

Flinching to myself, I gave the page a firm tug and yanked it free.

A priceless, fragile work of art, one of a kind and of holy origin... a book that had lasted a thousand years, and here I was defacing it like some teenager tearing out pages in the library. It felt dirty and wrong, and I couldn't help but frown to myself as I rolled up the page and then slid the tube of paper down the front of my tight dress until it nestled deep between my breasts and out of sight.

I felt rather than heard the step of soft feet behind me and tensed.

"Don't worry, honey. We've got you now," an unfamiliar, breathy female voice whispered in my ear. A hand touched my bare arm. Before I could turn, a disconcerting, vague feeling washed over me. My mind fuzzed, then went black, and the last thing I thought before falling into unconsciousness was that I'd been found.

By another succubus.

CHAPTER TWO

"A lot of people are afraid to tell you the truth in this business. Yes, you're going to have to suck a lot of dick. Yes, double penetration makes your ass look fat. Yes, that does look diseased. But I've always tried to be a straight shooter."—*The Absolutely True Memoir of Remy Summore*, by Remy Summore

~*~

Succubi don't dream. The few times I'd been locked in my own mind since I turned succubus, I'd basically existed in a conscious state while my body slept, my mind forming a "room" for me to inhabit to pass the time. Today's room was my favorite pub closest to Remy's place in New City. I drummed my fingernails on the bar as I sat on one of the tall stools, waiting to wake up. It had to be Remy or Dee who had knocked me out. Those were the only succubi I knew.

Don't worry, honey. We've got you now.

I replayed the voice in my head over and over, but didn't recognize it. They had me, all right. Whoever it was, this was *not* funny. We needed to get that page before some other immortal happened upon it and decided that they were going halo-hunting themselves. The Melledin Manuscript had gotten so much publicity in the last year that it was only a matter of time.

By the time I felt the shifting rubber band snap that told me I was zinging back toward consciousness, I was a nervous wreck, more anxious than furious. Oh, I was plenty mad, but I wanted to get the book taken care of first. I'd be angry later, when I had the page in my hand.

My eyes flicked open. I stared at the ceiling. Not cherubs. Okay, I'd been moved. I mentally assessed all my parts. No wounds. Still wearing the black dress and heels. On something soft. Couch? Bed?

I looked over.

A beautiful woman stood nearby, her tall, willowy height equal to mine. She had smooth black hair, lovely almond eyes, and wore a slim-fitting cheongsam.

"Awake?" she asked in a bright, cheerful voice.

I sat up and swung my legs down to the floor. I was definitely in a bed. I stood and eyed the woman. Her smile was friendly, but I didn't trust this. Unease grated on my nerves, and my internal tuning fork gave an anxious wobble.

"Where am I?"

For some odd reason, she looked hurt at my suspicious question. Then she smiled brightly. "Phryne told me you'd probably be suspicious when you awoke. I bet you have no idea what's going on." Her look became sympathetic.

It was true. I did have no idea what was going on. Of course, I wasn't going to tell her that. So I just stared at her.

She came to my side and linked her arm through mine. "Come on. Let's go wake up Remy. The others are dying to see her again."

Others? I let the woman lead me by the arm, staring at my surroundings. The room was lushly decorated, draperies and pale marble statues lining the walls. It looked rich, and the carpet under my shoes was thick and plush.

"Zane?" I asked.

"Phryne will explain everything, my love," she said sweetly.

Uh, okay. The woman clutching my arm led me down a hall. As we walked, I began to piece things together. Someone had knocked me out. That was clearly this chick. She was a succubus, then, and older than me. But what the heck was she doing, kidnapping us from a party? And who was Phryne? I eyed her, but she didn't look dangerous or unhappy or even angry. She looked sweet and lovely, and oddly thrilled to be at my side.

Which was just… weird.

Down the hall, she opened another door and led me into a bedroom. Remy slept on a huge king bed, curled up on one side, and the sight of her was jarring for me. I'd never seen her sleeping.

It was actually rather unnerving. I looked over at my companion.

"Whose house is this?"

She shook her head at me. "Phryne wants to be the one to explain."

"But—"

"I can say nothing until Phryne has assessed the situation, I'm afraid," she said with a soft grimace. "Come, let's wake Remy. It's been forever since I've chatted with her."

So she knew Remy? "Who are you?"

She smiled then, so genuinely and so warmly that I was taken aback. "My name is Yue. It's so lovely to finally meet you, Jackie."

And she hugged me.

I awkwardly hugged her back, utterly confused. What was going on? If she was so glad to see me, why had she kidnapped both of us and knocked us out? Better yet, how could this fragile woman have carried both of us? As I watched, she approached Remy and brushed her fingertips over the sleeping succubus's forehead.

Remy struggled awake. Her eyes flicked open, and I noticed they were blue. The sight of them made the Itch pulse through me, reminding me of my own need, now due.

We'd been unconscious for quite some time, apparently. Alarm flared through my body. How long had we been out? And where was Zane?

"Wake, sister," Yue said with a smile.

Remy stared up at Yue for a moment and then gave a girlish squeal of delight, jumping to her feet. "Yue, baby! How the hell are you?"

Yue opened her arms wide, and Remy fell into them, hugging and squealing as if seeing an old friend. Her arms went around Yue's slender body and she tugged her close. As I watched the two hug, Remy's gaze moved to me, making eye contact over Yue's shoulder.

Not good, she mouthed, and gave me a look of alarm.

Oh great. Not what I wanted to see. But Remy pulled away and gave Yue another bright smile as if everything were perfect. "Girl, look at you! You never change."

"Very funny," Yue said with affection, touching Remy's cheek. "I should say the same for you, Remiza."

"Where's everyone else?" Remy asked, moving to my side and linking her arm through mine. "Have they met Jackie?"

Yue shook her head gently. "I've just awakened Jackie. She has not met the others yet."

"They'll be so thrilled to see her," Remy gushed.

Yue smiled again, but I noticed she didn't reply. She simply gestured at the door. "Please come with me, sisters."

"Of course," Remy said cheerily, and her fingernails dug into my arm, and she more or less dragged me forward.

Yue glided past us, her steps smooth. She smiled and began down the hall, and Remy and I followed. Remy's steps were slow and deliberate, as if she were admiring our surroundings. When Yue was several feet ahead of us, she bent in and whispered. "We are *so* screwed, Jacks."

"Who is she? What's going on?"

"Nothing good," Remy hissed back. "Just be careful and tell them nothing. I'll explain later."

Yue must have heard our furious whispers. She glanced back at us as we walked, her eyes narrowing. I smiled back at her, and pointed out a statue to Remy, as if admiring it.

We acted as if we were sightseeing at a museum instead of finding ourselves kidnapped by another freaking succubus.

Yue opened the door to a long, well-lit hall. She continued down it, strolling past beautifully decorated walls adorned with ornate picture frames, end tables set with fresh flowers, and small, delicate knickknacks that I didn't have time to examine. The ceilings were arched, a faint peachy-pink that made me think of dawn and only added to the feeling that this place was owned by someone who had great taste and loved expensive things. It was not merely a home—it was a showcase. Yue led us down another hall, then another. Then another. I had no idea where we were, but the place was enormous and expensive. Still in Europe somewhere? How long had we been out? Was it daylight?

And where the hell was Zane? Fear prickled my skin, and I felt real panic claw through me despite Yue's warm smiles. I wanted my vampire.

Yue glanced back at us again, then put her hand on the handle of a door. "You're just in time for dinner."

Just in time for dinner, my ass. They'd woken us up when it was convenient for them. Still, I pretended like this was thoughtful and not a bullshit move. "Great," I said, my traitorous stomach growling to help my fake enthusiasm along.

Stupid supernatural metabolism didn't care about the situation. It just wanted cake.

Yue led us into a long room, mostly taken up by a long mahogany dining table. Eight places were clustered at the far end of table, though only four women sat before the plates. A spread of food was laid out on the table, colorful and aromatic, and my mouth watered at the sight.

Just how long had they left us out?

But before I could ask, all four women at the table stood. A girlish squeal erupted and they rushed forward, arms outstretched to hug Remy.

"Hey, girl!" one cried, and Remy moved forward to hug them, seemingly equally thrilled at the prospect.

"Oh my God. Ashara! How the hell are you? And Nefer, and Marguerite. And Phryne! You wench, you," Remy said, giving another pale redhead a playful punch in the arm before hugging her as if they were old friends that had been parted for far too long. "How have you been?"

The women finished with Remy and then enfolded me, too. The one called Phryne was the last one to embrace me, and I didn't miss the assessing look she shot my way as she hugged me. Another redhead, like me.

Actually, nothing like me, I reassessed. My skin was milk-white and pale. Phryne's was golden bronze, like a goddess. Her brows were low and winged above thickly lashed catlike eyes, and her nose was strong, her cheekbones prominent. My hair was fire-engine red and wavy, hanging to the middle of my back in a messy tumble. Not Phryne. Her hair was the delicate, rosy shade of sunrise, a red-gold that I'd never seen on anyone before, and it fell in a thick, straight waterfall to her waist. Phryne was golden and exotic and unique, even surrounded by beautiful succubi.

And sly. I couldn't help but notice the calculating look in her pale silver eyes. "Greetings, sister," she told me sweetly, and even her voice was husky and gorgeous. "We have waited so long to finally meet you."

As she moved forward to hug me, I stammered in surprise. "You... you have?"

She drew back and smiled at me. "Of course. I have heard tales of Remy's friend and knew that she was looking out for you. I've waited and watched over your progress from afar. But when I heard of your recent troubles, I decided it was time to step out of the shadows and introduce our little sisterhood."

Phryne clasped my hand and pulled me toward the dinner table.

"My troubles?" I echoed, glancing back at Remy. She shook her head at me and raised a pinky, as if swearing she'd never told them anything. So I asked again. "What kind of troubles?"

"Why, master troubles," Phryne said easily, moving back toward her place at the head of the table. "It seems that you have one master who's gotten into quite a bit of trouble with the Serim, and the other keeps you under his thumb." She tsked, giving me a sympathetic look. "Of course, you've been a very popular girl lately. My sources among the Serim told me that you've made an enemy out of Ariel. I've heard he tried to dispose of you."

"That's right," I said weakly, sitting down at the place they'd left for me. I tried to digest all that Phryne was tossing at me. Noah was in trouble? I was under Zane's thumb? I didn't know if I should correct her or not. Judging from Remy's wary look in my direction, it was best to let Phryne keep talking.

Yue moved to the corner of the room and pulled a rope, and a servant entered, refilling everyone's wineglasses. The women were silent until the servant left and then they began to fill their plates. I stared at the food in front of us. Seasoned chicken; delicate, flaky fish; rolls; vegetables tossed in a colorful steamed medley, dessert pastries, soufflé—it was a tempting smorgasbord. The succubi began to fill their plates, chatting. I took a bit of food, watching them carefully.

This was weird. This was beyond weird. They'd kidnapped us so they could hug us and serve us dinner? It didn't make sense. And where was Zane? I was afraid to ask. These women seemed to treat us like long-lost sisters, not enemies. So why the kidnapping?

Phryne leaned over to me again as I took a bite of chicken. "It's not often that a succubus gathers the attention of a Serim council. You must have done something quite terrible to incur Ariel's wrath."

"Oh, uh—"

Remy coughed.

I glanced down at her and she waved a chicken wing in the air. "Bone," she wheezed, then glanced over at me.

I looked over at Phryne's beautiful face with the strong features that were somehow so gorgeous on her, the catlike eyes. She leaned on her hand, as if fascinated by what I had to say. And she wasn't eating, if the few grapes on her plate were any indication.

A succubus with self-control? No such thing. I didn't trust her a bit.

I took a bite out of a divine potato casserole. "Um, well, it's a long story. I'm not sure that right now is the appropriate time to discuss it."

Phryne's eyes widened and she gave me a sympathetic look. "Of course."

Well dang. That had been easier than I thought. I smiled.

She reached over and patted my hand. "We will discuss it privately later."

My smile faded. Great. I took another bite, and someone made a blissful moan on the far side of the table. It immediately sent a jolt of lust through my body—and not lust for food. I was very Itch sensitive at the moment.

"It's been a while since we've had a new sister," Phryne was saying, but I barely heard her over the pulse pounding in my ears. I was suddenly acutely aware of my body… and how much I needed Zane. I forced myself to suppress it.

First, I needed some basic answers. Where we were. Where Zane was. And why we'd been dragged here. "Who are you? All of you?"

Phryne smiled at me, and I noticed for the first time that her smile never reached her eyes. They seemed cold—beautiful, but diamond hard. She looked to the other women with a little indulgent smile. "Shall we go around the table and introduce ourselves, ladies? Yue, darling, you go first."

One by one, the women introduced themselves. Yue was our escort, of course, and she smiled and laughed merrily as she spoke, telling us of how she had grown up in China during the Qin Dynasty. She had been a concubine and after being turned, served her vampire master for many years before Phryne had liberated her. She ended her tale with a glance at the other succubus that was half admiration, half desire.

Kinda awkward for me, sitting between them.

Nefer was a small, rounded woman with thick black braids and equally dark skin, her pale eyes eerie in her face. She'd been born in Nubia and sent as a gift to the Pharaoh Hatshepsut, who had been served by Serim advisors during her reign.

At her side, Ashara clasped her hand. She had wildly thick, curling hair, strong features, and olive skin. She told us that she was Sumerian and was the oldest one at the table. That was met by a laugh from Nefer and a tight little smile from Phryne, who didn't seem very pleased at the reminder. I noted that for later.

Marguerite was the melancholy blonde that sat at the end of the table. She didn't seem to be paired up with one of the others, smiled when spoken to directly, and seemed lost in her own sad thoughts when no one was looking. She was beautiful—pale skin and even paler hair, but she didn't seem happy in the slightest. When prompted by Phryne, she confessed to us that she'd been turned during the time of the French Revolution.

After Marguerite finished, Phryne looked back to me. "Do you have any questions, my dear?"

Oh, I had plenty of questions. I knew—I just knew—that if I asked about Zane, the conversation would die instantly. "Nope, I'm cool. Nice of you ladies to invite us over."

Her smile was knowing. "Shall you tell us about you? We know all about Remy."

"Not much to tell. I don't have the fascinating history like the rest of you."

She leaned forward, her expression fascinated. "But you are quite interesting. How was it that you were turned?"

I stammered through an abbreviated description of my turning—running into Zane in a dark alley, then meeting up with Noah and my subsequent turning.

"I see," she said, and her voice was all sympathy. "That must have been hard for you. Have you struggled with the turning?"

"It's been… challenging," I said, smiling cheerfully despite feeling like my face would break. Where was she going with this?

"And is there one particular master that you feel has used you and taken away your free will more than the other?"

I shook my head quickly. "Oh no, not at all."

"Ah," Phryne said with a knowing nod. "They are both equally terrible. I understand."

Uh… okay. I glanced down the table, looking for help. There was none to be found—Remy was chatting merrily with Yue, and Nefer and Ashara were feeding each other grapes and chatting quietly. Phryne kept watching me with those too-keen eyes, though she'd occasionally pop a grape to participate in the eating. I shoved a mouthful of fish into my mouth and began to eat like a woman starving.

"So how about you?" I asked, changing the subject. If there was one thing immortals liked to talk about, it was themselves. "Where are you from?"

Phryne leaned back in her chair, reclining in an elegant way that made my mouth go dry. She was incredibly beautiful. "You have not heard of me? Truly?"

I froze, fork halfway to my mouth. Was I supposed to have heard of her? "Um…"

She laughed softly. "I tease you, little sister. In my day, however, I was the most famous woman in all of Greece. My name was Phryne, and I was a hetaera without compare."

"Hetaera?" I prompted.

"Courtesan, of course," she said, inclining her head regally. The gesture must have been a rather practiced one, as her striking peach-gold hair slid over her shoulder in a sultry move. "Men paid fortunes for a night with me. And one could not get enough of me, so he turned me." Her indulgent smile tightened a little. "I was forced to serve him for many, many years. Eventually, I broke free from him."

And she'd founded the Vagina Sisterhood. Lovely. I stabbed at a piece of chicken on my plate. She was from Greece, then. Were we in Greece? Where the hell were we? Could I find out?

"Wow, this fish is terrific," I said between mouthfuls. "Is this a Swiss recipe? Maybe… German? Is there any schnitzel on the table?" Germany was right next to Switzerland, right? Maybe they'd smuggled us over the border while we slept.

Phryne gave me a coy smile, as if amused by my obviousness. "It's sea bass. I had it flown to New York." She stressed the city name, as if reassuring me.

Or threatening me.

So we were in New York? I took another forkful of the potato soufflé, pretending to savor it even as my stomach churned. So not only had they smuggled us over the border, but they'd smuggled us over an entire ocean. Was Zane still in Europe? Had they left him behind? Panic began to flutter in my breast. A vampire needed to drink blood daily. What if he had to drink from a stranger while I wasn't at his side? My hand trembled on the fork.

"New York, huh?" I repeated. "How… interesting."

Phryne tilted her wineglass as if studying it. She gave me another slow smile. "I enjoy visiting from time to time. I don't tell little Delilah about it, though. She doesn't enjoy my presence on this side of the pond."

No, I could imagine that Dee wouldn't. She envisioned herself as the head honcho of the US. "Is Dee here?"

"She is not invited," Phryne said smoothly, her expression unchanging.

Okay. If this was some sort of succubus slumber party, I didn't get why Delilah wasn't invited. Something else had to be at work. I gestured at the unused place setting at the end of the table. "That her spot?"

"That is Sophie's spot," Phryne said easily.

"Sophie?"

"Sophonisba," she said, as if that answered everything.

"Ah," I said, and took another piece of chicken, though I hadn't even eaten the first one. So there was another succubus somewhere around here? "And where's she at? Powder break?"

Phyrne suddenly smiled. "She will be along shortly, I imagine. Our Sophie is a good woman, even if her manners are a little less than we'd hope. She has a good heart and is eager to participate in your liberation."

"My... liberation?"

"Why, from your masters." Phryne's smile was brilliant. "The vampire's been neutralized, so it's simply a matter of tracking down the Serim one in order to obtain your true freedom."

Tracking down Noah? Neutralized Zane...?

My entire throat went dry. "My... master? You have him? He's here?"

She gave me a sympathetic nod and continued to rub my hand, those catlike eyes focused on my face. "Do not worry, little sister. The situation is under control."

My heart hammered wildly in my breast. "I—I don't understand."

"We know that if he commands you, you must obey. And we know a vampire's strengths and weaknesses, having intimate experience with them ourselves. As I said, he has been effectively neutralized," she said, stating that horrible word again. "He won't threaten you anymore. You are safe here with your sisters."

"Where is he?" I whispered, my mind full of horrible thoughts.

Phryne leaned back and tossed her napkin down on her plate, as if the very mention of a vampire made her lose her appetite. "I understand that your mind is focused, Jackie, but trust us when we say that you're safe. Sophie's likely handling him at the moment. She has interest in how this will be resolved, but I don't see a happy way out. It is a delicate situation."

And she gave a ladylike grimace.

My heart pounded at her frown. "Can I see him?"

She gave me a puzzled look. "Why? You are safe. Trust me, no one will let him harm you." The sympathetic look crossed her face again and she clasped my cold hand. "He's bound hand and foot. His wings are staked. The room is covered with the appropriate wards, so he cannot escape even if he tried. And he's gagged, so he cannot command you. You are safe, sister. Safe."

"But…"

"Jackie is thrilled that you guys have saved her," Remy said loudly. "Just thrilled. Aren'tcha, Jackie?"

I shook my head. "But—"

"Thrilled," Remy repeated.

But Phryne cast a sympathetic look at me. "It must be hard for you to grasp, I know. For so long, we are kept under the boot of our masters. It's a good thing for you that he got so careless with you—forcing you to go and steal priceless items in the midst of a crowd." She tsked, looking disgusted at the thought. "Abusive wretch. No doubt he forced you to feed him on a regular basis as well."

Phryne had it all wrong. Well, not about the feeding. "He didn't force me to do anything. It was my idea."

The catlike eyes narrowed at me. "Oh?"

"Jackie's constantly trying to think of new things to make her master happy," Remy chimed in. "Stay one step ahead of him and all that. If he's happy, then he doesn't abuse her."

Phryne's too-sharp expression relaxed. She nodded. "Clever. And I understand completely."

I looked down the table at Remy, who had a bright smile frozen to her face. Okay. She didn't want me talking about my relationship with Zane. For some reason, that would be bad. I'd play along, even though every nerve in my body screamed to go to him. It had been at least a day since we'd been captured. Was he starving for blood even now? Could I ask?

I forced myself to take another bite of food, pretend that I was still enjoying the meal.

"So, what were you after?" Phryne watched me eat, waiting.

My smile became a little more forced. "After?" I asked, feigning ignorance.

"Yes. Your vampire master. What did he seek at the party? It gave us the perfect opportunity to intercept the both of you, but it was a rather foolhardy sort of thing to do. The only thing I can assume is that he wanted that book for some reason. Why is that?"

I couldn't think of a good excuse. And I sure wasn't about to tell Phryne about the book. It led to a halo, and I was suspicious of all other immortals. They had a habit of stepping on each other for any kind of advantage. No one could be trusted.

She tilted her head, staring at me. Waiting.

"He didn't tell me," I blurted. "He liked to keep me in the dark about his reasons for things. It was one of his little games." I winced internally, hating that I had to sell my lover down the river for these crazy women. "It was probably just to mess with me. I used to be an archaeologist, after all. I just knew that he wanted it and when I saw it was going to be unveiled, I suggested we go for it."

"And it was his suggestion that you hide the page in your gown?" Her gaze flicked to my breasts, then back to my face.

I realized then that my chest wasn't crinkling. Shit. She'd stolen my page. Panic flared through my body and I set down my fork, my stomach churning. We'd worked so hard to get that page—and she'd taken it.

Shit!

We'd just have to get it back somehow. I touched my ear casually, looking for my small radio transmitter. It was gone too. We hadn't worn our phones in our dresses—too tight. Damn. We had no way of contacting anyone. "Something like that."

Phryne's smile didn't go to her eyes. "Of course."

She didn't believe me. Time to divert. I glanced down the table and clenched my hands, feigning confusion and timidity. "I'm sorry. This is all so new to me," I said, and that was the honest truth.

Across the table, Yue smiled and buttered a slice of bread. "I think you will like our sisterhood, Jackie. Our kind is tormented by those who create us. Our sisterhood works to keep each other free from the tyranny of our masters."

"A noble cause," I said, picking up my wineglass and sipping. It was a good idea—as succubi, we were created for our masters to use and abuse. We could turn down no command they gave us, and since we needed a steady diet of sex to survive, well, it didn't put us in the strongest position to bargain. A sisterhood was a noble cause, all right, with one tiny problem.

I loved my master. I didn't *want* to be separated from him. I didn't want to join their sisterhood, though I could imagine why it had appeal.

The average succubus—and incubus—hated their masters. And since we were unable to disobey an order given, it was far too easy to abuse a succubus. We were like oversexed, powerless genies, unable to resist our master's every command. The power balance was definitely skewed.

I guess I'd been lucky. I had Noah Gideon as my Serim master. And while Noah was bossy and domineering, he was also a good man. He gave his orders because he was trying to protect me; he cared for me.

And I had Zane.

Gorgeous, rakish, dangerous Zane who was never anything but wonderful to me. Who went out of his way to avoid commanding me, because he wanted me to have free will. Who loved me for my smart, bitchy mouth and my nerdy tendencies, and I loved him back. We made a good team, Zane and I, and I never felt as if he were abusing the power dynamic of our relationship.

"This is a really nice place you have," I said, staring at the paintings on the walls and the expensive furniture.

"Some of us have acquired a fortune over time," Phryne said, pleasure in her voice.

"But what about…" I hesitated, since it'd seem a crass subject to bring up at dinner. So I pointed at my blue eyes, trying to broach the subject as delicately as I could. "You know."

"Ah," Phryne said, and Yue smiled again, giggling as she took a bite of her bread. "That is another thing the sisterhood helps each other with. You need have no worries."

I looked down the table at Ashara and Nefer, still lovingly feeding each other bits of food. Remy shoveled vegetables and bread into her mouth, eating with an indelicate rapidity that made the others look like cultured goddesses next to her.

"Um," I said. "So no… men?"

"What Jackie is trying to say is that she likes cock," Remy said bluntly. "And she's young enough that she hasn't become bisexual like the rest of us."

"Ah," Phryne said delicately. "That could be a problem. A gender preference definitely makes things difficult, but that is a prudish sentiment you will discard in time." Her smile widened and she wagged a finger at me. "Or rather, I should say a prudish sentiment you will discard sooner rather than later. You see, no men are allowed here. It is our sanctuary."

Oh friggin' lovely. Not that I wanted another man. I wanted Zane. I guess men were all right as long as they were bound and tied and imprisoned, like Phryne had said.

But I figured it'd be a bad call to ask.

"Remy and I are both in need," I said, trying not to pull away when Phryne began to rub my hand again. I was sure it was just a friendly rub, and not a flirty one.

I hoped.

"It's cool, kid. Remember that time in Vegas? I can take care of you again, and you can take care of me." Remy gave me a lewd wink.

Time in Vegas? What the hell was she talking about? But she winked at me again, obviously. "Um, okay. Sounds good. Promise you'll be gentle?" I took a sip of my wine and played the innocent.

"I'll use my smallest strap-on," she said with great seriousness.

I spewed wine all over the table. "Great," I choked.

CHAPTER THREE

"You want to get ahead in this business? Pretend that you love clam."—*Business Advice: One Porn Star's Secret to Success*, by Remy Summore

~*~

Remy smiled brightly. "Now that that's settled, can you show us our rooms so we can get things taken care of?"

"Of course," Phryne said, and gestured to Yue. "Will you, my sweet?"

"Naturally." Yue pushed out her chair, stood, and gestured for us to follow her.

Uncertain, I looked at Remy, then back at Phryne.

Phryne gave me an indulgent smile, like a mother hen doting on her children. "Go on. Take care of your needs, little sister. You can rejoin us when your cravings have been sated. We'll be enjoying a bit of culture in the drawing room after dinner." She patted my hand, her fingers stroking my skin. "And don't worry. You'll get over your shyness soon enough."

"Thanks," I said. "See you soon."

Remy put an arm around my waist as I moved to follow Yue, and this time her friendly moves were a bit too meaningful. I had to fight not to pry her off me. Surely Remy had a plan... but what if she didn't? She was in need too, her eyes bright blue. And she didn't care nearly as much about these sorts of things as I did.

Yue led us up a flight of stairs, then a second one. I eyed our surroundings, trying to count how many doors we passed so I could remember in case we had to escape. She continued down a long hallway, through a foyer, then another hallway. Good lord, this place was enormous. And only the succubi lived here? It was a mansion, a dozen times the size of Remy's house. Remy had nice digs, but Phryne had set herself up in a freaking palace.

Yue glanced back at us as we walked, as if bothered by the silence. "How long have you been a succubus, Jackie?"

"Oh," I smiled cheerfully. "About a year now."

"A year in captivity is not so bad, then," Yue mused. "But don't worry. You are free now."

"Yippee. Thanks. You guys are my heroes."

Remy pinched my arm. Guess that didn't sound sincere.

Yue didn't comment on it, though. She continued to glide down the hallway, her footsteps soundless on the carpet. "And do you still have both your masters?"

My hackles raised at that one. Why did she want to know? So they could dispose of the one at hand without offing me? A chill coursed through my body. "Still have both," I said, and at Yue's nod of response, added, "At least, I think I do. I haven't seen Noah since the Serim punishment."

"That is probably wise," Yue said thoughtfully. "If they punished him, he is sure to take it out on you."

I doubted Noah would do that. Well, he might force me to have really dirty sex with him, but that wasn't exactly a punishment. Just thinking about that made my nipples hard, and I hated myself a little for that involuntary reaction.

I didn't want Noah. I wanted Zane.

Yue opened one door. "Here is your chamber, Remy. If it doesn't suit you, let me or Phryne know. We want you to be comfortable."

Remy glanced in, grunted, and then looped her arm around my waist again. "Let's check out your room, Jackie."

She pinched my side as soon as Yue turned further down the corridor.

"What?" I hissed.

"What's the plan?"

An outraged squeak erupted from my throat. "I don't have a plan—"

Yue turned and glanced back at us, and Remy and I fell silent.

"This way," she said with a graceful gesture and opened a door at the end of the hall. "Phryne saved the best room for you. She wants you to feel welcome."

"Gosh, that is really nice of her," I said, feigning enthusiasm. I slid out of Remy's clingy embrace and into the gorgeous room. A princess bed dominated the room, high upon a dais. A cream-colored canopy attached to the wall and then glided downward to the posts of the bed in a decadent swirl. A dozen fringed pillows topped the head of the bed, and the carpet on the floor was thick and plush and expensive-looking. Red draperies lined the walls, a stark contrast to the cream colors of the bed. There was an entertainment center on the far wall, fully stocked, and an adjoining bathroom that I suspected would be just as spectacular as the room.

It was a very pretty prison. And Zane was not here, which meant that I was not staying.

Remy began to play with my hair, her hand moving to the hooks in the back of my dress and beginning to undo them. "So," she said in a husky voice. "Where do you girls keep the sex toys? This one's going to be skittish unless I give her a good ride."

God, I wanted to fall through the floor. Especially when Remy slapped my flanks as if I was a horse she was gentling. "Quit jumping."

Yue smiled and gestured to a bureau nearby, turning her back to us. "Each room has a fully functional set of dildos and vibrators. Simply leave them out for the staff and they'll clean them for you and replace them."

As she spoke, Remy jabbed me in the back with her finger and gestured at the draperies dangling from the bed.

"What?" I whispered. What was I supposed to do?

She waved a hand wildly at them and stomped on my foot with her heel.

"Ow!"

Yue turned back to glance at us, raising a brow.

Remy reached out and tweaked my nipple—hard. I slapped her hand away, outraged, but Remy slapped me back, giving me a sultry grin. "Meee-ow. I keep forgetting you're a pain bitch." Before I could protest, she turned to Yue. "You got any nipple clamps in there?"

Yue turned back to the bureau and pulled open the first drawer, studying the contents. "I'm not sure, but I imagine it's a request we can accommodate."

Remy pinched my arm again, and I turned to her with a frown. What the hell did she want? But this time, she flicked her hand toward the door, and my gaze went there. It had opened just a crack, and a tall, bronzed figure in black leather strode in, a ponytail of wild black dreads high on her head. Her cheeks were covered with swirling designs, and the belt slung at her waist gleamed with metal weapons.

I froze at the sight of her, but she seemed to be heading straight for Yue. She glanced over at Remy and I noticed the odd, bright silver of her eyes in her dark bronze face. Another succubus. She gestured for Remy to be quiet.

Remy shoved past me, moving to Yue's side. "Well, what do you have if not clamps?"

Yue reached into the drawer, gesturing at something. "You could always try—"

The tall woman in leather moved up behind Yue, grabbed the other woman by the sides of her face. Yue's eyes widened with recognition for just a fraction of time before the tall woman wrenched her head to the side. Quick. Rough. There was an audible snap, and then Yue fell to the floor in a boneless heap.

My jaw dropped and I flinched backward.

Remy stepped to the side of the fallen woman and clutched her stomach, gagging. "Ugh. That was seriously gross, Sophie. I practically felt her vertebrae snap and I didn't even touch her."

The tall woman named Sophie stared at Remy with unblinking eyes. "That is why I am the assassin, Remiza."

"True, that," Remy said with a shudder. "Thanks for coming to our rescue."

"It is not your safety I am concerned about so much as my own," she said with a hard smile that showed even white teeth. Her voice had a musical, thick accent that I couldn't place.

I couldn't stop staring at her. I looked at Yue, crumpled on the floor, then at the woman standing over her. "Who are you? What the fuck did you just do?"

Sophie arched an eyebrow at me. "I broke her neck." She looked over at Remy. "Is this one touched?"

Remy shook her head, hands on her hips. "Nah. Just really new. Jackie, this is Sophie. I'm guessing she's on our side today."

Our side? *Today?* I moved to Remy's side, staring at the new succubus. They'd set a plate for her at dinner. Talked about her as if she were one of their sisterhood. Why was she helping us? I studied her—tall and beautiful, and strong. She wore a short leather vest that buttoned over her breasts and left her arms and abdomen exposed, and every inch of her beautiful bronzed skin was covered in darker, swirling tattoos. Henna tattoos, I realized. Her face had henna tattoos on the high cheekbones as well, and one across her forehead. Her thick black hair had been twisted into a nest of dreadlocks that had been gathered high and stuck out at odd angles. Her legs were clad in tight leather pants that showcased perfectly curving hips and a jillion weapons.

I shook my head, trying to absorb this. "I don't understand—"

The words died in my throat as Sophie rolled her eyes.

Remy grasped my arm and leaned in, her gaze still on Sophie. "Look, kid. Yue's a couple thousand years old and she's cute as a button, but she's also batshit crazy. All of them are. We have to get out of here, and you didn't have a plan. I'm glad Sophie showed up." She nudged the fallen woman with her shoe, wrinkling her nose.

Sophie inclined her head, taking Remy's words as a compliment. "It was clear you would not be saving yourselves."

"Double true," Remy said with a sigh. "So what's the plan?"

"You snapped her neck! You could have just put her to sleep!"

"Nu-uh," Remy said, stepping over Yue and heading to the closest dresser, searching the drawers. "Someone'd have to come back to wake her up, and I have a feeling Sophie's not going to be welcome after this."

"Yue will hold a grudge," Sophie agreed, studying her fingernails as if bored.

Well, hell *yes* she'd hold a grudge. If it was me, I'd be furious too.

"Do not feel too bad for her," Sophie said, arching an eyebrow at me and turning toward the door. "Yue is quite proficient in poisons. I have no doubt that once Phryne determined that you are not happy to have your master imprisoned here, she would have slipped you something that would have disabled you until they could find a delicate way to dispose of your master and remove your choice from you. That is, after all, how they pulled in Marguerite."

32

The sad-eyed blonde at dinner. I stared at Sophie.

"Besides," Remy pointed out. "I don't know if you noticed, but they're all gung ho for girl power and not so much for guys. So unless you'd like to spend the next millennia eating clams and watching men get tortured for fun, we have to move."

"Okay, okay," I said, raising my hands. "You win. Let's get out of here."

Sophie pulled a length of cord from a pocket and threw it at me. "Tie Yue's hands with this. Remiza, find something for a gag. We don't want to take our chances that she can heal before we get away."

I stood over the fallen woman, my skin crawling, rope in hand. "I still can't believe we just broke her neck."

Sophie's laugh was low, melodious. "You are quite young, aren't you? These people stole you for a reason, little one. They are not going to play nice. In fact, no one is going to play nice. If you do, you're going to find yourself quickly outmaneuvered."

I swallowed hard and finished binding Yue's hands. As I watched, Remy moved over and shoved a pair of socks into Yue's mouth, then tugged a frilly pair of thong underwear over the woman's mouth to hold them in place. "Come on, let's dump her in the closet."

We did. Yue was surprisingly heavy—she was deadweight and we were both wimps. Sophie didn't seem inclined to help, watching the hall through a crack in the door as we struggled with the body of her friend.

"Why is she helping us?" I asked Remy as we shoved Yue's bound legs into the closet.

"Long story," Remy hissed back. "Tell you later." She raised a pinky into the air. "Pinky swear."

Once Yue was situated, Remy grabbed a pair of candlesticks off a dresser and handed one to me. "Here. Weapon."

I looked at Sophie's belt, full of knives and throwing stars. "Can't we just borrow one of hers?"

An amused smile curved Sophie's full mouth. "No."

Well, fine then.

"Shall we go retrieve your master?" Sophie asked me.

"My page, too," I pointed out. "Phryne stole that from me and I need it." It was absolutely vital to finding one of the haloes, and the closest I'd come so far.

"Phryne has that page locked away. She thinks that holding it hostage will keep you here." Sophie tilted her head, dreadlocks bouncing. "Will you prove her right?"

I sighed heavily. "No. I want Zane and I want out of here, in that order."

Remy patted my shoulder. "We'll figure out some other way to get the page, Jacks. Don't you worry."

We fell in step behind Sophie. Armed with candlesticks, we crept down the hall after the tall succubus. She walked with quick, ground-eating strides. Confident. Unafraid. Meanwhile, Remy and I crouched and slunk down the hall after her. I glanced over at my friend as Sophie paused at the entrance of a door, cracking it open a hair, checking for occupants. She gestured for us to stay in place, and slipped into the room.

"How do you know Sophie?" I asked Remy quietly, wincing as I heard another too-loud crack come from the other room. God, I hoped that wasn't someone else's neck.

Remy jabbed me in the gut with the candlestick. "Be quiet."

"She's not going to leave anyone in that room to hear us, dummy. Just tell me."

She rolled her eyes at me. "This isn't my first run-in with Phryne and friends, Chatty Cathy. Trust me when I say they're assholes. If you see someone, don't hesitate to bash their brains in. They'll grow 'em back."

Right.

Sophie returned a moment later and gestured for us to follow once again. We crept through the house, and my heart pounded wildly. I kept expecting someone to happen upon us and sound the alarm. But there was nothing. All was quiet.

We cut through the kitchens and Sophie tugged open a door, flicking a hand to indicate that we should follow. She led us through a wine cellar and then down another flight of stairs. The walls were stone here, the air damp and cold. One solitary light flickered overhead, revealing a dark, narrow passageway.

"Where are we?"

"Dungeon," Remy replied grimly, and I shivered. The thought of being in someone's dungeon scared the crap out of me. Mostly because if someone had a dungeon, they were going to use it. And this didn't look like the fun kind of dungeon that leather fetishists liked.

My internal spidey-sense began to tingle and I turned down one hall, toward a door on the far end. "This is the right way," I told Remy. "I can feel him."

The knowledge that he was so close pulsed within me, a strange mixture of anxiety and arousal. I needed Zane. How badly did he need me—need blood—right now?

We moved to the end of the hall. The door was cold metal, no window. When I looked closely, I could see faint symbols traced into the metal, as if scratched there with a knife. The stain of wet liquid in the dirt at the doorway was likely holy water. If we got in, how would we get Zane out?

I tested the doorknob anyhow. It turned easily and I stepped inside.

One dim yellow light bulb hung from the ceiling here. The walls were bare, damp concrete. And there, on the only piece of furniture in the tiny room, lay Zane, stretched out on a plain wooden table, utterly still. His wrists were extended over his head and chained with cuffs, his ankles also manacled. His wings were tight beneath him, and as I stepped forward, I noticed that runes covered the manacles. Silver duct tape covered his eyes and mouth, symbols hastily scribbled on in what looked like marker.

I gasped, the breath escaping my body. Oh, God. He was so still. I'd feel it if he was dead, wouldn't I? "Zane?" I reached out to touch him.

Sophie pushed my hand away, her gaze hardening.

I looked at her in surprise. "What are you doing?"

"I must know your intentions, first."

Who the hell was she to question me? I pointed at the man on the table—so unnaturally still—and lifted my chin. "That is my master. And I love him. And I'm getting him out of here before they kill him. He doesn't deserve to be held captive like this."

She snorted at that. "You are a naïve fool," she said in that thick accent. "This one is not an innocent any more than I am." Sophie gestured at me. "But, very well. You may free him."

Was this a trick? A trap? I glanced at Remy, but she was staring down the corridor, watching for the others.

I took a step toward Zane. Sophie didn't move. I circled around him, and still she didn't move. She simply watched me with interested eyes.

My fingers touched his bare chest. It rose and fell underneath my fingertips, and I exhaled in relief. Thank God. I hadn't realized until now just how frightened I was. He was unnaturally still, but he lived. "Is he all right?"

"Does he look all right?" Sophie sounded amused.

I didn't know how to answer that. I glanced over at her, then back down at Zane. I tugged at the tape over his eyes, and carefully peeled it off.

Then gasped.

His eyes were entirely red—no whites showed. They flicked over to glance at me, the only movement in his too-still body. "What's wrong with him?" My fingers grazed his cheek lovingly and I began to pull the tape off his mouth.

Sophie watched me. "I imagine he is quite hungry."

My poor Zane. I looked at her in shock. "They're starving him? He has to drink every day."

"Or else he dies. Yes, I am aware." Her full mouth thinned a little.

Remy shut the door to the cell behind us. "Uh, Jacks, you might want to work a little faster. I'm pretty sure the others are coming."

I looked over at Sophie, but she calmly watched as Remy jammed her candlestick into the door, locking the handle in place.

I didn't need to be told twice, and since Sophie was just going to stand there, I'd work. When Zane's mouth was freed, he didn't move, though his lips were chapped and raw. I leaned in to kiss them, feeling the prick of his distended fangs. My fingers tugged at one of his cuffs, and to my surprise, it bent easily. I glanced down at it, and then twisted until it snapped under my grasp. It had been brittle, cheap tin. As an immortal, Zane's strength was enormous—it had to have been the magical wards holding him down.

And as if on cue, the other three cuffs fell away from his remaining wrist and feet.

Zane moved like a flash of lightning.

He was like a blur in my vision, all black coat and red eyes. As I watched, he leapt into a crouch on top of the table, studying his surroundings. His eyes flared red as his gaze lit on me, feral with need. Wild. Inhuman.

"Zane, baby," I said, holding my hand out to him. "Are you—"

Before I could finish the sentence, he barreled into me, shoving me to the stone wall. I felt every bone in my body protest as it met the wall, felt his hands grasp my long hair and pull it away from my neck.

And then his fangs sank into my neck as he fed ravenously.

All of that had taken the space of a brief second.

I moaned, instantly wet as his teeth pushed into my neck and he began to suck. A vampire's bite was an instant orgasm, and I felt the bursts of pleasure flood through my body in response. He continued to suck at my throat, pulling heavily on my blood, gulping down draw after draw, until I felt the blood from his mouth slide down my neck and over my breasts. The orgasm continued to crash over me with every flick of his tongue against my neck, and my eyes rolled back in my head. Zane normally drank from me, but not like this—not with this ferocity, this intensity. This need so thick and violent that he was going to drain me completely.

And I didn't care.

My arms wrapped around his neck and I cradled him closer, my legs wrapping around his hips as well. Bliss fogged my senses, a heady drug. I barely noticed Remy hammering at Zane's shoulders, shouting something. I saw a brown hand reach to Zane's hair, trying to tug him off me.

They were *totally* just jealous. I purred with each throb of the ongoing orgasm, my breath gone from my lungs. He'd taken every last whisper of it, just like he was taking my blood. He was welcome to all of it. Even when black began to cloud my vision, I moaned my pleasure. Zane's mouth on my skin was the most exquisite sensation I'd ever felt—would ever feel. I loved it. I loved him.

His head lifted, his eyes glittering with lust as he stared at my blissful face. Blood streaked his mouth, and he leaned in to kiss me tenderly. I could taste my own blood on his lips and felt his fangs graze my own mouth. He still struggled with control.

"Princess. I took too much blood," he rasped against my lips. Even now, they pushed against my lip, breaking the skin. "Sorry."

"Don't be," I said dreamily. "Whatever you need, I'll provide." My body existed in a pleasant haze. Problem? There was no problem, there was only Zane, holding me close to him, my body deliciously languid. I was his meal and lover all in one. I could be a fountain of blood for him. I raised a hand to caress his cheek.

But my hand wouldn't rise. In fact, when I tried to lift it, it just hung at my side, limply. The black continued to swim forward into my vision.

"Hold her," Zane rasped. "I'm getting us the fuck out of here."

I barely noticed when strong arms grasped me around my waist, supporting my body. In my dimming vision, I saw Zane rip his coat off and toss it to Remy. He glanced up at the stone ceiling.

And then he launched himself at it like a rocket. The ceiling collapsed in a rain of stone and cement.

And the world went black before my eyes.

CHAPTER FOUR

"The best thing about this business? The men. The worst thing about this business? The men."—*Looking Back on a Decade of Dong*, by Remy Summore

~*~

There were no dreams for me this sleep. Perhaps Zane had drunk too much, or perhaps something else was in play. Either way, I existed in a black, hazy limbo of pleasure, outside of time and space. It was almost like being human again—a deep, restful, drugging sleep like I hadn't experienced since becoming immortal.

A warm hand stroked my cheek, causing the black to recede.

"Wake up, Princess," a voice called softly, and I followed it. I knew that voice. I loved that voice. I pushed the darkness away and opened my eyes.

Zane hovered over me, his eyes dark, his thirst slaked. For now. His rakish hair swept over his forehead as he dipped his head, running his gaze over my body.

"Mmm," I said, stretching my arms over my head. I stifled a yawn, then glanced at our surroundings. A cheap, sparsely furnished room. A painting of a cowboy hung on the wall, and a TV sat atop a dresser nearby. The thick, ugly curtains were drawn over the window and I was lying on top of the world's ghastliest bedspread. "Where are we?"

"A motel somewhere in upstate New York," Zane said. "That was as far as we could get with you unconscious."

His mouth tightened, and I suspected he'd been worried about me. How… sweet. I reached up and brushed my fingers over his forehead, furtively sneaking a few of his memories as I did so. Zane wouldn't mind, after all.

One of the few perks of being a succubus was that we could push into the minds of others with a thought. It was supposed to be used to manipulate dreams, but I found I used my powers for snooping more than anything else. I pushed through his mind, sinking deep into the warmth of his familiar thoughts. His head was full of me in his arms, how delicious I tasted, and I had to drag myself away from those memories, seeking more.

In his mind, I saw Zane flying, carrying Sophie and Remy. Zane was a fallen angel, strong enough to crush a car with the flick of his hand. A vision of him punching through the floors of Phryne's mansion shocked me. Blood was dripping down his chin. My blood.

My unconscious body was cradled in Sophie's arms, and I could feel the bitter flash of Zane's thoughts—he hadn't liked that. It was jealousy—mixed with concern. His mind was focused on my body, crumpled to the floor, my neck wet with blood. He'd savaged my neck and I'd collapsed under it. A strong flash of remorse. *Too much*, he'd thought. *Drank too much. Wasn't careful with her.*

Aw. Such a marshmallow. I reached up and stroked my hand through his hair. "You're not hurt, Zane?"

He sat back on his haunches, still hovering over me. He patted his coat and pulled out a pack of cigarettes, taking one and lighting it. His eyes flared with emotion, his mouth a grim line. "I should be asking you."

"Immortal," I said, thumbing my chest. "We heal everything. Remember?"

The cigarette flicked and I watched his jaw clench, tensing. "Doesn't give me the right to hurt you. To take from you without permission."

Was that why I saw all the self-loathing in his eyes? He thought he'd taken without permission? He thought he'd hurt me?

Total marshmallow.

I hooked my hands into his coat and pulled him toward me. He resisted, just a little, and I reached up and plucked the cigarette out of his mouth, tossing it into a nearby ashtray. "Vampire, how would you feel if you woke up from your day-sleep to find me riding your hand?"

And I lifted my hips at that. They were still pinned under him, but even pushing against his immovable body felt incredibly good. The Itch stirred in my body. Mmm, how long had I been out? Didn't care, really.

His eyes flared with desire and he leaned in to kiss my mouth. "I'd find it incredibly arousing. And I'd do my best to help you along."

The husky timbre of his voice was arousing me too. I nibbled at his lip and gave my hips a suggestive flex under him once again. "So why would you think I would react any differently to your feeding?"

"Because I hurt you."

"You didn't," I assured him, and then licked at the seam of his mouth. "Unless an unending orgasm starts to hurt at some point."

He chuckled and then his tongue flicked to meet mine. "I should have asked first. I was just... starving. Crazed. I've... never been that close to the edge before."

"Poor baby."

"I hurt you. Was rough with you. I don't like that."

Mmm, rough. My nipples were growing hard at the feel of him over me, and I wanted to be out of this annoying gown like, yesterday. I also wanted my vampire between my legs. Deep inside me. Drinking from my neck again. Just the thought made my sex pulse with need and I gave a little whimper at the mental image. "Sometimes I like it rough."

His eyes flared red with immediate need. "Do you?" he asked hoarsely.

I licked his lower lip, then sucked on it. "With you I do," I said softly. "Because I know that despite all this strength, all this power, you'd never hurt me intentionally."

And then I took his lower lip in my own again and bit down. Hard.

He groaned, his eyes flaring red. I felt his fangs elongate against my own lips, and I raised my hips under him again, hoping he'd get the message.

I needed him. Right now.

His eyes had gone that dark, hazy red, and I quivered with need, anticipating the moment that he'd sink his fangs into my skin again.

"You want me to take you rough?" he said, his voice ragged.

"As rough as you want," I encouraged, squirming under him.

He looked incredibly aroused by the idea, and hell, that aroused me too.

He leaned in to kiss me, his teeth clashing with mine. The kiss was brutal and punishing, and his fangs scraped against my lips.

I loved it. A low moan rose in my throat.

His fingers went to the front of my dress and as his tongue thrust into my mouth, he ripped it away. My breasts bounced with the force of his movement. Zane lifted his head; his gaze fell there.

Immediately, my nipples puckered. I arched my back a little, pushing my breasts into the air. My hands went back to his hair.

He grasped my wrist, his eyes locking on mine, and ever so slowly, pushed it over my head, pinning my arm there. With his other hand, he captured my second wrist and then pinned them both above my head with one hand. I was trapped underneath him.

At his mercy.

I was so wet at the thought of it.

I licked my lips and shivered a little, noticing his gaze falling back to my breasts again. "Are you going to bite me, Zane?" God, was that husky, aroused voice mine? It practically sounded like a purr of need. "Sink your teeth into my breasts?"

"I am," he growled low, then leaned down and scored his sharp teeth over my left breast.

The breath caught in my throat, the sharp pain of his teeth raking my skin giving way to a fierce pulse of pleasure. As I looked down, blood beaded on my breast in a line. He leaned down and very gently licked it. "You taste sweet, Jackie. I could never get used to the pleasure of drinking from you."

"For all eternity," I added.

"I need to learn to pace myself," he said in a low voice, his free hand tracing a circle around the plump weight of my breast. "Lest you become immune to my touch and bored with it."

I laughed. "Never."

He gave me a wicked grin, then leaned in and sank his teeth into the curve of my breast. It was a fierce, hard bite, and my eyes rolled back in my head with delight at the sensation. Now he would drink. Now he would take what I was offering. He'd shove deep inside me and sink his teeth in as I came.

But he didn't drink. Blood welled on my breast, slid down the globe of it, and he leaned in and bit me again, right next to the other bite, his teeth sinking deep.

My mouth worked in a soundless gasp, watching as he withdrew again, only to bite once more. This bite wasn't the instant orgasm—he had to drink for that to happen. And once he drank, he'd send me to sleep, a magical side effect of his bite.

But I didn't go to sleep. And he wasn't drinking. Instead, he was painting my skin with bites, each one an exquisite burst of sharp pain followed by searing pleasure. He'd pull up to glance at me, his tongue licking my blood away from his fangs. Tasting me. My sex throbbed at the sight. God, he was sexy.

When he sank his teeth into the other breast, I moaned, jerking my arms against his hand. He held me tight, and I was helpless to do anything but writhe under him. This was torture. It was heaven. Each time, a sharp nip of pain was accompanied by an intense burst of pleasure.

"Do you want me, Jackie?" he rasped, even as he bit down again.

I moaned my need. "I do. Please, Zane."

"If you want more, then keep your hands on the headboard," he said softly, and released my hands. His own went to the waist of my dress, and with a loud tear, he tossed it away from my body. My panties snapped as if made out of cobwebs, and then I was bare under his gaze.

His mouth grazed down my belly and then he sank his teeth into the soft flesh surrounding my belly button.

I moaned, arching against him to sink his fangs further in. That bite was just a tease. I looked down to see the blood welling on my belly, my breasts streaked with crimson, and still he bit and snapped at me.

This wasn't rough sex. This was exquisite, biting torture, and my lover was my willing torturer.

My hips rose with need and I whimpered again, wishing he would slide downward. "Zane. Please."

His mouth grazed my hip, and he nipped lightly, just enough to draw blood. I watched him with hot eyes. "This isn't fair," I said, eyeing his bare chest and the erection that tented his jeans. "I want you naked too."

Completely casual, he ripped at his own jeans and they fell away from his body and landed on the floor. Well damn, that was a neat trick. His underwear soon followed and then Zane was totally naked over me. His body skimmed up mine, my blood painting his chest.

And he leaned in and gave me a kiss. "Is this what you wanted, Princess?"

I could feel the hot throb of him against my sex, long and hard and needing. I raised the cradle of my hips, bucking against him. "God yes. Please, Zane. I want you inside me. Right now."

"I'm not finished biting you," he said and sank his teeth into my lower lip, silencing me.

"You've already bitten me all over," I said between kisses, my blood mixing in my mouth. It was an erotic taste when one had a vampire for a lover. I didn't get off on the taste itself, but my body now knew it was a precursor to pleasure, and like one of Pavlov's dogs, the taste of my own blood made me pant with need.

"I'm not finished," he said, his voice husky. And before I could protest, he tugged my body against his and rolled in the bed. I was suddenly on top, my hands going to his bare chest, and he was below me.

"That's more like it," I said with a smile, leaning in to brush my breasts over his chest and rocking my hips against his cock.

"I want you on my face," he told me, red eyes gleaming.

A shot of lust pushed through my body. I actually blushed at his request. Not a command—never a command from my vampire. He was always careful to make everything my choice.

"Your face?" I said softly, sitting up.

He gave a short, jerky nod, his fingers reaching out to tease one of my tight, peaked breasts. "Still haven't bitten you everywhere, have I?"

Lust roared through me. Oh, God. Me, on his face, and he was going to… keep biting? I whimpered. His hands grasped my hips and tugged me forward. I fell toward him, my hands going to the headboard.

"That's it, Princess," he murmured. "The headboard. Do you want to put your hands there?"

He was deliberately forming his words, ensuring it wasn't a command. "All right," I said softly.

"I want your thighs here, though," he said, and patted the pillows next to his head.

I whimpered, but moved up his body. His hands went back to my thighs and he guided me forward. I clutched the headboard, digging my knees into the pillows next to Zane's head. This was really… vulnerable. We'd had all kinds of sex, but he never failed to surprise—and shock me—just a little. I was slick with need, though, at the thought of riding his face. My hips rocked a little as I hovered over him.

His big hands clasped my hips, dragging my body down toward him, and then I felt his tongue slide through the wet folds of my sex.

I moaned, trying to buck my hips. He held me pinned in place, and I felt his tongue slick along my clit, teasing, then he tilted my hips until his tongue thrust at my core.

My fingers dug into the headboard, and I pressed my cheek against it, needing something to hold on to. God. I looked down, watching his hooded red eyes gleam with pleasure as he tilted his mouth, licking at the cradle of my thighs. His gaze flicked up to me—pure satisfaction—and then he rocked me forward, shifting my hips and angling his face in response.

His teeth sank into the slippery, swollen flesh of my sex.

I screamed, clawing the headboard at the intense pleasure. Oh my fucking *God*. His fangs burned hot, buried in my skin. My hips tried to buck in response, but he still held me in place.

And then his tongue began to thrust deep inside of me.

Spearing me, over and over again, even as his teeth sank deeper into my folds. An orgasm ripped through me, hard and brutal and utterly delicious, and I screamed again, feeling my core clench tight even as he continued to thrust his tongue inside me. I wanted to rock my hips so badly, but he held me still, those fangs clamped on my softest flesh, bringing exquisite agony to my body.

As I came down from the orgasm, I felt his fangs slide out and then he tossed me backward onto the bed. I bounced hard, my breasts jolting at the sudden move. Then he was over me, my legs parted wide, and his cock thrust deep inside me, replacing his tongue. I moaned at the sudden move, at how full I felt. My hands reached for him even as he moved over me, his mouth nuzzling at my throat as he thrust into me again, hard. His teeth sank into my throat at the precise moment that he thrust once more, and I locked into another orgasm, yelling his name even as he pounded into me, his speed unnaturally fast.

Then he was growling against my neck, and his body shuddered against my own as my vampire came in my arms.

"I love you, Jackie," he murmured, kissing my throat and licking at the bite there.

"Love you too, Zane," I said with a soft yawn, even as I wrapped my arms around his neck. Another bite meant another rest for me, but I couldn't muster enough energy to care. I burrowed in against Zane's skin and slid into his dreams, where he kissed me and held me in his arms, even then.

~*~

Someone banged at the front door of the motel room. "You guys gonna sleep in there all goddamn day?"

I roused from my slumber, pushing my tangled hair out of my face. I peered blearily at my surroundings. Zane was lying in bed next to me, naked, his body curled around my own. I glanced over at the window. Sure enough, a line of sunlight gleamed under the curtain. Daytime. That meant Zane was going to sleep for a while.

The banging at the door came again. "Helloooooo," Remy called. "I know you're in there."

I got out of bed, dragging the sheet with me and wrapping it around my body. Zane had ripped my clothes off me earlier. It had been sexy at the moment, but now I looked at the pieces of my dress in dismay. I didn't exactly have a spare.

I opened the front door and Remy and Sophie stared back at me, both of them with eyes blazing bright blue in their faces.

Oops. Here I was, slaking my Itch with my master and they were still in need. "Good morning," I said brightly.

Remy glanced up and down at me in the sheet. "Damn, girl. You are a kinky fuck."

I glanced down. The sheet was spattered with blood, my skin covered with dried red lines. Awkward. "Oh. I tripped and fell."

"On his fangs? Over and over?" Remy said dryly, shoving her way inside the motel room, a notebook tucked under one arm. Sophie followed, her bronze face impassive despite the blue of her eyes.

Remy glanced around the room and shrieked at the sight of Zane, totally naked and sleeping in the bed. "Oh gross. Cover that shit up, Jackie. Like I want to see a vampire naked."

I rushed over to cover him with a blanket—I didn't want Remy seeing him naked either. Especially not when she and Sophie were in need. Remy I trusted. Sophie, I didn't know. As soon as he was covered, I turned around. "What are you guys doing here?"

Sophie picked up a piece of fabric off one of the tacky motel chairs and quirked an eyebrow at me. It was a remnant of Zane's underwear, now shredded. Blushing, I snatched it out of her hand and wadded it up, tossing it in the garbage.

"We brought food," Remy said, holding up a box of doughnuts and a jug of orange juice. She set it on the table and then sat down next to it, opening up her notebook again. "Sit. Eat."

"We also brought a change of clothing," Sophie added in an easy voice.

"Oh good," I said, sliding into the seat across from Remy, sheet wrapped around my body. I grabbed a doughnut and took an enormous bite out of it. "My clothing had an accident."

"Is that what you call it?" Remy said dryly. "Don't get too excited. Your change of clothing is my old dress."

I groaned. She'd been falling out of that dress. "Gee, thanks."

"You're welcome," she said cheerfully.

"We should move on soon if we are to evade Phryne and the others," Sophie said, her tone all business.

I sat at the table and crammed more doughnut into my mouth. God, I was starving. "How would Phryne possibly know where we are?" I looked uneasily at Sophie. I didn't know her. What if she'd sold us out?

But the warrior woman simply shrugged and pulled out a dagger, beginning to polish it. I wasn't sure if that was supposed to be a threat or just something she did when she was bored. It was impossible to tell with Sophie. "Ashara is a tracker. She knows a few tricks from days long past."

A tracker. Great. Just what we needed. I remembered Luc and his magic, and Dee and her voodoo powers. Damn it. I needed to learn some magic myself if everyone else was bringing it to the playing field. Totally unfair advantage.

I grabbed another doughnut and eyed Sophie. "Why are you helping us?"

Her too-blue eyes lit on my face, almost caressing, and I squirmed uncomfortably in my sheet. Was she into women? If that was the case, then why hadn't she and Remy hooked up to take care of the Itch? I knew Remy swung both ways. She had a preference for men, but she also didn't really care who she was sleeping with as long as she was getting something out of it, be it cash or pleasure. Or both.

At least, that was how she was prior to Ethan. Ethan's innocence and possessiveness made Remy rein in her natural ways to please him, though I knew it wasn't easy for her.

"She's cool, Jackie," Remy added quickly, not looking up from her notebook as she scribbled. "I know Sophie from back in the day. You can trust her."

I didn't take my gaze off Sophie's perfect face. "You were with Phryne, though. And they tried to kill my master."

Her mouth curved in the barest hint of a smile. "It is in my best interests to keep your master alive."

I narrowed my eyes at her. "And why is that?"

"Hey, Jackie!" Remy said in a too-loud voice, digging in one of the bags at her side. "You said you like bear claws, right?"

I took the one she tossed at me, licking my fingers to clean them. "Quit distracting me with food."

"You just need to leave Sophie alone," Remy said cheerfully. "She helped us. Don't be such a stick in the mud. For now, we need to get in the car and head toward Ethan. And we've got to find Sophie here a date."

"I am quite fine on my own," Sophie said calmly. "The Itch can be controlled, for now, with discipline." Her eyes skimmed the mess of our motel room. "And I am very disciplined."

Whoop dee doo, I thought, but said nothing. Instead, I grabbed the orange juice and swigged it straight from the jug. Then I took another bite of bear claw. "Remy, what are you writing down?"

She held up a finger, scratching away with the pen, then paused, staring down at the page. "Would you capitalize 'cock-gobbler'? It's not really a title."

Sophie snorted.

I leaned over the table. "What on *earth* are you writing?"

"My memoir. Duh, Jackie. Pay attention." She tapped the pen on her chin, thinking. "I can't decide what to call it. I need something catchy that rolls off the tongue. Like, *A Virgin's No-Holds-Barred Back-Door Entry into the World of Porn.*"

I held up a finger. "Number one, you weren't a virgin when you started in porn. And number two? *Gross.*"

"Yeah, but it's a proven fact that the word 'virgin' sells books. And this shit's not going to be totally autobiographical anyways. I can't mention the succubus thing. Just the sex and the cameras."

She shrugged and began to write again.

I watched her write for a moment more, then shook my head, trying to focus back on the topic. "I'm sorry, where did we say we were going?"

"Wherever," Remy said cheerfully. "Except not home, because that's where Phryne will be looking for us next. She stole your page, so she knows we're after something, and her curiosity is going to make her follow us to the ends of the earth until she finds out what we're seeking. She's a huge pain in the ass."

Sounded like it. "So how do we get rid of an immortal tail?"

Sophie gave me a hard look. "We go someplace that they cannot read us."

Remy snapped her fingers. "The monastery! There are so many immortal signatures there that they won't be able to track us. Plus, no succubus in her right mind would head straight to a house full of Serim."

"Uh, so why are *we* doing it, then?"

Remy grinned. "Because we're not in our right minds?"

CHAPTER FIVE

"Come on. What woman hasn't had to wrap her lips around something unsavory and sell it to the crowd?"—*Memoirs of a Flesh Peddler*, by Remy Summore

~*~

With the three of us working to carry Zane's limp form, we loaded him in the back of the rented SUV. I guess we weren't too worried about Phryne tailing us based on financial records, because we stopped at three drive-thru restaurants before leaving Pennsylvania. Remy drove the vehicle, and Sophie sat next to her in the front passenger seat. Her long legs were crossed on the seat and as I glanced up at her, she laid the backs of her palms on her knees, her eyes closing. Meditation? Yoga? She seemed oblivious to the country music that Remy had found and was currently singing at the top of her lungs.

I sat in the backseat, stuffed into Remy's too-tight black formal dress, Zane's head cradled in my lap. I stroked his hair as we drove. It was stupid to miss someone who was asleep half the day, and considering that we spent every day together, well, you'd think I'd get used to it.

But that just wasn't the case. I lived every day for sunset, and Zane's eyes cracking open, the satisfied look he'd give me as he gazed upon me. I was the first thing he saw when he awoke every day, and the last thing he saw when he went to sleep.

All in all, immortality? Not so bad with him by my side. It might even be fun to live a jillion years and never age, as long as I spent that jillion with Zane. I liked the thought of that.

We crossed several states as we drove, Remy speeding all the way. Ethan was visiting a monastery somewhere on the shores of Lake Erie, so that was where we were headed. As we crossed the miles, Remy began to bounce in her seat, her hands gripping the steering wheel.

"You okay?" I asked her at one point.

"Don't talk to me unless you want to reach up here and give me a handjob," she snarled.

I shut my mouth. Okay. Touchy. I glanced over at Sophie. Her gaze was on Zane's unconscious face, though it darted away when I caught her, and she went back to meditating.

The skin on the back of my neck prickled. Why was Sophie so interested in Zane? I didn't like it. How did we know that she wasn't going to betray us to Phryne?

I stroked Zane's hair harder, growing more and more upset at the thought of him being bound and chained in Phryne's basement. Yue had asked me how many masters I had left. She'd been planning on killing Zane, but wanted to ensure that I remained alive.

I'd never let her touch a hair on his head.

"Almost there," Remy said sometime later, and I glanced out the window. The afternoon sun was still high, the waves of Lake Erie rippling on the right side of the window. We drove up a long, winding path, seemingly deserted.

As we turned into the driveway, another car zoomed by and I frowned. Had I caught a glimpse of peach-colored hair in the Mustang that had just rolled past? Was Phryne on to us, even now? I shuddered at the thought.

"Yup, this is the right place," Remy said, dragging my attention back to her. She pointed out the car window to a privacy fence that ran through the thick trees and ended in an open gate. She revved the engine, frowned, and then revved it again. Our wheels spun in place.

My skin began to tingle with awareness even as Remy swore, pressing on the pedal.

"Sensor wards," Sophie said in a soft voice. "They know we are here, and they know we have arrived with a vampire. You will need to park here and continue on foot. Our car cannot move forward as long as the vampire's in it."

"Well, then we stop here," I said, my fingers clutching into Zane's coat protectively.

I waited for someone to protest, but Remy only sighed and shut off the car. "Come on, then. Let's go get my man."

"I don't know if we should go in," I said after a moment. "If this place is warded against vampires, I don't know that succubi are particularly welcome."

"I don't care," Remy said stubbornly. "Ethan won't let them hurt us."

The look Sophie gave her worried me. And I worried anew when Sophie glanced back at Zane. Damn it. Why couldn't it be late afternoon so he'd awaken? I stared at the distant monastery. Farther down the drive, a large, stately stone manor sat surrounded by trees. As I stared from the gates, the front door opened and several men stepped out and my hackles rose. They wore the monastic robes I'd seen on Enforcers, but these carried crossbows and the flasks strapped to their waists were not, I guessed, for wine. More like holy water.

In other words, they were expecting a fight.

I slid out of the car, shutting the door carefully to protect the still-sleeping Zane, and moved forward. Sophie did the same, though for once I was glad to see that she'd drawn her blades. Remy trotted behind us.

A man approached, his skin golden, his hair a dark shock of curls set off by a well-trimmed goatee. He wore one of the pure white monastic robes, but his belt was full of armaments. As he strode forward, he gestured for the others to stay back. He looked at me, then at Sophie. "You are not welcome here."

"Bullshit," Remy said, pushing forward. "Where is Ethan?"

"The Enforcer is being detained," the man said in a cool, detached voice. "Drop your weapons, and give the vampire over to us."

"Detained?" Remy said, her voice rising. "Oh *hell* no. Do you not see how horny I am right now?"

The Serim continued to stare at her impassively. "You may only enter the monastery if you are unarmed and the vampire is given to our keeping."

"Those terms are not acceptable," Sophie said in a calm voice. She drew her sword and brandished it.

Behind the front Serim, the other three drew up their crossbows, aiming at us.

"Look, we don't want any trouble," Remy said. "We just came here to pick up my man and hide out for a night or two."

"Ethan will not be joining you."

Remy's lips curled into a snarl. "You are kidding me."

"Hand over the vampire," the Serim said, "and you shall be our guests."

"No," I said, stepping in front of the car protectively. "You can't have him. We'll go."

"You're not going anywhere," the man began. He reached out to grab Remy.

Sophie danced forward, her blade slicing through the air.

The man's hand landed on the ground.

"Oh shit!" Remy said, just as I turned to stare at Sophie in surprise. The other three Serim approached, weapons ready, as the first one backed up and hissed, clutching his bleeding stump.

Sophie spun, tossing a throwing star at the first one and slamming it into his chest. He groaned and paused, digging the blade out of his chest. The other two continued to advance.

"You bitch," the man grated, holding the stump of his arm. "You'll pay for this."

"Behind me," Sophie said in that same cool voice, ignoring the man.

I didn't have to be told twice. I skidded to a stop behind her, keeping out of reach of one of her longer blades. If Sophie wanted to do all the fighting, I was totally okay with that.

Remy ran to my side. "Are you sure this is wise?" I called to Sophie.

"They will not take the vampire on my watch," she proclaimed, and began to do another little spin that marked the throwing of another star.

"Stop!" A hard, authoritative voice rose above the crowd.

I groaned. I knew that voice.

Remy gasped with delight.

"Put down your weapons," the man said, striding forward down the long driveway. The Serim parted to allow him a look at our party, and I got my first look at the newcomer, confirming my suspicions.

Noah. Goddamn it.

"Noah," Remy cried in delight, running forward to hug him. "It's so good to see you!"

He accepted Remy's hug, but his gaze remained locked on me.

Noah Gideon, my other master. Zane's rival. And he did not look pleased to see me.

The feeling was mutual. It wasn't that I didn't like Noah, it was that Noah wanted me to fall in love with him, and I couldn't.

I was in love with Zane. I cared about Noah, but in a friends-with-benefits sort of way. Noah wanted it to be more, and when I'd chosen Zane over him, he'd been furious and abandoned me. Delilah—my fellow succubus—had followed him, but I didn't see her around.

Noah seemed different. Hard. Gone was the warmth and understanding in his eyes. Though his thick, collar-brushing blond hair was the same, his tan looked deeper, his clothing a bit less crisp. As he moved forward, I gasped. His clothing shifted, displaying tattoos. They covered his skin at his collar, and I saw the hint of more at the cuffs of his long sleeves.

One hundred tasks of servitude, Ariel had told me with a smug smile on his face.

In exchange for the "sin" of creating me, Noah had been found guilty by the Serim council and sentenced to one hundred tasks to be meted out by his Serim brothers. Did Noah wear their promises like the one I wore on my wrist? I'd promised the Archangel Gabriel that I'd retrieve two haloes for him, and he'd tattooed his name on my wrist as a reminder of my promise.

Noah was... covered. I swallowed hard. I was guessing he regretted ever seeing me right about now. His hard gaze swept over Remy, who was still bouncing with excitement at the sight of him. Over Sophie, her tall, strong form bristling with blades, poised to strike. Over me, standing in front of the car as if that might somehow protect Zane. His cool, hard gaze didn't speak of friendship or kinship at all. He looked at me like a jilted lover.

"Is the vampire with you?" His words were clipped. Furious.

"He is," I said softly.

"Then why do you come to me?"

He thought we'd come to him for protection? "Remy's here to pick up Ethan," I began lamely. "And we thought since we were in the area..."

His gaze flicked over me. "So you did not know I was here?"

Boy, did I *not* know. If I had, I'd have suggested going anywhere but here. Old boyfriends made things a little awkward, especially when those old boyfriends could command me with a word. And since Noah was my master, I had to obey his slightest command. He wasn't shy about giving them, either.

"Why are you here?" He approached me, his voice going soft, his gray-blue eyes scanning me as if he hadn't seen me in years, instead of mere months.

"Remy and Sophie are in need," I blurted.

His gaze went to my bleached eyes. I was most definitely *not* in need. "I see," he said brusquely. "You are welcome here, but the vampire will not be allowed into the monastery proper."

"Will he be hurt?"

Noah gave me a hard look. "I would not wound you like that, Jackie."

And he turned and walked back into the monastery.

So he said. I hesitated, torn. I didn't want to leave Zane with these jackasses. He was too vulnerable while the sun was up. And I couldn't help but think of the car that had driven past, and the glimpse of brightly colored hair I'd seen as it had zoomed by. What if Phryne was here, just waiting for a chance to strike? "I don't know, Noah."

Noah paused as he passed Sophie, giving her a long look, eyeing her amber skin covered in tattoos, her weapons, her wild ponytail. She met his gaze with a frank, open one of her own that seemed to irritate him. He glanced back at me and saw I still hadn't moved. "Jackie, come."

Goddamn it.

Gritting my teeth, I moved to follow after him, compelled.

Remy followed close behind me, bouncing with every step, her eyes incredibly blue. "Can we move this along, already? I am Itching like mad."

The Serim glared as I passed by, and one moved forward to scoop his hand off the ground. The others didn't look thrilled either. Combine that with a pissy ex-boyfriend and the fact that Zane was unable to rise for hours?

"Promise me that Zane is going to be safe," I blurted.

Noah didn't turn around, didn't stop walking, which meant I had to keep moving forward as well. "I make no such promise," he said. "Nor will I. My brothers are free to do as they please."

That was *exactly* what I was afraid of. "I will hate your guts until my dying days if you let something happen to Zane."

"Undying days," Remy said helpfully, still bouncing in place, unable to contain her excitement at seeing Ethan.

"Undying," I corrected. "I'm not leaving Zane unguarded." Just the thought made me skittish as hell. Not that I could stop from following Noah after he'd commanded it, but sometimes you had to push him to get the point across.

"Do not worry," Sophie said in her calm, accented voice. "I will remain outside with him. He will be safe with me."

As I looked at her in surprise, she twirled her sword, as if admiring the way it gleamed in the sunlight. Or admiring its ability to lop off heads? Who knew with Sophie.

"You'll stay with him?" I glanced back at the car where Zane slumbered, then Sophie's tall, statuesque form. I wasn't sure that I trusted her, but I couldn't think of anyone better qualified to guard Zane than a six-foot-tall Amazon, bristling with weapons.

Who had also just cut off the hand of the nearest immortal. I had to admit, that had pretty much rocked my world.

She gave a firm nod, planting the tip of her sword in the ground in front of the car and standing straight and tall behind it, as if daring any to approach.

"You'll be cool out here?" Remy asked.

Another firm nod. "You may send someone my way to tend to my needs later." And she gave a blatant look at Noah's retreating back.

"Dinner?" I asked, because I was afraid of the mental image otherwise.

"Sex," Remy stage-whispered.

"Thanks for that," I muttered dryly.

Remy moaned, holding her own breasts. "Can we just go inside already? My body is dying here. *Dying.*"

"You're not dying because you're a few hours overdue," I grumped, casting one last look behind us at Sophie as we followed Noah into the monastery.

"Says the woman who we had to wait on this morning."

I was surprised to find myself blushing, especially when Noah turned back to glare at the two of us. Awkward.

All of that was forgotten as we entered the cool marble foyer and Ethan appeared at the end of the hallway, his long black hair pulled into a taut ponytail atop his head. He wore a plain white robe, belted at the waist—a far cry from the too-tight Diesel jeans and tees that Remy insisted on dressing him in.

She gave a little squeal at the sight of him and bolted down the hall, bounding toward him.

Ethan stoically put his arms out for her and she leapt into them. Her legs wrapped around his waist and she climbed him, breathless little pants echoing in the hall. A second later, her mouth planted on his. Her jeans rode low on her ass, exposing half of her backside as she rocked her hips over his. Moans of delight filled the air as she began to kiss him wildly, her hand tugging his long ponytail. "God, you sexy beast," she groaned. "Take me."

Ethan kissed her back, at first reticent, but under Remy's onslaught, he began to warm up, kissing her back with abandon. The acolytes behind him stared with shock at the two of them.

"She's overdue," I explained, then cleared my throat. "And they probably need a room."

"This way," said one of the Serim.

Remy and Ethan didn't look up as they staggered after the Serim, Remy dry-humping Ethan all the while.

Noah turned to me and gestured at one of the nearby doors. "I believe you and I should talk."

"Really? Because I'm pretty sure we're just here to pick up that one," I said, thumbing a gesture down the hall. "No time for the meet and greet. I imagine she'll be done with him in about ten minutes and then we'll be on our way."

Sophie could always pick herself up a nice trucker at a rest stop or something.

"I would like for you to stay for dinner," Noah said persuasively.

My stomach rumbled. Damn you, stomach. I crossed my arms over my chest, thinking. "I don't know, Noah." Just being here with him, with Zane so close nearby, knowing they hated each other... it made me edgy.

"Stay for dinner," he said in a harder voice, and it wasn't a request. It was a command.

Damn him. "Staying," I said in a flat voice. "What's on the menu?"

~*~

57

"This doesn't have to be awkward," Noah said, tucking my hand in the crook of his elbow as though we were heading to a dinner party.

"Doesn't it?" I said. "You're holding me captive, more or less. I told you I couldn't stay." The last thing I wanted was to be here this afternoon. "Zane will be up soon and—"

"Don't mention him again," Noah said in a cold, unfriendly voice.

Grr. A command. "You get more high-handed the longer I know you."

"I tried to do things your way, Jackie," Noah said. "Gave you a bit of lead, but you don't seem to want to cooperate."

"That was doing things my way?" I gave a bitter laugh. "That's rich."

His jaw clenched. "Since you refuse to listen to what I have to say, I'm forced to have you as a captive audience. If that's what it takes to get my point across, that's what it takes."

"And here I thought I was lucky to have two masters who were nice to me," I said. "Guess that was wrong on my part."

"Nothing so bad as that, Jackie. I merely want to catch up with you, not hold you captive."

So he said. "You promise?"

His gaze darkened, his mouth thinning. "Have you forgotten I am covered in promises?"

"Then you won't mind making one more, will you?"

"I promise," he said, his teeth gritting. He paused in the hallway, his gaze roaming over me. "I have missed you, Jackie."

I melted a little at that, my thorniness abating a little. Before Noah had left, we'd been happy. We'd been friends and lovers, and he'd supported and shared my enthusiasm for archaeology.

All of that seemed so long ago now. I smiled at him, relaxing and just a bit wistful. "I miss you too, Noah. We had fun together."

"But not enough?"

Sigh. "No, not enough for me to give up Zane. I'm sorry. That's not what I want."

Instead of digging into that, he simply studied me. "Are you in trouble, Jackie?"

"It depends." How much was Yue going to blame me for that broken neck?

"You're on the run again, aren't you?"

"Not me exactly," I hedged.

He gave me an exasperated look. "How does one lone immortal manage to find herself in so much trouble?"

God, I asked myself that all the time. "Maybe I was conceived under an unlucky star," I bit back. "You didn't think to consult my star chart before having sex with me that first night, did you?"

"What is it?"

I hesitated. I didn't want to tell Noah. As soon as he found out that I was seeking two more haloes, he'd stick his nose in and try to take over things. Noah wanted to help me. Sometimes too much. And the last time he'd bailed me out, he'd earned himself a body full of tattoos and indentured servitude.

I eyed the tattoos now, and I reached for his sleeve, tugging it. Words danced along his skin, written in an old script that no one could read but those who had fallen. "So why don't you tell me about all this, Noah?"

"You know what it is. My penance." His expression became grim. "A hundred tasks, remember?"

It had been three months. I stared at the tasks, my mouth dry. Each word represented another promise he owed. "How many have you done?"

"Six."

Six? Oh jeez. Noah would be serving the Serim for a decade at this rate. Maybe longer. Were they going to draw his penance out deliberately? "Noah, I am so sorry about all of this. It's my fault."

"You did not ask to be made, Jackie," he said quietly. "You can blame Zane for that. I know I do."

I rolled my eyes. "Here we go again."

"I am surprised you are here with Sophie at your side," he admitted.

"Sophie? Why?"

He gave me a long, hard look. "You don't know?"

I stiffened. Oh great. Another tidbit of information that Noah was going to dole out to try and wreck my relationship with Zane and my friends. Or both. "You know what? We can't stay after all. Let me leave."

"Not until you've told me what you're running from. What sort of trouble have you gotten into now?"

Not a command. I glared at him, refusing to answer. Knowing him, he'd get it in his head that he needed to find Phryne and get that page back from her, and I suspected that she'd want it for herself once she found out what we were after.

Damn it. Without that page, we were flying blind. That was the closest I'd gotten to the missing haloes yet. Damn Phryne and her twisted sense of helping me out.

"Jackie," Noah said in a warning tone.

Down the hall, a door opened, and I could hear the sound of cutlery scraping against plates. A man came down the hall, dressed in robes. He extended his hands toward me, his skin gleaming like mahogany, a wide smile on his sculpted face. "Ah, you must be our guest. Come, join us for dinner."

I looked over at Noah uncertainly. The last Serim I'd met had been a rapey asshole who'd tried to impregnate me.

Noah gave a tight smile. "Jackie, this is Samuel, one of my brother Serim."

Samuel smiled sweetly at me and took my hand in his own. "Noah has told me so much about you."

Had he? Well, at least I wasn't a dirty little secret. "I don't know if we can stay," I protested. "My friends—"

"It will be taken care of," Samuel said with another gorgeous smile. His eyes were a startling pale blue in his face. "Please give me but a moment."

As I watched, he took Noah aside. "One of their company is in need," Samuel said in a low voice, and I edged closer a fraction, listening in.

"I do not care," Noah said in a hard voice. "We're not here to service others. We're here for a measure of peace."

"It's very important to the council that succubi are encouraged to visit. If they know we will see to their needs, perhaps they will return to us when they need a favor. You know the council encourages such things."

I shuddered. So Noah was being asked to go sweet-talk Sophie in the hopes that she'd owe them a favor somewhere down the road? And then what? Have her bear an Enforcer baby? Manipulative jerks.

I could practically hear Noah's jaw clench at Samuel's words. "I am not the council's puppet."

"Are you not?" Samuel asked, touching a word on the side of Noah's jaw. It lit up as if on fire from within, the symbols darkly outlined against his tanned skin.

A pained expression crossed Noah's face.

"I invoke a promise from you, Noah Gideon," Samuel said quietly. "Seek out the succubus Sophie and see to her needs this day. Treat her as you would a treasured lover. It is a favor to all of us." When Noah said nothing, Samuel added, "I could tell that she appreciated your form. I am sure hers was equally pleasing. I will keep your friend occupied."

With a glance back at me, Noah gave Samuel a tight bow and then stalked back down the hall.

Leaving me alone with Samuel. Goody. The Serim was all smiles as he approached me, noting my apprehension. "Do not be alarmed, sister. You are safe in these walls."

"You'll forgive me if the last Serim I chatted with was a big fat liar."

He laughed. "We also are not so fond of Ariel."

"In that case, any enemy of his is a friend of mine," I said dryly.

"Come, eat," Samuel said, drawing me back toward the dining hall once more.

"I don't know," I hesitated. "We really should be going soon." Zane would be waking up at dusk, and Sophie's eyes were lit up like beacons—I didn't want her pouncing on my vampire as soon as he was awake. And Remy was likely slaking her thirst as we spoke.

"You and your friends must stay overnight. Let us refuel you before you head back out on your journey."

The delicious scents carried from the dining hall. Were those tater tots I smelled? Curse my succubus stomach. "I really shouldn't," I forced myself to say.

"Your friends are taken care of. Ethan has seen to Remy, and Noah will see to your friend Sophie. As you heard, I have requested that he see to her needs."

I stared at Samuel. "You mean you pimped him out."

"The promise I invoked is not compulsion," Samuel said with an easy smile at me. Too easy. "If Noah truly wished to avoid the succubus, he would ignore my request. Servicing her needs services his own."

Servicing? Gross. Poor Sophie was mad with the Itch right about now. Looking at Samuel's face, I decided that he was nice and smiley, but underneath, he was the same old asshole as Ariel. He didn't care about what Noah wanted, just what it could do for him.

To him, this was all hospitality, just like dinner. Invite the guests in, serve them an afternoon snack, diddle the succubi.

God, immortals were bizarre.

And Noah had looked furious at the command. I felt a twinge of pity for him. Weird that I wasn't jealous. I was simply relieved that Sophie wouldn't be digging her claws into Zane.

"Really should be going," I muttered again as Samuel entered the dining hall a few steps ahead of me. How fast could I get through this meal and back out of here? Not so fast that I would catch Sophie on Noah, or something. I wasn't jealous, but I also didn't want to see that. At all. But Phryne and her cronies would be looking for us, which meant we needed to keep moving if we wanted to get to that halo before she figured out what she had in her possession.

The thoughts died as I stared up at the ceiling of the dining hall. Ornate symbols lined the walls in perfect, familiar patterns. Seven perfect circles traveled the length of the arched ceiling of the hall, surrounded by ancient writing. A spiky crown lay at the cardinal points, and ancient writing looped all around the entire drawing.

I'd seen those symbols before.

On my freaking page that Phryne had stolen.

"You know what?" I told Samuel, forcing myself to look away from the ceiling. "I am just famished."

CHAPTER SIX

"Woe to the woman who falls in love in this business. It'll lead to nothing but heartbreak. You need to learn to fuck well and to fuck without emotion. Otherwise, you'll just get fucked in the end. Also, how cool is it that I just used 'woe' in a sentence?"—*So You Want to Be a Porn Star*, by Remy Summore

~*~

I forced myself to ignore the ceiling all through dinner, lest I give away my true motive. Instead, I played the sociable guest. I smiled and chatted with Samuel (who seemed nice enough, I supposed, for one of his kind) and the other Serim.

Three Enforcers ate dinner at the far end of the table, and it was obvious from the looks they cast in my direction that they didn't know what to make of me. That was just fine, since the sight of them disturbed me just as much. Three of them, not including Ethan. And this was not the only Serim monastery. How many Enforcers were there? I thought of Phryne and the others, and as Remy and Ethan entered the room and sat down to dinner, I compared Ethan's high cheekbones and almond eyes to Yue's beautiful, delicate features. Was she his mother? How many succubi had been forced to breed a son and had the child taken away from them?

Jesus. The more I thought about that, the more I thought Phryne and her "Girl Power" crew weren't so crazy after all.

I kept these thoughts to myself, though. Remy seemed happy enough, her eyes bleached a cheerful, sated silver. She fed hot dogs and tater tots to Ethan and cooed to him during dinner. Ethan was quiet, the look on his face alternately adoring and awed as he stared down at Remy. Someone's world had clearly been rocked just a short time ago.

The meal seemed to last an eternity. When dinner was over, I yawned hugely, hoping that the Serim would see my pretend exhaustion and assign us a room for the evening.

Remy stared at me.

The Serim stared as well.

Oops. I patted my mouth and smiled sheepishly. "Been around humans too much. Have to fake being tired and all."

They seemed to accept this, though Remy gave me an odd look.

"Will you be staying the evening with us, Jackie?" Samuel asked.

"Oh no," Remy began.

I kicked her under the table and leaned forward, resting my chin on my hands. "*Love* to."

"I'm pleased to hear that. Noah will be happy to see that you've decided to stay for a short time. He has many things he wishes to talk to you about."

Oh, I could just imagine. And he hadn't even had time to order me to do anything but stay for dinner. "So do I get a room? What about my vampire?"

Samuel shook his head. "I'm afraid the grounds are warded. He won't be able to enter."

"That's okay," I said quickly. "Sophie's with him so I'm sure he'll be fine."

Remy stared at me, jaw slack. "Who are you and what—"

I kicked her under the table again, smiling. I needed alone time with this ceiling, and I was not going to get it if Remy kept sabotaging me.

She gave me a puzzled look, then shrugged and turned back to Ethan, wiggling another tater tot at him. "Open wide, snuggums."

~*~

Soon enough, the Serim retired. I was shown to a room, Ethan went back to his own room with Remy, and I could hardly contain myself with excitement. The symbols were on the ceiling. All I needed to do was take a picture of it with my phone…

Shit. I hadn't had my phone in my dress when Phryne had

stolen us. We'd left it back at the hotel, so it was probably long gone. I chewed my lip, thinking. Maybe Remy had hers. Or Sophie.

Actually… Sophie carried swords. And knives. A phone might not fit in that weapon belt of hers. I rummaged through the guest room looking for pen and paper instead. If I couldn't take a picture, I'd just have to recreate it myself with my limited artistic skill.

Pen and paper tucked into the cleavage of my borrowed dress, I smoothed my hair and then peeked out my door. An Enforcer stood at the end of the hall, holding a staff. Not Ethan. This one had the gangly form of a teenage boy and probably had not hit maturity yet. Well, that was a good thing—that meant my admittedly wimpy succubus powers could probably take him out.

I didn't hesitate to use those powers, brushing my fingertips on his skin and watching with satisfaction as his eyes rolled back in his head. He went down quickly, crashing into a heap, and I waited a moment for a telltale snore. Satisfied, I knelt at his side, keeping my fingers pressed to his forehead to see what I'd learn. He didn't have a phone in his pockets and to my annoyance, he didn't know anything about the large painting on the ceiling in the dining hall, other than that it had always been there. Not helpful.

Out of curiosity, I tried to find out who his mother was. I'd met quite a few succubi in the last few days and looked for their faces, but it was a no-go. Just as well. Propping him up against the wall, I clutched a hand to the paper shoved in my bra and tiptoed down the hall. Now if I could just avoid seeing anyone else…

Other than my acolyte guard, the place was deserted. The Serim were in their night-sleep, and Zane would be awakening. Any minute now, he'd be calling for me, shouting my name at the top of his lungs. Sick with fear for my safety.

Any minute now.

Actually, it was kind of strange that we hadn't heard anything from Sophie or Zane. I was starting to worry. What if Phryne had pounced on them while I'd been in here schmoozing the Serim? I'd never forgive myself. Anxiety clenched my stomach and I forced myself to calm down. Getting a copy of that design on the ceiling of the dining hall was the most important thing right now. Zane would understand.

I pushed open the doors to the dining hall and entered quietly, wincing at the creak of the door. No one sounded an alarm.

Emboldened, I flipped the light switch and stared up at the mural in triumph.

How the eff had I gotten so lucky? Did they even know what they sat under every night? I stared up at it in awe, mentally comparing it to the page I'd had in my possession for so short a time. There it was, just like the last one. Seven haloes, each ring interrupted by ancient writing. Each one dotted with symbols for the sun, the moon, and other divine markings. There were subtle changes—the center of the ring was empty this time, and not a pyramid. The colors of the rings and the text on the edges of the mural looked different, but I'd worry about that later. And edging around the outermost halo was a three-pronged crown at each of the cardinal points—north, south, east, and west.

Those crowns meant something. I had no clue as to what.

I wasted no time in copying down the information. I didn't know how long it'd be before someone came upon me here in the dining hall, so I'd make use of the time I had. With my pencil and paper in hand, I began to sketch, taking extra care with the strange, slashing writing that decorated the edges of the circles.

A few minutes later, the door behind me creaked open. I jumped and turned quickly, hiding the paper behind me.

Remy poked her head in, glancing around the room before her gaze landed on me. "There you are!"

I put a finger to my lips, motioning for silence even as I waved her forward with my other hand.

She tiptoed in, Ethan two steps behind her, their hands clasped together. Remy's hair was disheveled and tumbling around her face, her eye color reset to a pale silver. Ethan had a dazed expression, and his long hair was even more snarled than Remy's, his robes askew.

"Reunited?" I asked dryly.

"And it feels sooooo good," Remy agreed, She leaned over and tugged at Ethan's hair until he bent down, and she kissed him again. "My snuggums missed me terribly. We had to make all the bad memories go away fast."

I rolled my eyes. "Have snuggums shut the door. I'm trying to do a sketch here."

"What are you drawing?" Remy asked, pulling away from Ethan to come stand by my side. He gave her an adoring look before going to close the door to the dining hall, his eyes flashing with a good deed. Though created from a succubus and a Serim, Ethan's kind seemed to get none of the drawbacks—they were immortal, healed fast, didn't sleep, didn't have the ravening need for sex. Instead, they fed off good deeds. A small favor might feed Ethan for a few hours. A big deed? For days. Helping Remy with her succubus curse? Kept him sated in more ways than just one.

Ethan clearly adored Remy—that much was obvious. My own lover should have been awake. He'd be hungry and needing to drink blood. It made me a bit anxious to think that he was out there, awake, and not looking for me. How codependent was that?

"So that symbol," Remy said, turning down one corner of my paper. "What is that, like a vagina or something?"

I pulled the paper away from her, scowling. "It's a series of circles."

She tilted her head, staring at the picture, then at the ceiling. "Huh. You suck at drawing circles. I'm not kidding. It looks more like a vagina."

"I'm in a hurry," I said, resisting the urge to smack her in the back of the head. "This would be a lot easier if that jerk Phryne hadn't messed things up for us."

"So you're drawing vaginas in her honor?"

I glared at her. "Can I work on this?"

"That's fine," she said, waving a hand at me. "I'll just be over here, cranky pants."

"Give me ten minutes," I said, trying not to be too anxious. "I'll finish this and then we'll go get Zane. I'm worried that he's so quiet out there."

"Mmm," Remy said.

I lifted my head from the paper again. "What's that mean?"

"Hmm? Nothing."

"You mmmed. That's not nothing. That's an 'I'm deliberately being quiet but I know something Jackie doesn't' sort of mmm."

"No it's not."

I sighed and bent back over my paper again. Goddamn it, it did look like a vagina. My concentric circles were not so concentric. I picked up the pencil again.

"I was just going to say," Remy began, distracting me all over again. I looked up to see her trailing a finger over the table. "He's probably being quiet because of Sophie."

My heart slammed into my throat, pounding so hard that I

couldn't breathe. "You think she would hurt him?"

Now Remy looked confused. "Huh? No. Not at all."

"Then what? I don't understand."

She chewed on her lip, clearly torn. "We're BFFs and all, girlfriend, but some shit is not mine to spill, you know? Zane and Sophie just have a… history." She gave me a meaningful look.

Oh. Was that all? I shook my head. "If they had history, it's in the past. I trust Zane."

"That wasn't quite what I meant," she said, then waved a hand. "Never mind. Finish drawing your vagina."

I gritted my teeth and went back to sketching, trying to be as accurate as I could. The light in the room was low, and I wasn't gifted with super vision. Couple that in with Remy and Ethan nearby, and Remy's soft giggles as she played "tickle monster" with Ethan, well. It was making me think about Zane more and more.

A sudden flash of bright light caught my attention. I looked up sharply, only to see Remy with a phone in her hand. She took a picture of the ceiling, then squinted at the phone.

"Where did you get that?" I reached for it, and she snatched it back out of my hands.

"From my lover." She made a kissy face at Ethan. "He promised to sext me while he was gone and he never did."

"I sent you pictures as you requested," Ethan said in his stuffy tone.

"Yeah, but you were clothed, babe. Ain't the same." She winked at him and lifted the phone to take another picture.

"Can I borrow that?" I put my hand out.

Remy tossed it in my direction. I caught it and folded up my drawing with a sigh. "I can't believe you didn't tell me you had a phone."

"It is a penis move," Ethan agreed in a stiff voice.

"*Dick* move, baby," Remy corrected, then grinned over at me. "I'm teaching him street slang. Isn't it cute?"

"Word," Ethan said, then looked to Remy for approval.

Oh lord. "It's something, all right."

~*~

We finished recording the ceiling with some grainy pictures on Ethan's phone. I figured between that and my sketches, we'd have

68

it covered. With that, we tied up the teen Enforcer that I'd knocked out, left him in my bed, and then woke him up before we made our getaway. We quickly left the monastery, heading for the gate. Now I was really worried about Zane and Sophie. They'd been utterly silent. Not one call for us? Not even one shout? One attempt to bust down the front doors?

I didn't know what to make of that.

There, out at the front gate of the monastery where we'd left it, sat our rental car. Sophie sat on the hood of the car, cross-legged in a meditation pose. Leaning against the car, Zane smoked a cigarette, his gaze flicking back at the house, and then at Sophie, and then back at the house.

"We're here," I announced as we raced down the steps of the monastery. "Let's get going."

Zane threw down his cigarette, relief lighting his features. "Good. Let's ditch this joint."

You didn't have to tell me twice. I moved to his side and lifted my arms to wrap around his neck, raising my mouth for a kiss.

"We need to talk," Zane rasped before slanting his mouth over mine in a hard, possessive kiss. "Later, when we're alone."

A shiver of foreboding crept through me. "Can we talk now?"

My heart thudded slowly as Zane looked over at Sophie, who sat, serenely ignoring us. Her eyes, I noticed, were bleached silver. So Noah *had* been out here. If that was the case, why was Zane acting so odd? I immediately turned to look to him, but his eyes were still red with hunger.

Waiting for me. I relaxed. God, how silly of me to worry about such a thing. Zane loved me. Had given up everything for me. He'd never look at another woman. It was just me being neurotic.

But when he gave Sophie another black scowl, I couldn't help but worry. Something was off.

"All aboard," Remy said, pumping her arm in a mimic of a train whistle. "Let's get this party started."

Zane looked at me. "Where are we going?"

I pulled the crinkling paper out of my pocket and handed it to him. "I was hoping you could tell us. This is like the book, but the symbols aren't all the same. Check it out. The crowns are on the outside this time."

He peered at the drawing, then back at me. "You said this is the same?"

I nodded enthusiastically.

He tilted the paper, studying it. "It looks like a vagina."

I snatched the paper back from him. "You suck."

He clicked his teeth at me with a fanged grin, and my heart fluttered at the flirty move.

I pushed the drawing at him. "Can you decipher this? Does it tell what we're looking for?"

He shook his head at me. "I can't read it."

I grimaced. "Is it my drawing? I took pictures of it, if those will help."

"No, it's not the drawing. It's the language. I think it's Phoenician." He held the page out to Sophie. "Can you read this?"

I wanted to snatch it back and tell him she could look at it later. But I bit my tongue, glancing over at Remy. She was whispering something in Ethan's ear, and his eyes widened, his gaze moving to Sophie and then to Zane.

Goddamn it.

As graceful as a ballerina, Sophie got up from her seated position and moved to Zane's side, taking the page between her thumb and forefinger. Her fingers flexed on the paper, long, elegant brown fingers covered in swirling tattoos. She looked down at the page, then raised her silver gaze back to my face. "It's an ancient Scythian dialect. I can read it." Her voice was smooth, melodious.

I wondered if Noah had enjoyed his "duty" with her. Ugh. Then I hated that I'd even thought about it. I wasn't sure how I felt about the whole thing. I didn't want Noah, right? So why did I have this "Don't play with my toys" sort of mentality around Sophie? Was it because she was an unknown quantity, and I'd learned not to trust those?

"Well?" Zane said, impatient.

With a bored sigh, Sophie tilted the paper. "In the stone crown of the sun, only one shall bear the kiss of the eternal. He must first pass the madman's way and the measure of the unknowing before finding the truth deep in the belly of the lake. Those who push to succeed shall end up with the spoils, or with none."

Remy jingled the car keys. "What is that, some sort of shitty haiku?"

"It's a puzzle," Zane said grimly. "A key to where a halo is, but only part of the message. The other page was written in angelic script. *That,* I could read."

"And this was in Scythian," I said thoughtfully, taking the page from Sophie when she held it back out to me. The Scythians were an ancient race that had lived in what was now Iran. Nowhere close to here, yet the entire thing looked so familiar that it was driving me crazy. Where had I seen it before?

"The crown of the sun," Ethan repeated. "And the picture is of a sun. If we find that symbol, will we find the halo?"

Good, helpful Ethan. I thought hard. "Maybe. It would have to be someplace old. As old as the Scythians," I said, looking over at Sophie. Was she Scythian? Her lovely oval face and tall, lean body could have been from any time, any place, but her coloring and thick, lush black curls could be Middle Eastern—or the predecessor to it.

"Do you know of any sun crowns, Sophie?" Remy asked helpfully.

"I do not," Sophie said. "I have no use for kings, alive or dead."

Sun crowns. The words rattled in my mind, trying to jar something loose. I stared at the picture and the writing. Sun. A crown of the sun. I didn't know what that was. I stared at the crowns surrounding the circle of haloes. It looked so damn familiar. I knew I'd seen that somewhere before. I knew—

My stomach sank like a rock as I recognized the symbol. I tilted the picture. Those weren't crowns around the circle. Those were flames surrounding the circle of haloes. The entire picture was one big sun symbol, and I knew exactly where I'd seen that same symbol before. "Oh, damn."

"What?" asked Remy. "What is it?"

I groaned. "I'll explain on the way to the airport."

~*~

"So?" I asked, keeping my voice light as I flipped through a rack of sweaters at an all-night Target. I grabbed a green one and tossed it into the cart, along with a few dark tank tops and some shorts and travel toiletries.

Zane picked a red bra from a nearby table, eyed it, and then dropped it into my basket.

I plucked it back out again and gave him a frustrated look. "Are we going to talk about this?"

"Out here?" He gestured at the store. At three in the morning, it was nearly empty of all shoppers. The circular racks of clothing in the clothing section were currently being replenished by an old woman in a red smock who stood fifty feet away, hanging sweaters and yawning.

"What's wrong with here?" I asked.

"It's not private," Zane said with a frown, eyeing my neck. He hadn't yet had a chance to feed, and the bloodlust had to be driving him crazy. "We should leave."

"We need clothes," I told Zane. "That includes you."

"The clothes here won't fit my… appendages." He wiggled his eyebrows at me. "I think you know what I mean."

"Oh, I think I know, you naughty man."

He leaned in as if sharing a secret. "I meant my wings."

"I didn't."

He grinned.

"You're still naughty. And I don't know about you, but I am not going to Colorado in this trampy dress."

"I like you in that trampy dress," he mused with a smile, eyeing my figure. "Reminds me of when I first met you."

Man, I sure did spend a lot of time dressing up in scanty clothing around him, didn't I? I was probably setting women's lib back fifty years. Oh well. I'd be around for it to catch up.

"So why's the clothing so important?" he asked.

"You'll see," I said. "Don't change the subject. We need to talk. Now."

"It can wait for the plane, along with my feeding."

Sophie was at the airport, chartering a private jet for us. I made a face, just thinking about the henna-covered assassin. I didn't like her. I certainly didn't like her smug attitude, or the fact that she seemed to know quite a bit about my vampire lover.

As if reading my thoughts, Zane pulled a black sweater off a rack and put it in the cart. At my raised eyebrow, he commented, "It's for Sophie. In case she needs to cover up. I can't imagine that leather is warm and her tattoos catch the eye a bit too much."

Fuck Sophie. I stared down at that black sweater and ground my teeth. What was the deal with him and her? It was making me anxious. "What's going on that you can't tell me about?"

He shook his head. "Later."

I didn't want later. Sophie would be back later, and that was precisely why I wanted to talk about it *now*. I shoved my cart past him and stalked toward the dressing room.

Zane trailed behind me, his leather duster swishing as he walked. "Are you really going to try those on?"

I parked the cart at the dressing room and pulled the red bra out of the cart, then glanced over my shoulder at him.

He rubbed his lip, grinning, and I saw the barest hint of fang. As I sauntered into the dressing rooms, I headed for the back. Someone was in the front stall, and I could hear a lot of shifting and clothing rustling. I picked a dressing room and slid in, shutting the door behind me, and waited, counting the seconds.

Seven passed before there was a soft knock at the door. "Come on in," I said softly, and opened it for him.

His eyes were blazing red as he entered the small room, his gaze on me. "Going to model for me, Princess?"

I tugged at the knot at the back of my neck. The dress top fell to my waist, my long curls bouncing over my now-bare shoulders. "Maybe."

He sat down on the bench in the dressing room across from the mirror, his long legs sprawling out. "Keep going, then."

I grinned and gave a little shimmy, the dress pooling at my ankles and letting my breasts bounce free. At his rapt gaze, I took a step forward, brushing the tips against his mouth, his fangs prominent. He gave a low groan in his throat and laid a hand at the small of my back, tugging me against him until I had to brace my hands on his shoulders for support. My breasts were now crushed against his face, and as he glanced up at me, his teeth elongated.

"No drinking," I whispered, feeling the pulse of desire flooding through my body. "Not until the plane."

He raked his fangs over the swell of one breast, not breaking the skin, just a reminder. His red-eyed gaze remained hot on me, and I felt my sex grow wetter with need.

God I loved this man. My fingers twined in his hair and I leaned forward to kiss him, sucking at his upper lip. My legs slid over his until I was straddling him, feeling the hard length of his cock against my thighs.

And then I rolled my hips atop him.

He groaned, tilting his head back against the wall.

A fist banged on the wall behind us. "Get a room, you two."

I stiffened in surprise. "Remy?"

A pause of silence, and then I heard a male groan in her room. Was that Ethan? I stifled the laugh in my throat. Looks like she and I had the same idea.

I glanced back down at Zane, my lips quirking. I swerved my torso slightly, letting my nipples brush past his face. "I'm not sure I can do this with Remy ten feet away and listening," I whispered.

"I can," he said, his tongue snaking out to lick one nipple.

My breath caught in my throat at the pulse of pleasure it sent through my body. I forced myself to pay attention to the reason why I was here. "Sophie?" I asked quietly again.

He shook his head. "Not here. Remy and Ethan—"

Another louder groan punctuated the air. I brushed my fingertips over Zane's jaw. "Sounds like they're busy. Just tell me."

He gave me an agonized look. His hands went to my waist and he pulled me close, wrapping his arms around my naked body, hugging me. Just hugging me. His black head was nestled against my breasts.

That pang of foreboding hit me again. "What is it? Who is she? Why won't you say?"

"I want you to know that I love you, Jackie," he said softly against my skin. "Nothing has changed that since the day we met. You know that."

"I do," I said, brushing my fingers over the shell of his ear. I caught his earlobe between my fingers and then tugged, hard, trying to get his attention. "But just *tell* me."

He paused, looking as defeated as I'd ever seen him.

"You're scaring me," I told him softly, anxiety making my entire body tense.

He shook his head and looked up at me. "You should know that she wasn't my idea."

"I don't understand," I said softly. "What do you mean, she wasn't your idea?"

He heaved a sigh, glanced away, then back at me. "Sophie's mine."

I wasn't following. "Yours?"

His gaze was solemn. "I created her. She's another succubus that I made."

CHAPTER SEVEN

"Did he introduce something into the relationship that you're not keen on? Whether it's an anal plug the size of a football, a pair of lick-happy twin blondes, or a wedding ring, the response is the same: If you want this to work, you've got to loosen up your muscles and just trust your partner."—*The Bad Girl's Guide to Dirty Sex*, by Remy Summore

~*~

We weren't speaking.

Or rather, I wasn't speaking to him. I had nothing to say. What could I possibly say that would relieve my seething jealousy? How could I possibly blithely explain away my sudden hatred of Sophie?

I couldn't. So I said nothing.

I'd gone stiff in his arms, and Zane had quickly tried to explain that he'd never had a romantic relationship with Sophie. That she'd been a meal back in the days when meals had been scarce, and a Serim friend had wanted a companion. So Zane had helped turn her, and had thought nothing more of it. She'd dropped off his radar millennia ago.

Until she'd arrived with me.

So that was why Zane had been so quiet and secretive since he'd awoken. And that was why Remy and Ethan were constantly whispering. No one had wanted to tell me the truth—that Sophie was just like me.

That I was no longer special to Zane.

It hurt. It wasn't rational in the slightest. I was the one that he loved. But it still hurt to think that she had that same special connection with him that I did. Worse, it hurt that no one had told me.

And so I didn't talk to him on the flight to Denver. Zane had taken me to the private room in the back of the plane, had tried to talk about it with me. But I hadn't wanted to talk about it, even when Zane had peppered my skin with affectionate kisses, speaking words of love. Even when I'd returned his caresses, and he'd had his teeth sunk into my neck, his cock sunk deep into my body.

I still kept thinking about it.

We were supposed to spend eternity together. Me and him. Zane and I. And now there was Sophie to think about.

~*~

By the time we disembarked from the plane, the sun was rising. We went to the rental car parking lot and Remy squinted at the sun. "It's almost daylight," she pointed out helpfully. "Are we going to keep on or should we stop for the day?"

Zane's eyes were already heavily lidded, as if he struggled to stay awake. "I need to crash somewhere safe. It can't be helped. You can go on ahead."

"Then who's going to protect you?" Remy asked.

"I will remain by his side," Sophie said in her smooth voice.

That broke me from my silence. Like I was going to leave her with him. Alone. "We're waiting for Zane."

Sophie raised an eyebrow at me.

I scowled, ignoring her amusement. "It can wait a day."

"If you say so," she said sweetly.

~*~

We ended up at some tourist trap motel on the side of the road. We sent Ethan for food, and Remy tagged along. She wanted him to use some of his new "slang" and greet everyone with a hearty "'Sup, bro?"

I stayed behind, because that was where Zane was.

After Ethan and Remy left, Sophie turned toward me. I watched her with wary eyes as she crossed the room and moved to her sheathed sword. She pulled it out along with a whetstone and began to sharpen the blade.

I crossed my arms over my chest, frowning at her movements. Every motion of the whetstone emphasized the muscles in her arms, the delicate henna designs that she'd covered herself with. She was beautiful. Tough, deadly, and beautiful. I was neither tough nor deadly. That sucked. Since we were created to be the ideal of feminine beauty, I had little to no muscle, my body soft curves. Sophie, however, was toned and sleek and strong. That seemed unfair.

"Why do *you* have muscles?" I asked, hating the petulance in my voice.

She looked up, arched a black eyebrow at me. "Muscles?"

Despite myself, I moved forward. "Succubi don't get super strength. How come you're so strong?" It wasn't that Sophie was overdeveloped like a bodybuilder. It was that wherever I had softness and curves, Sophie had muscle. She could take care of herself.

Sophie ran the whetstone along the edge of the blade, eyeing the metal. "You know that a succubus must be the ideal of femininity in her master's eyes, do you not?"

I'd been rather plain and plump before I'd been turned, with reddish-brown, frizzy hair. Now I was curvy with a long, gleaming riot of bright red hair, and I was downright beautiful. Remy had told me she was fat when she was turned, so I guessed that all succubi went through some change like that. "Yes, but how did you get *muscle*? I'd freaking kill for some muscle."

"When I was turned, it was considered a female beauty." She gave me an amused look, as if titillated by my question. "Is it so hard to believe?"

"So nothing changed for you?" That hardly seemed fair.

She shook her head, the ropy dreads bouncing on her shoulders. "My breast grew back."

I stared at her, aghast. "Grew... back?"

"Have you ever heard the legends of the Amazons?" she asked, sharpening the blade again and raising it to look down the balance. "Warrior women who cut off a breast as an offering to the goddess Artemis? So that they might draw their bows more easily?" Her mouth twitched at my horrified expression. "One breast is apparently not an idealized look for a woman. Mine grew back overnight. I had to learn a skill other than archery. I took up swords instead."

Dear lord. She was just a fountain of information, wasn't she? "So you're an Amazon?"

"The Amazons were not a true tribe. I am Scythian. The legends were simply built off us."

"And the henna? Is that a Scythian thing too?"

"It is not," she said, sheathing her blade again and pulling out one of her throwing stars.

I eyed her decorated arms. It must have taken hours and hours on end. "I don't understand. Then why do it?"

She carefully laid one of the stars on the table and reached for another, grazing her thumb against the edge of the blade. "When I became a succubus, many choices were taken from me. My appearance was changed without my consent. I cannot change that. No spells or charms work. So I do what I can to make this body my own."

I sat at the foot of the bed, my hand automatically going to Zane's ankle, as if I felt the need to touch him even though he couldn't touch me back. My mind slipped to his, reaching for a connection. His thoughts were frenzied, tortured. I traded them for a soothing dream of us together, sitting at a lake at sunset, watching the water ripple in the breeze.

Sophie glanced askance at me. "You truly care for him?"

My hands tightened on Zane's ankle. "I love him."

She studied me for a minute longer. "That is a foolish path. He is not a good man. No vampire is."

"You don't know Zane."

Her smile was sad. "Don't I?"

That made me furious. "Not like I know him."

Sophie glanced back down at her weapons, then at me. "I believe you. I only seek to caution you that it is not a wise path. Those who can control you will never stop abusing the power. Love does not come with conditions, and you cannot have a relationship when such things stand in your way. You must love someone that you cannot control—and who cannot control you—or else you are doomed to fail."

I said nothing. She was wrong.

"I see my words offend you," she said with a slow, carefree smile. "I am glad to hear of your love for your master, though. It would make things difficult between us if you tried to kill him, as I would be forced to stop you."

"Kill him," I sputtered. "Are you crazy?"

Her blue eyes blinked at me, so bright in her dark face. "It is not so crazy. I killed my Serim master. Did Zane tell you that? He enslaved me because he was bored." She sneered the words. "And I served him for many, many years. When I broke free, I destroyed him and vowed to never be another man's puppet. I would have killed Zane as well, except I found out that if his existence ended, so did mine. I find that I rather like existing. As a result, I will take down anything that threatens that existence, be it Phryne or Serim, or you."

"I told you, I love him."

She shook her head. "I am in your shoes, sister. I know there are only two emotions when one refers to their master. And only one is love. Hate can be a strong companion as well."

"I don't hate him," I said softly. I crawled over the bed to where he slept, his face so peaceful. My fingers brushed over his cheek and I resettled in the bed, pulling his head into my lap. "He's everything to me."

She gave me a pitying look and picked up a dagger and began to sharpen it. "And that is why you are doomed to heartache."

"I don't think—"

Sophie grew instantly alert, her gaze swiveling to the door.

My protest died in my throat and I stood up slowly. "What is it?"

She put a finger to her lips and moved to the door of the motel room. As I watched, she jerked the door open and reached out, grabbing someone and pulling them inside the room.

The woman tumbled in, all dark braids and unnaturally blue eyes. She rolled on her feet and hissed in response to Sophie's narrow-eyed gaze, brandishing a pair of thin daggers. "Sister," she spat. "Or shall I call you 'traitor'?"

"A tail?" Sophie asked, unconcerned. She shut the door behind her and ran a hand down the shades, ensuring they were shut. "You, Nefer? So Phryne begins the great chase after all?"

"Begins?" Nefer said, backing up against the wall with a mirthless laugh. "We are already two steps ahead of all of you."

What? How was that possible? "Wait—"

"She bluffs," Sophie said in a cool voice and sprang at Nefer.

As I watched, the two women locked arms. Nefer tried to stab at Sophie, only to have her wrist captured. Sophie gave a short, jerking motion and I heard the snap of bones. Nefer screamed and fell back, clutching at her hand.

Sophie moved in, grasped Nefer by the jaw, and quickly broke her neck with an efficient snap.

Bile rushed into my mouth as the other woman dropped to the ground. "Sophie, what the fuck?"

The other succubus turned to look back at me, raising one eyebrow. "You wished to question her first?"

"No! You can't go around just snapping people's necks."

The other woman's expression became indulgent. "I am an assassin. That is what I do. She was in the way. I stopped her." She brushed off her hands as if done with a messy issue. "Do not worry. She will return soon enough, and by the time she wakes up to warn Phryne, we will be long gone from this area. Unless you would rather warn your enemy and give away your presence?"

I scowled. "I hate you sometimes."

"You're welcome."

"I wasn't thanking you."

"No, but you should have." She waved a hand at Nefer's fallen body. "Now, come, we should move her into the closet and hope the cleaning crew doesn't find her after we leave."

~*~

We pulled up to the Mesa Verde park entrance just as the sun was setting. The cliffs were high in the distance, bleached tan dotted with green scrub trees. At the front of the park entrance, two tollbooths sat side by side, but only one lane was functional. I pulled the car up to the booth and held out my money.

The park ranger held up his hand, refusing my money with a smile. "Park's closing in five minutes."

I gritted my teeth and forced a smile. "We're with Mrs. Brighton's team."

He peered into the car at our motley assortment. Zane, in sunglasses and leather duster. Sophie, covered with henna tattoos and weapons, her arms bare thanks to a tank top, her dreads piled high, her eyes shining unnaturally blue. Remy, scrawling notes in her notebook as she leaned on Ethan, who was easily the biggest man anyone had ever seen.

"'Sup," Ethan said in greeting.

Remy giggled.

I sighed and ran a hand down my face. "Look, we just need to go in for a bit, okay? We've got something to drop off and then we'll turn right back around."

He shook his head. "I'm sorry, park rules—"

I waved a hand casually. "I know, I know. Just give me a brochure, I guess."

When he reached out to hand me the pamphlet, I grabbed his hand. At the contact of my skin to his, I slammed my succubus powers through him. He shut down, his eyes rolling back, and collapsed, falling partially out of the booth. I peered in the rearview mirror to see if anyone else was nearby and threw the car into park.

"So much for subtlety," Sophie murmured.

"We don't have time to waste," I said, opening my car door and stepping over the fallen guard. "Besides," I said, tugging on the man and dragging him back inside the booth so no one would see him. "You wanna talk about subtlety? How about you strap thirty less of those daggers to your waist? Nothing screams subtlety quite like a six-foot-tall tattooed woman covered in weapons."

Sophie said nothing.

"That's what I thought," I muttered, and pressed my fingers to the guard's forehead again, pushing through his mind. Past dreams, past consciousness, looking for stored memories. Aha. Using his stolen memories, I flipped the appropriate switch that activated the gate-bar. It crawled into the air slowly in response. I tapped the guard to wake him up (since I didn't need him anymore), slid back into the driver's seat, put the car into drive, and sped down the road.

Zane looked over at me, impressed. "You're very much a woman of action tonight, Princess."

"I want that halo," I told him. "I can feel it's here. Can't you?"

He nodded quietly, his face strained with tension. He could feel it, too.

We traveled over the winding park roads and as we drove, I chewed on my lip, looking for landmarks. A few minutes into our drive, I found our goal. A small archaeological dig had been roped off on the far side of the road, a couple of tents set up in the distance. Bingo. I pulled up to the dig site and parked the car. The majority of the tents were small, individual dome tents, several of them with a light on inside. One larger tent stood slightly apart from the rest, big enough for several people. That would be the tent we were looking for. Nearby, floodlights were hooked to a generator over what looked like a pit of rock, and at the sight of it, my stomach gave an odd wobble that I hadn't felt in a very long time. As we all piled out of the car, I heard Ethan ask, "What is this place?"

Remy pulled out her map and squinted at it, turning it in the dim light as Ethan helpfully clicked on a flashlight. "We're close to the Luminary House, Mesa Verde," she said helpfully. "Sounds boring."

"Mesa Verde?" Zane inquired, glancing over at me. "How are you sure it's here? How did you know this place out of all of them?"

"It's a city of rock," I murmured. I stared up at the canyon walls, feeling the thrum of something decidedly supernatural—and strong—in the area. The cliffs were dark with the light of the setting sun gone, and the area at our feet, brushy. The oppressive heat of the day had disappeared, the night breeze soothing and cool. "You can't see it, but on the side of this cliff, there's a city. Just like it says in the Scythian writing. And in that city, there are sun symbols. A circle surrounded by flames. I've seen that before. That's how I knew."

"That's where it'll be, then," Zane said, coming to my side. His hand went to my lower back, a soft touch. A reminder of support. "It's amazing that you knew to think of this place."

Well, not *so* amazing. I turned and gave him a hesitant smile. "Just let me lead tonight, okay?"

He quirked an eyebrow in my direction, then reached for a cigarette and lit it, shielding it from the breeze. He dragged on it for a moment, then studied the tents, the fabric backlit by lanterns within. I could hear the faint sounds of chatter in the distance—no doubt they were trying to make out who would come here after dark, and why we hadn't approached yet. Camping here on-site seemed bizarre, but I looked at the floodlights, and the generator, and wasn't surprised. They didn't want to leave the dig site, so they stayed. Uncomfortable, but sensible for a workaholic, I supposed.

"Is this going to be a problem?" Zane asked me quietly. I noticed Sophie's hand at her sword, ever at the ready to defend.

"Not in the way you think," I said wryly. "Like I said, let me lead. This won't be fun."

He nodded. The others looked at me expectantly.

I sighed. "You guys stay here until I give the word." I headed through the brush, toward the scattering of tents.

I could hear people moving around inside the smaller tents, the soft murmuring of conversations. About fifty feet away, floodlights shone on the sunken dig site, where someone still crouched, hard at work despite the fact that it was dark outside and getting late.

I knew who that would be. Steeling my shoulders, I turned and strode forward, crossing the brush to stand at the edge of the pit. Then I squatted at the side and looked down. "Hey, Mom."

Suzanne Brighton squinted up at the light, then turned back to the piece of pottery that she was delicately brushing out of the sandy soil. "I'm busy. Who's there?"

I sighed. "It's your daughter. Who else would call you Mom?"

"Jackie, honey, it's good to see you, but I'm very busy—"

I rolled my eyes. "I know. I'd have called but there wasn't time. Can you just come out and say hello?"

She paused, sighed, and then pulled herself away as if greatly peeved. She climbed up a small wooden ladder, grumbling under her breath. When she got to my side, I held my arms out for a hug.

She gave me a quick one and then wrinkled her nose at my appearance. "Something's different."

I waited for the inevitable outrage. I'd been transformed into a succubus since the last time she'd seen me. *Everything* looked different.

But she only tilted her head so she could squint at me through the bifocals resting on the tip of her nose, ugly chain dangling from the sides of the glasses. "Did you dye your hair?"

Lord. I'd been changed into a succubus and my mother thought I'd just dyed my hair? "Something like that," I said. "Good to see you too, Mom. Do you have someplace private we can talk? I have something I need your opinion on."

"If it's the hair, it looks tarty," my mother said, wiping her dusty hands on her jeans and heading over to one of the tents. "I thought you were trying to be a serious archaeologist? No one's going to take you seriously if you look like a tart and not an academic."

I gritted my teeth and followed her, glaring when Zane and the others appeared in camp.

So much for staying back until I gave the word. Now they were all going to meet my crazy mother. I winced and followed closely behind her as she entered the big tent. Inside, there was a wooden table with an attached bench, and maps and printouts were spread all over it, as well as open books, candy wrappers, notes, and pictures. My mother went to a cooler and pulled out a water bottle, twisting off the cap and drinking for a long minute before turning her baleful eye on my entourage. "Who are you all?"

"They're my friends, Mom," I said, then forced myself to shut up when I realized that I sounded like the whiny teenager I'd been far too long ago. I tried to see my mother through a stranger's eyes—her brown, lined face streaked with dirt, her gray hair ragged and disheveled under the oversized straw hat. The tank top she wore with the rings of sweat under the arms, the cargo shorts and hiking boots. Mom was a mess. Always had been. She simply didn't care how she looked because it wasn't important, like so many other things in her life weren't important – husband, house, and child included.

Only the work mattered. I'd been jealous of it as a bored teenager, but as an adult with the weight of the world on my shoulders, all I felt was annoyance.

Zane stepped forward and took my mother's hand in his, leaning down to kiss the back of it. "Delighted to meet you, Mrs. Brighton. Your daughter has told me so much about you."

Actually, I'd never mentioned her. I narrowed my eyes at Zane's charmer act.

To her credit, my mother snorted. "Now I see why she dyed her hair like a tart," she said acerbically, casting me a disapproving look and then gesturing at the table. "Well, sit down, all of you. Don't just stand there like lumps."

Well, wasn't this fun. I crossed my arms, waiting, as the others sat at the table like dutiful children, Zane's mouth curving into an amused smile as his gaze flicked back and forth between myself and my mother. I was glad someone was getting a kick out of this at least.

Remy pulled out her notepad and began to make notes again, and my mother gasped, dragging away the maps that Remy had put her arms on top of. "What are you doing? Are you writing a thesis? This is my discovery." Her voice grew hard and brittle. "Jackie, I'm warning you—"

"Mom, calm down," I began. "Trust me, it's not a thesis."

"I'm writing a book," Remy said brightly to my mother. "I'm going to write a memoir and pad my bank account since I'm not working anymore."

My mother's brows drew together. "Not working... in archaeology?"

Zane snorted. I could have sworn Sophie's lips twitched.

Remy wrinkled her nose. "Archaeology? Yuck, no. I'm a porn star." At Ethan's glare, she added, "*Former* porn star."

Mom's gaze swung to my hair, then back to my friends, and then her mouth thinned into a frown.

"Hey, Mom, I brought you something," I said, pulling out the drawing I'd made of the ceiling. I had to distract her before my mother decided that we were just drawing her away from her precious dig and wasting her time. That, or I got a lecture about hanging out with the bad kids at school. I waved the paper at her. "Come check this out. I think you'll find it interesting."

My mother moved across the tent to my side and gave me a concerned look. "Jackie, honey," she said in a low voice. "I'm concerned that you're not hanging out with the right people."

"You don't know the half of it," I said, giving her a one-armed hug and glaring at Zane over my mother's head. He gave me an innocent look, grinning and showing his fangs. Oh, he was getting a kick out of this. "I'm not twelve, though. I can take care of myself just fine."

"Actually," Sophie began.

"Hush," I barked.

Silence fell. Then Ethan spoke. "Word to your mother."

"When you said you were going to teach him slang, Remy, you should have stuck to one decade," Zane said dryly.

Ethan frowned, glancing over at Remy. "That was not appropriate? It is her mother. One says 'word' when one is agreeing with another. Is that not correct?"

She patted his arm. "You did just fine, baby."

"God, I am ditching all of you at the next hotel. No lie," I said, passing my sketch to my mother. "Now go on, tell me what you make of that."

She adjusted the bifocals on her nose, studied it, and then shrugged. "It looks like a vagina."

I snatched the page back from her, ignoring Remy's not-so-muffled snort of laughter. "It's the circles. The circles." I stabbed my finger into the paper. "I was drawing on a warped surface. They're supposed to be circles. Haloes. And these spiky things around the outside are supposed to represent the sun. If you hold the paper up, it looks just like one of the windows in the Luminary House."

"Of course they do, dear," my mother said soothingly, patting my back. "But you didn't have to draw it, honey. You're a bit too old for me to be hanging this on the fridge."

"I don't want you to hang it on the fridge," I said, clenching my fists. "I brought it to discuss. This is the only drawing of this particular ceiling and it's very important—"

She snorted, interrupting me. "This is a bad copy. The pictures in the gift shop do a much better job with it."

I straightened in surprise. "Pictures in the gift shop?"

"Of course. Luminary House is very popular even if they won't let anyone go up and visit the dig site. It sells lots of postcards, I'm told."

"They won't let anyone go up and visit the site?" I cried in dismay. "But I need to get up there. Tonight. You can't get me in?"

"You can't go tonight," she said. "It's dark outside. You'll fall off the ladders and break something."

"Oh, that's okay," Remy said cheerfully. "Zane can fly up there."

"Fly?" My mother's eyebrows rose.

"Fly!" I repeated quickly, thinking hard. "You know. Zoom up there. Because he's fast. Like a ninja." When she looked over at Zane, I winced and gestured for someone to help me.

Anyone.

They merely sat there and grinned at my discomfort, hateful beasts. I loathed all of them.

Sophie got up from the table and approached my mother, taking the piece of paper from me. She pointed at one line of the carefully copied writing. "We found this inscription along with this drawing. Have you come across any Scythian language in the ruins?"

"Scythian?" My mother said, baffled. "The Luminary House is only twelve hundred years old. Scythians existed much, much earlier than that, young lady." She shook her head, glancing over at me. "This generation is so uneducated."

"She knows when the Scythians existed, Mom," I said. Seeing as how she *was* one. Of course, I couldn't tell my mother that. "So no other languages?"

"Bob said he thought he'd seen an Egyptian symbol for Ra," she said thoughtfully. "But we all thought he'd been drinking on the dig again, and sun symbols aren't exactly rare."

An Egyptian symbol? Lots of the angels who had fallen had settled in Egypt. The queen of the vampires was Egyptian, after all. I bit my lip, excited again. "Can we see it?"

"In the morning, dear. My benefactor will be by early to see how things are going. You can go with his tour group."

I groaned. "Can't you just show me there now?"

"It's too late at night, Jackie. You'll fall and hurt yourself."

"Can you point out where it is on the map so we know where to look in the morning?" Sophie asked.

For a moment, I was almost grateful that Sophie was here.

Almost. It was a feeling that faded pretty fast.

"Not until morning," my mother insisted. "But if you want, you can all camp here tonight. We can catch up. You can tell me all about how your dig in the Yucatan went."

Oh hell. The dig I'd abandoned? I smiled tightly. "Fun."

Across the room, Zane grinned.

CHAPTER EIGHT

"Rule number one of a porn star: never let your family know what you've been up to. They won't understand. Tell them you went into finance or some shit. No one ever asks questions when you tell them you work with spreadsheets."—*Remy Summore's Tips on Life and Love*, by Remy Summore

~*~

My mother chatted for hours, seemingly full of energy despite being in her sixties and spending a full day in the sun. As she talked and told us about the dig, the weather, her arthritis, my no-good father, and then more about the dig, I sat next to Zane, who played with my hair as he watched my mother in amusement.

Mom had taken a shine to Ethan, it seemed. He seemed impressed at everything she showed him, so she'd been digging photo albums of digs past out of a trunk and was pointing to a particularly exciting bit of wall that they'd excavated in Cappadocia, Turkey.

Zane leaned over to me. "You never mentioned your mother."

"Nope."

"Strained relationship?"

"If by strained you mean nonexistent? Sure."

"Nonexistent? She seems to have affection for you."

"She does now," I said. "I'm grown and no longer require much attention. Also, I went into the same line of work she did and I'm not any good at it. That tells her that she was a good mother, but the fact that I'm bad at it makes it safe for her to tell me what she's working on. She doesn't have to worry about me 'scooping' her digs and stealing her thunder. That's why she and my father divorced. He was an archaeologist too. She didn't like the competition."

"And where's he at?"

"Last I heard, somewhere in Turkey," I said, swigging from my water bottle. "We don't keep in touch."

He nodded at one of the photo albums my mother was pulling out. "So I take it I won't find one of those full of pictures of teenage Jackie?"

"Only if I'm standing in front of a dig site," I said dryly.

He brushed my hair away from my cheek. "That's very sad, Princess."

I shrugged. "That's our family. We're not close. I don't feel sad about it because that's just how it's always been for me. And probably why I'm not the slightest bit inclined to settle down and have a family."

His face grew grim. "I can't give you a family. The only way we could have a child is unnaturally, and that child would be like Ethan, but worse. Dark. Unnatural."

I shook my head. "You're all that I want, Zane. All I ever wanted. The only reason we're here tonight is because my mom has information that I thought might be helpful." I sighed. "And we're stuck waiting for some tour group in the morning because she is hiding said helpful information."

"We could go up there on our own," Zane suggested.

I shook my head and pressed a hand to my forehead, wishing the vein in my temple would stop pounding. My mother always caused that reaction. "I have no doubt that if we try to go up there on our own, my mother would call the cops and get us kicked out of the park for trespassing. It'd be a bigger mess than it already is. Let's just wait for morning."

Zane dragged a finger down my arm suggestively. "We could always go find a nice private backseat of the car and misbehave, if you'd like?"

My skin tingled and my breath caught at the hot, heavy-lidded look he gave me. "I'd like that very much."

~*~

Though I didn't like waiting for sunrise, we didn't have much choice. We bunked down for the night with mom's archaeologists. The night was spent pleasantly—in Zane's arms in the backseat of the car as we took care of each other's needs. I suspected that Remy and Ethan were off somewhere doing the same. Where that left Sophie, I had no idea. We gathered early in the morning for a midnight snack and to make plans, and I noticed Sophie's eyes were over-blue again, a sure sign that she was in need, though she didn't acknowledge it.

Must be nice to have that much control over one's body. I started Itching like mad when I was overdue by a few hours.

We breakfasted with the small encampment, my mother making comments about how much I ate (some things didn't change), and then we waited impatiently for the "benefactor" to arrive. I kept checking my watch. The last thing I wanted was for Phryne's girls to show up and turn this into a brawl.

We had to get going, and quickly.

Unfortunately, that meant I'd be going without Zane, since the sun was now up and he was struggling to stay awake. I kissed Zane as he dropped into sleep in one of the tents. His fingers laced with mine, and he looked up at me. "You'll be careful? I wish I could be there with you."

"I'll be fine," I said softly. After all, it wasn't me that Phryne wanted to off. Which worried me—Zane was vulnerable in the daylight hours.

He sensed my unease and pressed a kiss to my palm. "Leave Sophie with me if you're worried. She'll guard me."

My mouth puckered as if I'd bit into something sour. "Yeah, and I don't know if you noticed, but she's currently overdue."

He rolled his eyes. "I'll be asleep, Jackie."

"So? I've totally molested you in your sleep before."

His eyes flared with red, his smile wicked. "I had pleasant dreams that day."

My cheeks flushed red and I pushed at his cheek playfully. "Very funny."

"You don't have anything to worry about, Princess."

I knew I didn't with him. It was Sophie I had to worry about. She was rather single-minded about her survival. Where I had found a core of strength in my immortality, Sophie seemed to be made of steel throughout. She'd use my boyfriend and think nothing of it. Just something that needed to be done in order to survive, like eating or drinking.

Man, I hated having other succubi around. Well, except Remy. She'd rather make out with *anyone* other than Zane.

This jealous streak of mine sucked.

Car tires grated on gravel and I jerked around.

"That'll be your tour group," Zane said, a yawn in his voice. "Go get 'em, tiger."

I gave him one last, lingering kiss and then strode out of the tent.

Remy immediately grabbed my arm, intercepting me as I walked out, practically shoving me between a pair of tents. I stumbled, clinging to her arm for support. "Remy, what—"

"Mayday, mayday," she hissed, grabbing my arm and crouching low.

I huddled behind one of the tents with her quickly. "What is it?"

"Guess who your mom's benefactor is?" she whispered. "It's Noah."

I groaned.

"My reaction too," she said. "I found out about two seconds before you did. We have to ditch him. I love Noah, but he's not exactly going to let us waltz in and steal shit from right under his nose."

Not if he was here. Him being here meant either one of two things—he was tracking me because he wanted to drag me back to his side… or he was after the halo as well.

Neither of these situations was ideal. I stiffened, glancing back at the tent where I'd left Zane. Shit. *Shit*. He was vulnerable in daylight hours. No matter how badly hurt, he'd never awaken. Someone could murder him while he slept and he wouldn't be able to raise a finger to stop them.

"We need a distraction," I murmured.

The gravel crunched to my side. "Did someone say distraction?" Sophie asked, all dulcet tones.

I looked up at the Amazon and her blue, blue eyes and grinned. She'd had sex with Noah before. She needed sex right now. I explained the situation to her quickly. "Think you could get Noah off our hands?"

She licked her lips like a too-pleased cat. "Perhaps. You're going after the haloes?'"

"We need to go before Phryne gets here," I said. "We can't afford to wait."

She glanced around the tent to the clearing, where Noah stood shaking hands with my mother, exchanging greetings. "I will distract him," she said. "You will need to go on."

"Got it," I said, standing up. "Thank you, Sophie. Can you keep guard over Zane, too?"

"Of course," she said, giving me a puzzled look. As if I was ridiculous for thinking that she'd leave his side. To my surprise, she reached behind her and tugged a gun out of her belt, and offered it to me.

My eyes widened and I shook my head.

She jiggled it at me. "Take it. I'd offer you one of my knives, but those require skill. Any fool can shoot a gun."

I scowled and snatched the gun from her. The last time I'd used one of these, I'd shot Zane by accident. Any fool, indeed.

Sophie pointed her finger and thumb like a gun and poked me in the forehead. "Aim for the head. Shooting a limb will not slow an immortal down much. A bullet to the brain will slow them down for several hours."

"Like in the zombie movies," Remy said helpfully.

I pulled the gun out and eyed it thoughtfully, and then handed it to Remy. "If my master's here, this might not be any good in my hands."

Sophie nodded. "Wise choice."

Remy took the gun and did a little hopping step, then struck a pose. "Look, am I totally Lara Croft or what?"

I glanced over at Sophie. "You were saying?"

"I was wrong," she said dryly. "Stay here while I go and distract your big blond Serim."

I didn't like the husky way she said that, but I said nothing. Instead, I watched as Sophie strolled out from between the tents, her hips rolling with an amazing, sensual fluidness that I'd never noticed before. Every step was a suggestion. She sauntered through the camp, as if heading for a set of tents across the way. As she moved, her gaze flicked to Noah, and the cerulean intensity of her gaze swept over him. She licked her lips again, and then kept sauntering. She was fucking gorgeous.

Hell, I wanted her in that moment.

Noah wavered, his conversation faltering. As my mother gestured at the cliff, I noticed Noah's gaze straying over to Sophie, where she continued past the tents, disappearing from view.

Noah excused himself from my mother and followed where Sophie had gone, frowning.

"He doesn't look happy," I commented, a little pleased to see that.

"That's because Sophie just went all Pied Piper on his ass and his dick is a rat." She frowned. "That sounded better in my head."

I elbowed her. "Maybe we should get Ethan to teach you some slang."

She pushed me. "Shaddup. Let's go before he decides not to pork Sophie after all."

~*~

"Dude," Remy complained for the third time in the last fifteen minutes. "These ladders are fricking ridiculous."

I paused at the top of the one I stood on, wiping my brow. "You can rest at the top, Remy. Just remember we're in a time crunch here."

"Oh, sure, time crunch," she panted. "I don't know if you noticed, but we're practically scaling a friggin' cliff here?"

Oh, I had noticed. I hauled my shaking legs over the ladder and knelt on the narrow, slanted path, wiping my sweaty brow.

After we'd found Noah's human assistants gathering near the base of the closest cliff as they'd waited for their leader, I'd quickly introduced myself to the first one, sticking out my hand for him to shake. After that, it was too easy. We put them all to sleep and left them under the closest shade tree. One of them had information on the Luminary House, and I picked through his memories, getting the information I needed. There was a locked gate and he had the lock code. Perfect.

We'd raced back to the cliffs only to find that getting to the actual Luminary House involved ladders. Lots of very tall ladders, and then narrow, rocky paths so steep that even a mountain goat would pause. But we climbed, because I lived in fear of turning around and seeing Phryne's shining head two steps behind us.

Ethan followed, bringing up the rear, his bo strapped to his back. He wore a baseball cap to blot out the bright sunlight and didn't seem to be sweating the arduous climb at all. Figured. When Remy got to the top, I took her hand and helped her haul herself onto the rocky ledge. She panted, glaring up at me as if this was somehow my fault.

"Let's keep going," I said with a nod to the gate that I could now see at the top of the path. It cordoned off an immense rocky overhang, and I knew that our little Luminary House would be found there.

"Come, Remiza," Ethan said gently. "I shall carry you."

"I thought you'd never ask," she said.

The big Enforcer knelt and Remy piggybacked on him, pressing her chin against his hat and grinning at me. "I feel a second wind suddenly."

I shook my head, hanging on to the railing as we moved forward. The little gate was shut with a numerical padlock and I quickly began to enter the combination that I'd stolen. The gate swung open and we stepped forward, going down the rough steps hewn into the side of the cliff.

The Luminary House was gorgeous. Thick adobe walls lay nestled under the rocky overhang, dotted with circular windows, so unlike the rest of the ruins here, which boasted square windows. The adobe walls seemed to make up one large building, and as I stepped toward it, I could see that the building started smaller at the edges of the cliff and increased in size toward the middle, where there was the most room. Each of the round windows was bisected with a smooth wooden rod. Odd.

"It looks like a crown," Remy observed.

My breath caught in my throat. It did look like a crown. Like the one mentioned in the writing? The page was tucked carefully away into my pocket, along with Ethan's phone, but I could pull them out and reference the drawings—or the notes I'd scribbled on the page—if I needed to. As we walked closer, I noticed the cliff had given way abruptly. Some enterprising person had rebuilt a crude wooden bridge to cross the ten-foot gap.

We made our way over it and hopped to the other side. As I stepped forward, I noticed the round windows were surrounded by swirling designs. Each window was like a little sun, except the center was dark instead of full of light.

I touched one window in surprise, thinking hard.

"Why's this called the Luminary House?" Remy asked behind

me, wrinkling her nose. "It's so dark."

"I don't know," I told her, moving forward into the ruins. I touched the solid wall, made of adobe. It felt cool under my fingertips, and I glanced around. "Let's find a way inside. Maybe it'll become obvious there."

We searched several empty rooms before approaching the biggest one. Someone had laid a woven blanket over the doorway of the room, as if to keep out the wind. I flipped it up, and sucked in a breath.

The largest room of the Luminary House was lit in sunlight, despite being buried into the side of the cliff. I stepped inside in wonder, staring up at the ceiling. A star-shaped hole had been cut through the cliff and sunlight streamed in from above. I squinted as the edges of the morning sun showed up in the corner of the hole and then blinked at my surroundings.

"Hey, this is pretty cool," Remy said, staring up at the ceiling. "You think they carved that?"

"I don't know," I said, putting my hands on my hips and frowning up at it. I didn't know of anyone who could carve rock like that, but the sunroof was definitely in the shape of another sun, just like the windows outside. It had to be connected.

"I don't see a halo anywhere," Remy pointed out.

"It won't be out in the open. It'll be hidden somewhere." I glanced around, but I didn't see anything that screamed "hidden room." "The halo doesn't feel any closer now than it did before, though. Where's Ethan?"

"Guarding the ladder. He's going to make sure no one comes to disturb us." Remy closed her eyes and tilted her face back, as if concentrating. She took a step forward, then backward, then to each side. Then she opened her eyes again and looked around. "The pull of the halo is strongest to the north."

North was the rocky cliff wall. I frowned and closed my eyes, following Remy's example. In the dark, I concentrated on the vibration of the internal tuning fork that alerted me when something big and powerful was nearby. I turned in a circle and stopped when I felt the tug even stronger.

Sure enough, it was to the north. I moved to the wall, running my hands along it. The cliff was solid rock here, "Well shit," I said. "How are we supposed to get to it if it's inside the cliff?"

"Maybe there's a secret door," Remy said, running her hand

along the wall. "We just need to find a way to open sesame."

I drummed my fingers on my lips, thinking hard. Luminary House. The sun symbols were the only thing that set this place apart from the other ruins scattered throughout Mesa Verde. But what did they mean? I tugged out the paper and stepped into the sunlight streaming down through the portal above. I stared at the drawing, wishing I had the other piece of the puzzle. Somewhere out there, Phryne had the other half of the answers. Damn her. I'd just have to do this on my own, with nothing but the smarts of my team.

I glanced over at Remy. She had her hand raised up, making shadow puppets on the wall.

We were doomed.

As I studied the paper, Remy moved to my side. "Huh. Look at that."

My heart tripped and I looked over at her. "What?"

She gestured at the ceiling. "There are seven sun symbols there."

"What? Where?" I stepped out of the blinding circle of sunlight and moved into the shadows, shielding my eyes from the sun and staring up at the ceiling.

Sure enough, seven Egyptian sun symbols had been carved into the ceiling. They surrounded the center sun where the light streamed in and looked to be reflective mirrors. I'd almost missed them because of the contrast with the blinding light in the circle.

"Holy crap, those must mean something," I murmured.

"Duh," Remy said. "Jeez, I thought you'd be the Velma of this Scooby Doo group. I'm the Daphne here. I just stand around and look pretty."

I smacked her arm. "Har de har. Now be quiet while I try to figure out how these mirrors play into things."

She shrugged. "Well, in my movie *Panty Raiders of the Lost Ark*, we had to angle mirrors to make them open a secret door. You had to flip a switch that looked like a dildo," she said helpfully. "By rubbing up against it."

I stared at her.

"What?" She said defensively. "It was a good plot line."

"That's the answer," I said, tucking the paper back into my shirt. We had to activate something. Of course.

She wrinkled her nose. "You wanna rub up against a dildo?"

I pushed back out of the Luminary Room. "Just stay in there," I called to her. "I'm going to try something."

"Okey doke," Remy called cheerfully.

I paced back to the front of the ruins, my gaze going to the circle windows. Not all of them had sun symbols around them. I passed each crumbling house and counted the windows with the sun design around them.

Seven.

My heart thudded with excitement. This meant something. I knew it meant something... except, what? The sunroom had no windows of its own. What did these windows mean? I approached the first one and studied it closely, running my fingers over the lines of the sun symbol. There was a slashing character at the tip of one that I recognized, but it looked upside down.

I thought for a moment, then grasped the wooden rod in the center of the window, and pushed on it, hard, trying to move it.

It didn't budge.

"Hey!" Remy called. "The sun's getting brighter in the hole here! What do you want to bet there's some sort of timing mechanism?"

That's what I thought too, and if that was the case, we didn't have much time. I tugged on the wooden bar, hard, pushing to the left, trying desperately to get the window to turn. It wouldn't budge.

A large brown hand clasped the wood next to mine, and Ethan's shadow fell over me. "Allow me to do this for you, Jackie Brighton."

"Thank you, Ethan," I said, panting, and stepped to the side. "I thought you were guarding the ladders?"

His eyes flashed silver and he braced both of his hands on the wooden bar. "I saw your puny attempt and realized I must intercede. Please step back."

Gee, thanks. I stepped backward and waited.

He heaved, bracing his enormous body against the wall, and I saw the corded muscles in his arm strain. I winced, waiting for the rod to splinter into a thousand pieces.

It didn't. I heard the sound of rock grating on rock, and then the entire thing turned. I gasped in shock as he continued to turn the entire thing, slowly. The sun symbol rotated in the wall itself.

I tapped my finger to the faint Ra symbol at the base of the sun. "Stop here. We'll know when this reads properly."

A shout came from within the ruins. "Holy fuck, you gotta see this, Jackie!" Remy shouted. "It's *so* cool!"

"Be there in a second," I called, and turned to Ethan. "Quick! Help me turn the other ones!"

We raced to the next window, and then the next. Each one turned, though the symbol marked on each one was slightly different. They matched up with my drawings, though, and I consulted it as Ethan turned, his big arms straining to move the rock. Each successful turn resulted in another delighted squeal from Remy.

When Ethan was on the seventh window, I raced back into the room with the sunroof, and gasped in shock.

Remy stood in rainbow streams of light. The entire room was lit up with sunbeams of different colors. I glanced down. In the center of the room the floor had become an enormous mirror. Each of the suns above was reflecting the light it beamed back up, shooting it down with different beams of color. It was like standing in a kaleidoscope.

"How did they do this?" Remy asked in wonder, raising her hands into the air as if to touch the brilliant beams of light.

"I don't know," I said, staring at my surroundings. "It doesn't make sense. The mirror in the floor—that's not Anasazi. And these lights—"

"They're not Anasazi," Remy said with an exasperated sigh. "We're hunting an immortal, Jackie. The rules don't apply."

Well, she had me there.

Something cranked and the final sun flicked into light—a brilliant blue. The light seemed to refract and fix upon one spot on the cliff wall, and to my shock, the beams of light lined up and made the outline of a door.

"No fucking way," Remy breathed, grabbing my arm with excitement. "This is like some Lord of the Rings shit! We're about to enter Mordor!"

Cautiously, I moved forward. Sure enough, the lights had formed a pattern that looked like a door. Sucking in a breath, I pushed on it.

Runes lit up at my touch, and the wall slid away in a crunch of rock.

The door opened.

CHAPTER NINE

"If you push hard enough, there's always a way in. Trufax."—*Fuck Like a Porn Star: The Basics*, by Remy Summore

~*~

Remy clutched my arm as I stared into the deep shadows on the other side of the opened door. The room we stood in was all brilliant lights and splendor, but through those doors, it was inky darkness.

And somewhere within, power pulsed, making me jittery and nervous. It felt like when I'd touched Joachim's halo, except ten times stronger.

"They must both be here," I told Remy, stepping forward. "It feels so strong."

"Wait," she yelped, grabbing my arm. "Are you sure you want to go down there?"

"We don't have a choice," I told her. "I'm not about to let Phryne get that halo and destroy Zane or Noah, or both. I can't let it get into her hands. They could be following us even now." I thought of Nefer, who'd shown up at our hotel room to take us down. They knew what we were after, and I was positive she was not more than a few steps behind us. But Remy looked rather stricken at the sight of the gaping black tunnel. "You don't have to go."

She chewed on her lip, thinking. "But who will be your fashionable sidekick if I don't? And besides, I have the gun."

99

"You do," I admitted, feeling relieved. I wasn't looking forward to going in there alone myself. "This won't take too long. We'll zip in, grab the haloes, and then zip back out again. How deep can this cave thing be?"

"Dunno," Remy said. "But I'm thinking we need flashlights."

She was right. I hadn't brought one in with me. I hadn't thought this would turn into a cave journey. I glanced anxiously around the kaleidoscope room. "I don't suppose that *Panty Raiders of the Lost Ark* offered any helpful tips for this?"

"Sadly, no. Just more dildo jokes."

"I can make you a torch," Ethan said, ducking into the room and studying us.

"You can?" I turned to him in surprise. "Really?"

Remy pinched his cheeks. "Of course you can, you adorable Boy Scout, you."

Ethan ignored her cuddling and gave me a dismissive look. "Fire making is quite an easy skill to learn, Jackie Brighton. It is a valuable skill if one intends to—"

I waved a hand at him. "Just skip the lecture and make me a damn torch so we can get going before that door closes."

Ethan pulled out a Swiss army knife and proceeded to tear strips from his shirt.

Ten minutes later, both Remy and I held torches. The end was wrapped with Ethan's shirt, and the green wood sticks had been pulled from a nearby tree. He'd searched for the perfect tree and then rubbed resin all over the end before wrapping fabric around it, and then lit it.

As Ethan handed Remy her torch, he leaned in and gave her a fierce kiss. "Good luck."

"You're not coming with us?" she asked, glancing back at me in alarm.

"I will stay and guard the door so that your enemies do not pass."

"Good idea," I said, then smiled at him. "Thanks, Ethan."

He nodded, "Return safely," he said, and brushed his fingers along Remy's jaw. "Or I will pop a cap in your ass."

Remy grimaced. "Babe, do you even know what that means?"

"I do not know what any of it means," he admitted. "I did it wrong?"

"Baby, see, you tell someone you want to pop a cap in their ass when—" she began.

I gestured at the door, interrupting them. "Can we just go already? Please?"

"Hater," Remy muttered, giving Ethan one last quick kiss, holding her torch aloft, and then stepping next to me. "Let's go then, cranky pants."

"I'm not cranky," I hissed. "I don't know if you noticed, but we're pressed for time here." I held my torch aloft and stepped into the doorway. The flickering light revealed a narrow hall, carved into the rock, the ceiling no more than two feet over my head. The walls were rough, as if no one had bothered to finish the tunnel, and when I raised my torch, it didn't seem like that long of a tunnel. "Come on," I told Remy. "It's probably just at the end here."

We crept forward, our torches brushing along the low ceiling, leaving sputtering sparks in our wake. I glanced back and Ethan stood at the entrance, his big body haloed in sparkling light.

"I see something up ahead," Remy said, pointing past me. "We're almost there."

There was a plain wooden door at the end of the tunnel. Thank God. This tunnel was making me claustrophobic. I picked up speed, and when I got to the door, I put my hand on the handle and tugged. It creaked and fell open easily, and we were hit by a musty gust of air that ruffled our hair and made our torches flicker.

The scent of deep, wet cave hit me, and I stared ahead in shock. A staircase had been cut into the rock ahead of us. It curved to the side beyond the door and descended into the darkness. A carved railing framed the edge of the stairs, which were made of stone that was far more delicate than anything I had ever seen.

"We're going... down?" I said, disbelieving. The room was so vast and open. I held my torch up and stared at the stalactites overhead. There was no place to go *but* down.

"How far does it go?" Remy asked in a nervous voice.

I had no idea. I glanced over at her. "Give me one of your earrings." She handed it to me and I tiptoed closer to the rail, mindful of the slick steps. Pebbles and rocky debris scattered as I moved to the railing, and I held her jingly earring over the side and dropped it, waiting for the clink that would tell me it had landed.

It never came.

"That *sucks*," Remy said softly.

"I know," I said grimly. "Who knows how far down this goes?"

We weren't dealing with mortals—anything was possible.

"Worst of all, that was my favorite earring."

I held my torch out, eyeing the steps. "Well, they're not going to climb themselves, as my mother always said."

"Yeah, but your mother's kinda crazy."

"True enough."

We began to descend the stairs. At first, we picked our way cautiously, as the steps were slick with mist and the drip from the cave walls. After about five flights of stairs, we were just stomping down, heedless of how much noise we made.

After ten flights, Remy started to grumble.

After fifty flights, I started to grumble, too.

"Jesus fucking Christ, how many stairs are there in this place?" Remy complained for the eleventh time that hour. "We've been going down these steps for forever."

I wished I had a phone so I could see the time. "I'm sure we're almost there."

"Really?" Remy said sarcastically. "You said that twenty flights ago. And they just keep going down."

It was true; they did keep descending into darkness. I wondered how deep these stairs were carved into the earth. Would they just keep going down? How much longer?

"I don't know if you've thought about this, Jacks, but what goes down must come up. We're going to have to climb all this shit to get out of here, dude."

I grimaced, switching my torch-holding arm again because it was tired. "I thought about that, yeah."

"Have you thought about what you would wish for if you got the haloes? Because I'm thinking you should wish for an escalator," Remy said.

"Ha ha." I thought for a moment, then said, "Noah. He's covered in the tattoos—the markings. It's changed him. He's become hard, cynical." It hurt me to see. I knew it was my fault that he'd been indentured to the Serim. "I guess I'd wish that Noah would be freed."

"You could wish for anything, and that's what you'd want? Really?"

I thought of Zane. I'd offered the wish to him, but he hadn't been interested—all he'd wanted was to stay with me. "I have everything I need."

"Girlfriend, I have seen your bank account. You do not have everything you need, and that vampire's flat-ass broke. Unless you want to get yourself a job, I'd suggest you ask the archangel for money."

"You have money," I teased. "I'll just use yours."

"My bank account is pretty low, thanks to Moochy McVampire and our little 'round-the-world jaunts. And since I'm not doing porn anymore, I need to replenish my bank account."

"That's why you're writing your memoir," I said, pausing on the stairs to look over at her. "Right?"

She rolled her eyes in the flickering light and pushed past me, clearly annoyed. "It is going to be the shortest memoir ever. Ethan has been helping me edit it down."

"Taking out all the dirty stuff?"

"No! That's the worst part. He's taking out everything that he thinks might point toward us being immortals, and things that he feels might violate my privacy. He's being protective, which is cute… but you're supposed to spill all in a memoir. Who's going to want to buy a book that doesn't talk about the juicy shenanigans?"

I muffled my laugh.

"It's not funny," Remy complained. "I worked hard to build my empire and now I'm leaving it all behind for a guy. The gossip magazines are totally going to have a field day."

"No one will care, Remy," I began, then squinted ahead of us. "Is that a light?"

"Damn, I hope so," Remy said. "Either that or a bathroom."

"Yeah, right." Succubi didn't have those kinds of needs. My steps slowed and I shushed Remy as we moved forward. There was definitely a faint light below us. It was hard to see beyond the torches, but the glimmer below seemed greenish and faint. "Maybe we're coming to the bottom."

"I think I hear water," Remy commented.

I heard it too, and that worried me. I said nothing as we traveled down another flight of twisting stairs, except this time, when the stairs turned, we landed on a platform. All around us, inky black water lapped around the tiny round platform. Across from the base of the stairs, an ornately carved torch holder stood empty. I moved past it, frowning at the edge of the water. Other than the torch holder and the stairs we'd come down, there was nothing.

It was like we'd been stranded on an island in the middle of an underground lake, the bottom of the stairwell barely big enough for Remy and me to stand close together.

She put her free hand on her hip. "What now, fearless leader?"

I turned, holding my torch high, trying to see around us. The pulse of the halo definitely felt closer, but how much closer? We'd felt like we'd been right on top of it for hours. I peered into the black water and then glanced over at Remy. "How deep do you think this is?"

She clutched her remaining earring protectively, hiding it from me. "Don't know, don't care. I didn't pack a swimsuit."

I stared at the green smear of light in the distance. We were level with whatever it was now, but no closer. How incredibly frustrating.

I handed Remy my torch and began to roll up my shorts.

"What are you doing?"

I gestured at the water. "Gonna see how deep it is. Maybe we can wade across."

"Maybe not," Remy said desperately. "What if there are cave sharks or something in there? Or alligators?"

"We're in Arizona," I pointed out.

"We're in the side of a mountain and we got here because some sparkly shit opened a door to the tomb of an archangel. I don't know if you noticed that, but I'm not ruling anything out right now."

She had a point. I slid off my shoe, rolled off my sock, and then dipped my pinky into the water. When nothing bit it off, I shrugged. "It's either that or go back up the stairs again. Empty-handed."

She sighed. "Okay, but don't come crying to me if you lose a leg."

"I'll just grow it back, right?" I slid one leg into the water, flexing my toes and feeling for the bottom. It was ice cold.

I also couldn't feel the bottom. I stuck my leg in further, and then accidentally fell off the slippery rock, dunking in. I clawed for the surface, hissing with cold, my teeth chattering.

"Did you hit the bottom?" Remy asked.

"N-no," I chattered, dragging my wet body back on the rock. I shivered and pulled the phone out of my pocket. Water dripped from it. Well, hell. I tugged the wet paper out of my bra, grimacing at the smears of pencil. I needed someplace to lay this paper flat, just in case I needed it again.

"So what do we do?" Remy asked me, handing me my torch back.

I frowned at the bitterly cold water surrounding us, my teeth chattering. My nipples felt like rocks in my now-damp bra and my clothing stuck to me. It felt awful, but it wouldn't kill me. "I don't know. The translation Sophie gave us didn't say anything about any of this."

"Maybe it said something on the paper Phryne has," Remy said helpfully.

Yeah, but that wouldn't help us, and I wasn't waiting around for her to arrive. I eyed the sculpted torch holder in the center of the small island and shoved my torch in to free my hand.

Rock immediately began to scrape, deafeningly loud. Remy grabbed me in alarm as the waters boiled around us. Smooth stepping-stones rose up from the previously calm lake surface. After a long minute, the scraping stopped, the stones locking in place and making a perfect path.

I glanced back at my torch. "Well, that was obvious. I need to return my Indiana Jones card."

Remy still held her torch aloft, peering over the edge of the water. "Do you suppose they're trick stones? Isn't that how it is in the movies?"

God, I hoped not. But I was already wet. "One way to find out, I suppose." I carefully stepped forward onto the closest one and squeezed my eyes shut, waiting.

Nothing. It felt solid. I could barely make out the outline of the next and stepped forward on it, then looked back to Remy. "You'll have to step behind me. Give me your torch so I can lead the way."

She handed it over to me without a word of protest. The darkness was almost overwhelming in the huge cavern. Our voices echoed when we spoke, and it was freezing . I wished we'd brought more lights or warm clothes, but none of this had been planned.

Going one by one on each step took time. Each surface was barely the length of my feet, so stepping carefully meant taking my time because the rocks were slippery and wet. We made our way forward cautiously. We'd check our balance, test the rock ahead before moving on. I was shivering and quaking with cold, my fingers like ice. The torch shook in my hands, and there was nothing I could do to warm up.

"No scenes like this in *Panty Raiders of the Lost Ark,*" Remy muttered as I stepped forward again, on what must have been the hundredth step.

I giggled at the absurdity of the comment, and my foot slipped. My body plunged forward into the water and my chin banged on the rock ahead of me, cracking my jaw. Remy screamed as the cave went dark.

My entire head was awash in sheets of red and black agony. On shaking, weak arms, I dragged myself onto the next rock and sat, shivering. My teeth wanted to chatter, but even the thought sent nightmare waves of pain through my jaw, so I remained still, trembling instead. Everything was pitch-black, that smear of green in the distance not nearly enough to light our way.

Trapped. Underground. In the dark. In the middle of a lake.

I tried not to panic.

Remy's hand reached for mine, and she felt my arm blindly in the dark. "You okay?"

I tested my jaw. It felt broken, but it'd heal eventually. I patted her arm as an answer.

"What do we do now?" Remy said, and I heard her shift on her rock. "Should we swim for shore?"

I didn't know. I didn't know anything. Why did I think a halo would be just up for the taking? How stupid was I? I was a newborn immortal. Why had I ever thought I could do this?

A light flared in the darkness behind us, and Remy and I both turned at the same time. Despite my jaw, I gasped in shock at the face haloed in golden light, standing on the platform behind us.

Noah Gideon, a lantern in hand.

~*~

Well, shit.

As always, the sight of Noah was stunning. He stood a hundred feet away, back on the platform, awash in soft, golden light that cast his stern face into shadows. He was beautiful, the angelic tattoos visible even through the loose white button-up shirt he wore over a white tank top. His blond hair was mussed, and I'm sure mine didn't look too hot after being in a cave all morning.

"Ladies," he said in a no-nonsense voice. His gaze moved over the rocks, then in my direction, as if he could see me in the darkness. "You don't look thrilled to see me, Jackie."

There was no humor in his voice, no playful affection.

"It's true," I admitted, and winced at the pain in my jaw, putting a hand to it and falling silent again.

Seeing Noah down here made even more curse words rise to mind. Not just the regular ones, too. He needed a whole string of them. *Shitfuckdamnitalltohell.*

He must have come here for the same halo. Damn it. That would be the only explanation as to why he'd kept showing up. Unless… someone had sold us out. Someone with peach hair and cold eyes, I suspected. Either way, the Serim knew we were after the halo and they'd come to snatch it first.

And who better to send than the one man that I was unable to disobey? I watched, guarded, as he stepped forward on one of the stones, and began to calmly make his way toward us.

"We don't need your help," I called, pressing a hand to my cheek. It throbbed something awful, but I ignored it. "You can go back. We're cool."

He made it to us in no time at all, which I kind of hated. Soon enough, he was at the stepping-stones beside us, holding the lantern out to peer at the two of us. Remy got to her feet, dusting off her wet jeans and I got to mine as well, my entire body shivering, my jaw a black ache that wouldn't go away. I'd scraped and bruised the hell out of my leg on my fall into the water, but that was trivial. A nice, long, thorough round of sex with Zane and I'd heal fast. I just had to endure until he awoke.

As Noah's gaze slid over me, I knew he took note of my bruises, my shivering, my swelling jaw. I said nothing, just crossed my arms over my wet chest and glared at him.

He glanced at Remy, then at me. "I'm not here to rescue you."

"You're here to stop us," I said through my tight, throbbing jaw. I looked back at that smear of green light, so faint in the distance. So close and yet so far.

He tilted his head, studying me, and then stepped forward onto the next stepping-stone. "No, I'm here to retrieve the halo myself."

I swallowed the gasp that threatened to rise in my throat and gingerly moved onto the stone he'd left. "What? Why?"

He continued to move forward, taking the light with him, leaving us no choice but to follow close behind. As I hobbled onto each stone he vacated, Remy followed.

"Because I am compelled, of course," Noah said without turning around, and I could hear the bitterness in his voice. "The council wishes to have the halo and the Archangel Gabriel's favor for themselves, and I am their willing puppet."

I said nothing to that. He carried the burden of those tasks because he'd accidentally turned me. What was I going to do, apologize for existing? I couldn't say I was sorry to be an immortal, only sorry that Noah was the one paying the price for it.

But somehow, I guessed that "sorry" wouldn't make things better.

So I said nothing.

Noah was remarkably surefooted on the flagstones, as if they weren't slippery with water or incredibly small. His strides were long enough that he walked on them without hesitation, unlike the anxious, slow steps forward that Remy and I did. With him in the lead, we made it to the other side, crossing that immense underground lake.

The "other side" proved to be a rounded nook, no more than fifteen feet wide and about that long. At least there was firm, solid ground to stand upon. We moved to the rock and stared at our surroundings. The luminescent green moss I'd seen from across the lake covered the small alcove like a film, setting the entire area aglow. A ten-foot-tall wall, heavily carved, blocked the way between us and the rest of the cavern. A stone door with a circular carving rested in the center of the wall, covered in more moss. As I looked overhead, the ceiling rose high into the darkness, and I was unable to see the top of it. The cavern seemed endless. The cold, black water made gentle lapping noises at the lip of the stone platform.

I reached up to touch one of the walls and the moss came off on my hands, so I was careful not to brush anything else. I didn't want to be stuck in the dark again. I hugged my wet T-shirt close and looked over at Noah, waiting.

He turned the lantern off, testing the light. The green glow from the moss was dim, but enough that we could still make out each other's outlines and the door ahead of us.

"So if you're here going after the halo, should we just turn around?" Remy asked. "Jackie's a little busted up."

I glared at her.

"No," Noah said quietly, shrugging off his shirt. "Stay."

Well that settled it. A command. Not that I was planning on

leaving. I'd find a way to get around Noah and get that halo for myself. "So what is this place? Since you got here without a map or anything."

He glanced back at me. "This is the final resting place of the Archangel Azazel."

"Then what's with all of this?" I gestured at the door, which was as beautifully carved as everything else in this weird place. "What's with all the stairs and the stepping-stones? It's not like it's a maze. Just a lot of walking. Why go to so much effort?"

"It was a labor of love," Noah said softly, running a hand down the carved circular door. "Azazel was the best-loved of all the archangels. I imagine someone built this for him to show how much they loved him. An homage to him, even in death."

"Well, as tombs go, this one hasn't had a single booby trap," I pointed out. "So either we're doing something wrong, or these guys didn't have much imagination."

Noah glanced back at me. "This is the entrance to the tomb proper. Behind it lies a madman's way, the measure of the unknowing, and the light of the eternal."

He'd known what I was after all along. I gritted my teeth. "So what was all that other crap? The stairs and flagstones and everything?"

Noah smiled faintly and glanced over at me. "Foreplay."

"Foreplay!"

"Only those truly devoted to Azazel were meant to come this far. If you make it this far in, then the real tests begin."

Oh goody.

"What does the council want from Gabriel anyhow?" I managed to grit out.

"I don't know," Noah said in a grave voice. "Nothing good, I'm sure." He held the shirt out to me. When I hesitated, he said, "Take off your shirt and put this on."

Burning anger flashed through me and I tore the wet shirt over my head, flinging it to the ground with a wet slap. My breasts were covered in nothing but a filmy bra, my hard nipples evident even in the low light. I took the shirt as I'd been compelled to do and buttoned it loosely. I didn't want to admit, even grudgingly, that it was a lot warmer than what I'd been wearing.

It was the fact that Noah had swept back into my life and thought he could just control everything again.

He seemed to know my mutinous thoughts, taking a step toward me. There was a hint of a hard smile on his face and he reached out to brush a thumb over my busted jaw. "I can help you with this, you know."

I slapped his hand away. We'd been lovers for a long time, but I was with Zane now, and Zane and Noah hated each other. Sleeping with Noah without coercion meant that I was betraying the man I loved.

And while succubi had questionable morals, I wasn't heading down that road.

A hard, wry smile twisted Noah's mouth. "Spurned by my own creation," he said softly.

"Why can't we just be friends?" I grated through my aching jaw.

He chuckled, the sound low, as he turned toward the door. "Why Jackie, I thought we *were* friends."

Yeah, 'cause this was so friendly.

Remy cleared her throat. "I hate to cut all this palpable sexual tension here, but, Noah, how did you get down here?"

As he moved toward the wall, he glanced over it, assessing. With one hand, he brushed his fingers over the carvings. "I came down the same way you did. Through the room of lights and down the stairs."

"But what about Ethan?" Remy asked, a note of worry in her voice. "He let you pass?"

"I told Ethan that I was here to help you. He was enthusiastic about the thought. Good deed and all."

I clenched my fists. Curse him for turning our Boy Scout against us. "You suck."

"I did what I had to," Noah said. He moved to the door, studying it for a moment. The center of the door was covered in moss and he wiped it away with gentle fingers, revealing a series of buttons in a circle. Another halo symbol? Noah placed his fingers over the center carving and pushed. The symbol of Ra, I noticed.

It depressed inward. He turned it over and then began to depress the circular buttons on the edges of the carving in a very slow, deliberate pattern, as if he were working an ancient combination lock.

"So I suppose you're just going to swoop in here, snatch the halo, and ignore the two of us working so hard to get it for ourselves?" I asked him, getting annoyed when he didn't even look up from the carving. He just continued to press the buttons in combinations of two and three at a time, pausing, and then pressing a button again.

"Hello, Noah? Earth to Noah, come in please." Remy said impatiently. "We're trying to lecture you here. You can play Connect Four with the wall some other time."

"You can lecture me afterward," he said after a moment, and I heard a click, then a rumble as the door's symbol depressed and began to twist on its own. He'd unlocked it. With a satisfied look, he turned to me. "I'm sorry if you're angry, Jackie. You know I don't want this for myself."

"It doesn't matter if you want it for yourself or not. The point is that you're still pushing ahead of us. That makes you a big jerk, just like that asshole Phryne," I pointed out.

"You say the sweetest things," a cool, familiar voice whispered behind me. I heard a splashing sound at the edge of the platform and then the sound of a gunshot and Remy's cry of pain as she pitched forward. I barely caught sight of Ashara's dark, dripping hair as she lowered a gun from behind Remy. Phryne was here?

A second gunshot went off. My head exploded.

All went dark.

CHAPTER TEN

"The sad truth of the business is that someone's always going to step over someone else to get ahead. Or give head to get ahead."—*A Porn Story*, by Remy Summore

~*~

Warm kisses pressed to my skin, dancing along my breastbone and stomach. Hands traced my hips and slid my shorts off.

A tidal wave of pain rushed through my head, nearly blacking me out again. I existed in that weird space without dreams or consciousness, only vaguely aware that someone crouched over me, running hands over my body. A mouth descended on my sex and began to lick, and I whimpered. No, not Noah. I didn't want Noah.

I wanted Zane.

"Don't fight me, Princess," a voice whispered against my thighs. "Just lie back and heal."

Zane. I relaxed. That tongue pressed to my clit and then I felt teeth sink into my slick folds, even as the tongue pressed to my clit again.

The orgasm that shot through me knocked me out again.

When I next awoke, it was to the feeling of warm hands stroking my breasts, teasing the nipples erect. My head throbbed and ached, but the pain was being quickly drowned out by the sensations flooding through my body.

"That's it, Princess. Come back to me," Zane said softly, whispering against my neck and then pressing a kiss there.

'What... where am I?" The words were soft, difficult to speak, my gaze fuzzy. My senses were drowning in Zane, his warm, naked body pressed against my skin. My legs were parted underneath him, but he wasn't deep inside me. His cock pressed against my belly, a hard bar of need as he continued to kiss and stroke every inch of my skin. "Zane... how?"

"Shh," he said softly, moving up to kiss me into silence. His tongue stroked into my mouth, sending a bolt of lazy pleasure through my body. Then he lightly nipped at my full lower lip, letting me feel his fangs. "Still in the tomb. Don't worry. You're safe with me."

His thumb traced small circles on my nipple, teasing the peak erect as my topsy-turvy senses tried to align themselves. He continued to kiss me, softly, gently, languidly, slow, sensual kisses that drugged my senses and made my body pulse with pleasure. We had all the time in the world, those kisses told me, and he was going to spend it loving me. His lips captured mine again, his tongue licking at the seam of my mouth before breaking the kiss again.

God, he tasted amazing. I whimpered when he pulled his mouth away from mine, needing more. His hand brushed my cheek and he kissed down my throat, pressing light, firm, tasting kisses to my skin.

My eyes began to focus in the low, greenish light, and I noticed the spread of Zane's black wings over the two of us. God, that was sexy. I always loved the sight of those feathers, the thick sweep of them. I reached up to touch one, run my fingers through the weave of feathers the way he liked, but my arm was sluggish to respond. Before I could raise my arm, Zane was there to press it back down again, then brushed his knuckles over the skin. "Just relax. Let me love you."

And he nipped at my nipple. It sent a shiver of delight through my body and I relaxed again, letting him work my body as I watched with dazed, sleepy eyes.

"My beautiful Jackie," he whispered, then lapped at my erect nipple, coaxing the peak to stand taller. "Gorgeous, sexy princess."

"Zane," I murmured softly. "You feel so good."

"I know," he said with a grin. His mouth dipped back to my nipple and he circled it with his tongue.

"Bite?" I asked softly. I loved it when he bit my nipples.

But he shook his head at me and gave me the lightest of teasing flicks on my breast. "Not tonight, Princess. You need your wits about you."

Wits seemed to be the last thing I had right about now. My world was full of Zane's delicious skin, his rippling black wing feathers, the weight of his body over mine. I felt so languid that all I could do was enjoy the sensation.

When his mouth dipped to my navel, I caught my breath. "I want you inside me," I told him. "In me, possessing me."

His red eyes flared with need and he ran a hand down my thigh. He hooked his hand behind my knee and tugged it open further, exposing me to him. Then his hand skimmed back down my thigh and brushed against my sex with his knuckles. "You're so perfect. Look at how wet you are for me."

I felt his finger dip into my sex, felt it slide deep and I was indeed wet with need. I moaned, my gaze rapt on him as he lifted that slick finger to his lips and tasted it. His eyes grew even redder with lust, his fangs elongating. "Taste so sweet."

"Taste me," I begged. "Bite me."

"Later," he promised huskily. His hand went to his cock and he guided it to my entrance, where I was aching and ready. I whimpered as he began to push in, loving the sensation. Normally he thrust into me with speed, knowing that it excited me to be quick and dirty—and okay, a little rough. But tonight, he was exquisite in his tenderness for me.

Inch by inch, he pushed deeper into my body, his red eyes watching me as he pressed forward. When he was seated fully within me, he let loose a hissing breath and then leaned closer, gently kissing my mouth again. His movement was slow and exquisite. The stab of him deep inside me, along with the matching thrust of his tongue—I moaned, feeling my body tighten in an oncoming orgasm.

"That's it, Princess. Come for me," Zane murmured, kissing me again. He continued to rock into my body, sinking deep with each careful, prolonged thrust. My movements grew more frantic, though. I writhed under him, needing him, unable to articulate just how much. When the orgasm shot through my body, I whimpered my release, feeling my sex clench around him, deep inside me.

He groaned, about to lose control, and his soft, seductive kisses stopped for a moment. Teeth scraped at my lower lip and he groaned again, then pulled back. Zane lifted his head from mine and watched me with intense, burning eyes. Then he sank deep inside me, rocking forward and thrusting once more, beginning the delicious, rhythmic torture again. I raised my hips a little with his movements, my hands sliding to his ass to cup those delicious bundles of muscle and holding him tight against me, deep inside me.

"I want you to come again," he said, and began to thrust harder into me. It was a slow piston of his hips, and I felt the answering flutter deep inside me, so deep and needy that I almost missed it. But at that flutter, I gasped.

"Perfect," Zane said. His hand went to my hips and tilted them, holding me pinned against him at an angle.

When he thrust again, I felt that sensation in every nerve ending of my body. My eyes widened and I gasped. "Zane—"

"I'm here," he rasped, thrusting again, harder, hitting that perfect spot once more. He was rubbing a spot deep inside me that was exactly what I needed. My moans grew louder, my nails digging into his shoulders as he continued to rock into me, his intense gaze devouring my every response, watching me intently.

That heated gaze seemed to focus everything in my body, my muscles tensing with need. When he hit that perfect place deep within me in his next thrust, I cried out and came again, clenching hard around him, my legs quivering.

Zane bit out a curse, and I felt him lose that measured control. His slow, measured thrusting became hard and wild. The orgasm racing through my body didn't stop, just cascaded around me, growing in intensity as his body driving into mine stroked us to a fever pitch. My cries became a keening moan.

When he finally stiffened on top of me, shouting my name, his fingers digging bruises into my hips, I was lost in the intensity of the orgasm, my limbs locked around his. I felt him shudder, felt him come deep inside me. He rocked hard against me one more time, then slowly fell forward, panting, his sweat-slicked body covering mine.

I languidly wrapped my arms around his neck and kissed his face like I always did, my body twitching after the orgasm. I wasn't tired after marathon sex. I usually felt pumped; energized. I did right now, but Zane's sweating skin and heavy breathing implied that he'd need a moment to recover. So I brushed my fingers through his wild hair and tried to pull my thoughts together.

The ceiling above our heads was the first thing I noticed. It was the same soft green of the moss from the tunnel, but it seemed low. As if I could reach out and touch it. That didn't make sense. I glanced over to my side and noticed that the cave we were in had a lip, and when the lip ended, I could no longer see the floor.

That... didn't seem right.

As I turned my head, I noticed that it was propped on something. I reached behind me to feel... fabric. Wet fabric. Pain pulsed in the back of my head at the slight touch and I jerked my hand away, remembering.

A crack like a gunshot, and Remy had gone down. Then a second shot and darkness. I hadn't even seen if Noah had gotten into the tomb or not. Those bitches had shot me in the back of the head. I made an outraged noise in my throat.

Zane pressed a kiss to my neck, breathing hard. "Glad to see you awake."

Anxiety swept through me. Phryne was here. She was after the halo, and she was too damn close. "Where is she? We have to stop her." I struggled to get up.

"Don't," Zane said, pressing a hand to my shoulder to keep me down. "Let your body heal. You were out for a long time. It was a bad shot."

It must have been if Zane was awake. I knew we'd been down in the cavern for a while, but surely not an entire day? "Remy?"

"Still down there. I couldn't grab you both."

True. And he couldn't heal her. Well, not unless he offered her sex, and while I adored my best friend... she could wait a few hours for her own lover. I brushed my fingertips over his mind, diving into his thoughts to pull the information. I had so many questions, and I knew the answers would be quickest this way. I pressed past the collage of current thoughts, images of my breasts bouncing as he fucked me, the softness of my lips, real fear as he'd found me unconscious in a pool of my own blood, and dove deeper.

In Zane's memories, I saw him awaken at dusk.

Both he and Sophie had been concerned that no one in our party had returned, and white-hot fear had shot through him when he'd found out that Noah Gideon had followed them.

He'd rushed up the cliffs, following the traces of my power signature, and found Ethan collapsed near the secret door, fast asleep. Someone—and he had a nasty suspicion as to who—had been here before him and put the Enforcer to sleep. Zane had pushed on through the tunnel and bypassed the stairs, gliding down to the bottom with only his wings fanning out to slow his drop, and then flown over the lake. It had only taken a few minutes for him to catch up to the others.

There, at the stone door that stood as the entrance to the maze, he'd found Phryne and another woman—Ashara—running their hands over the circular door, trying to find their way in. Noah Gideon was nowhere to be seen—he must have gotten through the door and trapped Phryne and Ashara on the other side.

The sight of Jackie's limp, bloodied form had driven him to action. As he'd descended, rage had overtaken him, especially when he saw the gun in Ashara's hands. A shot to the back of the skull on an immortal would put them out for a while. It was clever... and evil. That they'd done it to his woman filled him with fury.

My mind filled with rage—Zane's rage. I watched the flash of memories become choppy, watched Zane attack the two succubi, Ashara's gun going flying as she slammed into a wall. He grabbed her face and pounded her into the rock, her head crushing like a melon. Turnabout was fair play. And when he saw Phryne—the crafty one—run for Jackie's unconscious body, he grabbed Jackie and hauled her into the air. There'd been an alcove high in the ceiling, away from everything, and he'd taken her there. He'd propped her up with his shirt and then set about to bringing her pleasure, since succubi healed through repeated flare-ups of their curse.

In other words, orgasm.

My mind flashed back to his brutal punch of Ashara, how her head had shattered under his hand as he'd pushed her into the wall.

"Don't, Princess," Zane said softly, jarring me out of his thoughts. He rubbed a thumb over my nipple, distracting me. "If she hurts you, I'm going to hurt right back."

I nodded, not surprised or upset. Just... startled at the brutality of it, I supposed. Zane had so much strength, and he never used any of it against me. I sat up slowly, wincing at the pounding in my head. My jaw felt better at least.

"Here," Zane said, moving close, and his chest was all I saw as he loomed over me, tying a strip of fabric around my head as a bandage. "That'll stop the worst of the bleeding."

I smiled up at him. "You're a good man."

He laughed at that. "I am anything but good, Princess, and you know that."

Well, that was true. I did know that. I looked over at the ledge of our small cave and moved toward it to peer over the edge. Zane put a warning hand on my back but I only peeked over, wanting to see everything.

We were so high up that everything below seemed like it was occurring in an ant farm. Up here at the top of the cavern, I had a better idea of just how vast this cave network was. I felt dizzy staring down at the floor far, far below. How had the cliff been so very hollow? This was big enough to house a city. Far below, the tomb stretched and curled in a riotous mess of walls and small rooms. I stared over the ledge at it, frowning. It seemed to stretch on for miles. "What is all that stuff?"

"A maze," Zane said with a hint of amusement. "Old Azazel did like his games."

Of course. A maze. That must have been what all the notations on that first page had been. At the time, I'd had no clue. Now it all made sense, and it filled me with panic because the maze had been on the Melledin Manuscript page that had been stolen from me. "Where is Phryne?"

He pointed off to the right and I had to crane my neck to see in that direction, which sent a stab of agony down my spine. "Over there. You know that door where she shot you? She can't get through it. She must not have the code that Noah did."

It had to have been part of the monastery wall, or the Serim had passed it along to Noah. Phryne's page had information about the maze, but it seemed like she didn't have the key that would enable her to even get to it. Well, thank God. I breathed a sigh of relief at that. "And Noah?"

"Dunno." He gestured at a far end of the maze. "But there's a ward pulsing in that direction, so my guess is that he's using an arcane shield of some kind to hide his location while he's vulnerable."

Huh. "How did Noah get an arcane shield?"

"My guess is that the Serim dragged their favorite warlock out of hiding and forced him to make them some toys."

I grimaced at the thought of Luc Stone, an old frenemy of mine. He was an incubus created by the Serim named Ariel… also not a friend of mine. "So what I'm hearing is that if we can get past the door where Phryne is stuck, we can make a clear run for the halo?"

Zane chuckled. "Princess, we can simply fly over all of it."

"Oh." I stared down at the dizzying maze below. "Well, that's handy."

Zane's fingers brushed over the curve of my naked buttock. "But first, I think you need a little more healing."

I couldn't argue with that.

~*~

We dressed and left the alcove a short time later. Zane had to skip his shirt since it was trashed, and he shrugged his coat on over his bare chest. He scowled at the sight of me buttoning Noah's shirt back on. "I see that bastard didn't wait five minutes to get his hooks back into you."

"He was just being nice, letting me borrow his shirt. Nothing more. He won't force me to return to him," I said. "You know that."

"Won't he?"

I shook my head. Noah was hard around the edges—more now than ever—but he didn't want to force me to be at his side. He wanted me there of my own free will. "I don't think he means me harm. He just wants the halo."

"We have to stay away from him, Jackie," Zane said, straightening and handing me his coat. His wings shuddered, a black waterfall on his back. "If you get that halo, all he has to do is snap his fingers and you'll be forced to hand it to him. We do not want that kind of power in the hands of the Serim council. They'll use it to wipe out all of their enemies—and I'm betting that both of us are counted in those ranks."

I tugged his coat on over my shirt. Nice and warm. "I know. I'll be careful."

Zane pushed a lock of hair behind my ear and smiled down at me. "You will, because I'm going to tear into anyone who tries to touch you." His fingers dug into the belt loops of my shorts. "Now, hold on to my neck."

I clung to him, wrapping my legs around his waist and my arms around his neck. He pressed a quick, hard kiss to my mouth and then raced for the edge of the ledge. There was a brief moment of free fall and a scream lodged in my throat.

Zane spread his wings.

Our abrupt fall dipped and then we were gliding through the cavern, the enormous maze passing below us. He flapped his wings, getting altitude, and I kept my gaze on the sights below. On the far side of the maze, the ground cut away sharply into darkness—a gorge. A tiny rope bridge crossed it, and I swallowed hard at the sight of it. That would have been a problem to cross on foot, but with a winged vampire to carry me? It was a mere afterthought.

Past a room full of squares—I didn't even want to know what that entailed—and toward a pair of double doors at the far end of the cave network. Flames danced in braziers. I had no idea how they'd been lit, and a sweep of stairs led to a massive, carved door. Zane dropped me at the foot of the stairs and I clung to him even as I stood at the base.

Power pulsed here, so thick and heady that it made my brain swim.

"No turning back now, Princess," Zane said, reaching into the pocket of the coat I was wearing. He fished out a cigarette and lit it in one of the braziers as I stared at the intricate doors ahead of me. Zane took a drag, then glanced over at me. "You ready?"

I nodded, unable to tear my gaze away from the doors. "Ready." I took a step forward, and when Zane didn't, I glanced back at him. "You coming?"

He grimaced. "Can't. Beyond those steps, it's holy ground."

That meant I was on my own. I moved back to him and lifted my hands to his face, tilting his mouth toward mine for a long, searing kiss. He tasted like fresh cigarette. "I won't be long. Wait for me?"

His red eyes burned into mine and his voice went husky. "You know I'd wait for all eternity for you."

"I know," I said softly, pressing my forehead to his.

Zane kissed me again. Quick. Hard. "Be careful."

"I will." I turned back toward the steps. There were six of the thick, broad slabs of rock that made up the stairs, and I slowly dragged my feet up each one, taking my time, the power pulse making my body more sluggish the closer I got.

The doors opened as I took the final step and my heart sank into my stomach. Nerves shot through me. This was it. The power inside throbbed even harder, making my still-healing head ache even more.

Behind the doors was a small chamber, lit from within. The entire room was cast into golden light, the walls covered with carved murals. In the center of the room lay an enormous altar, and the pure golden light was beaming from the altar itself, almost as bright as the midday sun.

Holy shit, there it was.

I stepped forward, shielding my eyes with my hand, my gaze on the murals covering the walls. They were stylized renditions of Azazel's life. The panels started with his life as an angel, then as they crept across the room, they told the story of his fall. Later panels showed him worshipped by primitives—the ancient, long-ago natives of this area, I supposed. The next few panels showed him side by side with another tall figure and them embracing. His love. The next panel made my blood run cold. It showed another man, a sword raised high over his head, destroying Azazel. The next seven panels depicted his rather graphic decapitation, the burning of his body, and the scattering of his ashes. Lovely.

So this was the murdered Azazel's tomb, clearly. But there were no signs of a second immortal. Where was the second halo? None of this made any sense.

I moved forward, squinting at the altar. It was so brilliant with light that I couldn't tell where its surface was—it seemed to have been swallowed by the shining light entirely. I closed my eyes, laying my hands on the altar. Cool. Stone. That was the only impression I had before the bright glow flared like a supernova, lighting up behind my eyelids.

And then it died away.

The pulsing grew heavier, more ominous. I opened one eye, testing. The light in the room had fallen to a mere greenish glow—more moss on the ceiling. In front of me, at the center of the plain stone altar, lay a circlet of banked orange light, now gone dull.

The halo.

My fingers closed around it. It felt like liquid fire, and my hair started whipping around my face as if I were standing in the midst of a tornado. I jerked away, then realized that it didn't burn—the heat, the brightness—it didn't harm me. I grasped the halo again and raised it slowly.

It was gorgeous. Flames licked along the circle, looking as if I'd caught the sun. The halo itself was pure power, made of nothing but the angel's will. It rippled and spun like it was made entirely of fire, of magma, of heat and light. The light of the eternal, the puzzle had called it.

It was beautiful.

It was *mine*.

The power pulsing in the tomb died down, the light fading the longer I held the halo, as if it were recognizing me. My hair stopped whipping about my face, landing in tangled waves around my shoulders.

"Fancy," I said softly, pleased. I held it aloft, then frowned. How the heck was I going to carry the thing? It felt wrong to put it on and wear it like one of the angels. I looped my arm through it and it immediately began to shrink. Alarmed, I pulled my arm back out again and it expanded. It resized itself.

Huh.

I put it over my ring finger and sure enough, it resized itself once more, becoming as small as a golden band. Pleased, I flexed my hand and examined the altar, and then the murals. Sure enough, there was only one halo. Well, rats. Where was the other?

As if responding to my thoughts, the halo on my finger pulsed. My mind suddenly raced, flying through the skies, winging over oceans and heading toward a thick, vast jungle. *Let me show you,* a voice whispered in my ear, more suggestion than actual words—

Who are you? I asked.

A creepy, soft echo of a laugh in my mind, but no answer. I shook my head to clear it, more than a little alarmed. Okay. I'd go mental-exploring for the other halo later, when I could control it a little better, and when I had time to chat with that new voice in my head. If it even *wanted* to chat.

I left the tomb, shutting the doors behind me. Zane paced at the bottom of the steps, agitated.

"I have it," I told him, raising my hand in triumph.

His gaze lifted at the sound of my voice, but his eyes remained unfocused, as if he couldn't quite see me. "Where are you?"

Oh, no. He couldn't see me because I wore the archangel's halo. Serim couldn't see demons, and vampires couldn't see pure angels. It was a little cosmic insurance to prevent all-out war, I supposed. Hide the enemy from each other.

It was also damned inconvenient. But I wasn't ready to take the halo off just yet. I moved forward and touched my hand to Zane's chin, leaning in to kiss him. "Right here."

He hissed in pain and jerked away from me. Where my fingers had touched him, his skin reddened as if burned.

"Oh, Zane. I'm so sorry." I ripped the ring off my finger and pushed it into my pocket. Immediately, my pocket began to surge and grow, stretching to halo-size.

"Shit!" I quickly yanked it back out again and stuck it on my finger before it could rip my shorts from me. "I don't know what to do with this thing."

"Don't worry about it." Zane's voice was agitated.

"It was stupid of me. Sorry about that. I wasn't thinking—"

He raised a hand to silence me, and I looked at him with surprise. But his head was tilted, his gaze vacant, focused on something I couldn't see. Then, his face went stark with despair.

"What is it?" I whispered.

"Jackie, Princess," Zane said hoarsely. His gaze swept over where I stood, his eyes focusing on nothing. "Do you trust me, love?"

Love?

He never called me love. "Of course," I said softly, but a tremor of fear was beginning to vibrate deep in my belly.

"I need you to keep the halo on. Don't take it off for anyone or anything. It's yours as long as you have control of it. They can't touch you as long as you wear it."

Dread curled in my stomach. "They who?"

"They're here. I don't know how they're here, but they've found us." Hollow despair showed in his eyes. He reached for me, then hissed as the skin contact burned his hand. He shook it, frowning. "I want you to promise me that you'll stay back."

"Who's here, Zane?"

"The queen," he said harshly. "She's come for the halo."

Oh, *no*. Someone must have tipped her off. How in the hell did all these immortals show up at the same spot at the exact same time when this thing had been sitting here for millennia? Something wasn't adding up. Either we'd tripped some sort of cosmic booby-trap… or someone had sold us out.

My eyes narrowed as I thought of the peach-haired succubus with the cold, dead eyes. I had a few guesses as to whom. "What do we do?"

My vampire's eyes were full of sadness. "You trust me, don't you, Princess?"

"Oh no. Zane, you can't sacrifice yourself." I reached for him, only to pull away again, mindful of hurting him. "Goddamn it, Zane."

"There's no other way, Jackie. Use the halo to mask its power signature. Quickly."

I closed my eyes, readying myself for a struggle with the voice. But as soon as I thought it, it happened. The flaring pulse of power died, and then I felt... nothing. I glanced down at the ring on my finger. Still there.

"Good," Zane said, dragging a hand through his hair, agitated. "I can distract her. I'll tell her that you've already sent the halo back to Gabriel. If she has me to torture..."

"No," I said, and tears began. "Zane, please no. Don't do this. Not when we've got each other now. I need you."

A faint smile tugged at his mouth. "No you don't, Princess. You're strong. With that halo, you're as strong as she is. You don't need anyone or anything. Just watch yourself. And when you can... come and save me. I'll hold on for you."

Hold on? "Oh God, Zane. Please. *Please,* don't do this."

"Will you give me a kiss good-bye?" He closed his eyes, tilting his face toward my voice. "We haven't got much time before they fly in here and I need to intercept them."

"But—"

"Kiss me," His words were a quick snarl.

I moved forward, pressing my hands to his cheeks, ignoring the sizzle of his skin in response. I pressed my lips to his, crying. His lips felt warm against mine, dry. Wonderful. I could taste the faintest hint of cigarette as his tongue stroked briefly against my lips and then he pulled away.

Too brief, I thought, aching for him already.

"I love you," he whispered, pressing his forehead to mine. Then he stepped away, his skin red from my touch. His throat worked as he studied where I was standing. "Wish I could see you one last time."

"Zane, don't."

"Stay there, love," he said softly, a command. "Stay in the tomb for an hour. If I don't come back, I want you to send it up and go after the other. Remy'll take care of you. And if you need more help, get that prick Noah."

"Fuck Noah," I said, tears in my throat. "I want *you*."

That brought a smile to his face. "Good."

And with that, he launched himself into the air. I had no choice but to stay, because Zane had given me a command. The lover who had promised to never make me do anything I didn't want to do... was using my weakness against me for my own good.

CHAPTER ELEVEN

"There are boundaries, of course. Every person has them. But be prepared for people to try and push you past those boundaries. Not because they want you to grow as a person. Mostly because sticking your finger up your partner's ass looks great on camera."—*If You Put the Tip In, It Counts as Sex*, by Remy Summore

~*~

I went back into the tomb and closed the door, as I had been compelled to do. I slid against the cool stone door, my eyes wide, my entire body straining to hear something, anything, from outside. My thoughts were racing, frantic with worry, imagining the worst. The queen would be furious if she found out Zane was alive. I remembered his dream of the ripping feathers. Was she torturing him even now?

That only made my chest hurt with imagined pain, and I pressed my hands to my breast, fighting to keep the tears down. I couldn't cry. Wouldn't cry. Crying wouldn't help Zane. I felt the warmth of the golden band on my finger. Of course! I could use the ring to see what was happening. I pushed my thoughts outward, using the ring's powers, testing to see if I could feel Zane.

An intense cry of pain went up, rocketing through the cavern, and I bit down on my fist at the visual that accompanied the image.

The queen, standing over him, two other vampires holding him down, faces grim. The queen's unnatural, claw-like nails were sunk deep into Zane's chest, around his heart, and she hovered over him, her black eyes furious.

Torturing him.

"Where is the halo?" the queen asked.

"Gone," Zane had said hoarsely. "You're too late. It's already been delivered to the archangel."

Her snarl of fury was drowned out by the psychic wave of pain coming from Zane.

I snapped the tether and cut the vision. I wouldn't peek again. I couldn't.

The minutes ticked past so slowly. The hated compulsion seemed to take forever, and then I was suddenly free, the weight of the promise lifted.

I slid the heavy door open and stumbled down the steps, heading to the rope bridge, hurrying. I needed to help Zane. He was out there, somewhere, being tortured. Remy was still out there too, unconscious and alone and wounded. Noah was hidden in the maze, hibernating. Vulnerable if anyone found his shields and disabled them. We were all separated and in danger.

But all I could think about was Zane, and the queen's claws sunk into his chest, the burning agony he'd felt. The sacrifice he'd made for me.

I stumbled over the rope bridge, ignoring the chasm below. I raced through the room with the square panels, expecting spikes to fly up from the floor. Nothing happened. No traps went off—I didn't know if it was the ring or because I was going instead of coming. I didn't care. I just had to get to him.

The next trapped room didn't spring, either, and then I was in the maze.

"Show me the way," I whispered to the halo, and it tugged me forward, through the miles of catacomb, leading me along. We moved past a warded room and I felt the pulse of Noah's energy. I had no idea what time it was—would he be safe down here? I'd come back for him, I decided, just as soon as I figured out how to keep the halo and not have him know about it.

The halo led me to the entrance of the maze, the door still sealed on the other side. It gave a throb then went silent, and I heard a soft clicking from the other side, and then a softly muttered curse word. Phryne was still trying to work out the combination of button presses that would unlock the doors.

I paused on my side of the massive door and glanced up. The wall to the maze was ten feet high, and I wasn't strong enough to scale it and surprise her.

But I felt her still, on the other side, and she'd noticed me too. "Who's there?" she asked. "I have holy water."

"It's me," I said softly. I used the ring to stretch my mind, but all I felt was Phryne. "Where are the vampires? And how did you get here, anyway—what did you do to Ethan?"

"I didn't touch your little Enforcer. That was all my darling Ashara. As for the vampires, they're heading up with their captive," she said over the wall, her voice echoing in the cavern. "You should have left him with me. The death I gave him would have been a merciful one."

"He's not going to die, because I'm going to save him," I said, clenching my fists at my side. "He's waiting for me."

"You're a fool if you're going to go after them," she said through the door. Then, she paused. "The halo?"

I decided to use the same lie Zane and I had agreed upon. "I've delivered it to the archangel already. There's nothing left behind these walls."

Phryne sighed heavily, as if defeated. I heard her slump against the stone wall. "You foolish, foolish girl. Why would you give up power so easily?"

I said nothing.

"Well, this has proved to me one thing, Jackie dearest," Phryne said in a conversational voice, and I heard her moving around on the other side. "There's one halo left and it seems like I'm going to have to slow you down if I plan on getting it."

As she spoke, something landed on my head with a splat. I shrieked as bright yellow paint splattered all over my clothing and stuck in my hair. Paint ran down my face. "You bitch. What was that for?"

"For this." A bottle wobbled over the wall and broke at my feet. Sugar spilled on the floor. I stared at it in confusion.

"Sorry, darling, nothing personal," Phryne said, her voice receding as if walking away. "Oh, and I invoke the demon Mae."

No! Horror shot through me—how had Phryne known about my promise to the demon?—a moment before I was flat on my stomach, and the burning-hot foot of a demon pressed into my back.

"Well, well," the demon purred. "We meet again, my dear."

I lay frozen, my hand tucked under my body. My heart

hammered, my body plastered to the ground as if held down by some massive force.

This was not good, not good at all.

"Looks like you've been making enemies since last we met, little one," Mae said thoughtfully, her voice smoky and dark. That high-heeled shoe ground into my back, digging into my spine. Her foot was so hot I could feel it through the sole. "Didn't you learn your lessons?"

"Let me up," I said, gritting my teeth. I had to act casual, lest she figure out what I held in my hand.

"Not yet," Mae purred.

Goddamn that bitch Phryne. In the distance, I could hear the sound of splashing and knew she'd retreated, moving back over the underground lake. I hated her so much.

The demon leaned over me, dragging my attention back to her with alarm. As I looked over my shoulder into her face, I saw her eyes flicker red and black, like flames. Her smile widened, showing rows of sharp, dagger-like teeth, at odds with her neatly tailored gray business suit and stuffy bun atop her head. "Demons have long memories, dearest. And I seem to remember our little bargain. Don't you?"

I stilled. When the incubus Luc had kidnapped me months ago, I'd called the demon forth to save my own skin. I'd promised her anything. At the time, it had been worth it.

But now?

"Plate's kind of full at the moment," I said, forcing casualness into my voice. "Take a rain check?"

"No," Mae said, "but you do have something I want."

My limbs grew cold and I kept my hand pressed under my body, willing the pulse of the halo to remain quiet. "What's that?"

"I know what this place is," she purred. "And the fact that I can't see anything but the paint you're wearing means that you're holding a little something I want very, very badly."

Goddamn it. "I don't have anything."

She laughed merrily. "Nice try, but I'm not stupid. You can't live thousands of years and not pick up on the obvious. And you are very, *very* obvious." Her heel came off my back and I rolled away a few feet, turning to face her and watching her warily. She stood in front of the only exit from the tomb. Shit.

Mae dusted off her hands. "The nice thing about a bargain with a demon? It can't be broken." She extended her hand and flicked a finger, beckoning me. "Come and give me the halo."

A compulsion as dark and horrible as any I'd ever been given clamped down on my brain. I struggled, but it was no use. As if my body were not my own, I walked forward and pulled the ring off my finger, holding it out to her as it expanded.

The demon's eyes glittered with avarice, and she snatched the halo from my grasp. It dissipated into thin air, as if absorbed by her, and she arched her back in delight. When she opened her eyes, they gleamed golden with power. "Delicious. Who would have thought that you would prove to be such a fruitful little catch?" She reached out and caressed my cheek, her skin burning mine at the touch.

I hissed and jerked away. Damn it. I'd just blithely handed immense power over to a demon, and there wasn't a thing I could do about it.

She curled her claws and grinned at me. "As a reward for you, I think I'm going to let you watch as I smite my enemies."

"Enemies?" I echoed, taking a step backward. That uncomfortable, bone-deep fear heightened, my breathing quickening. There weren't many in this tomb other than Noah, myself, and the vampires...

She tsked and gave me a sad look. "Not you, little one! You are currently my favorite." She grinned and winked at me. "All we need is a little pulse of power to bring my old friend running," she said, and her eyes flared with golden light.

I felt my internal tuning fork twang wildly, felt the halo's surge roll through the air, thick and heady.

But the demon didn't move; instead, she watched me, her intense gaze unnerving.

I looked around the maze anxiously. I could disappear back into it... and then what? Be lost for days? Find Noah and have him berate me for losing the halo? That wouldn't get it back. I had to stop Mae before she left here.

"They're coming," she said after a long moment, golden eyes unblinking.

I had to do something. Had to act.

I lunged for her, desperate. She only laughed loudly at my clumsy attempt, neatly sidestepping. A burst of power knocked me to the ground, and she planted her shoe on my back again.

"Naughty pet. Trying to distract me?"

I struggled, but she sent down a casual wave of power, flattening me. I could barely lift a finger—it felt as if a massive weight had landed on me.

I was useless. Despair overwhelmed me. The halo. I'd lost it.

And Zane…

As if on cue, the sound of wings filled the cavern, and my stomach flipped in anxiety. *No, please no.* I closed my eyes, praying that this wasn't happening.

The vampire queen landed in the maze a few feet away, her leathery wings flicking. Her black eyes gazed down at me, but her dark anger seemed focused on one of the other vampires that fluttered to a landing next to her.

Zane was flung to the ground in front of me, his wings destroyed. Blood poured from his nose and mouth, and he slumped, crumpled on his side. At my sharp intake of breath, his head lifted and his gaze focused on me. He tried to crawl forward, pushing to get to me.

The queen stepped past him, taking care to step on one of his broken wings. I saw his mouth clench at the pain, but he said nothing. His gaze was on me.

We lay on the floor but feet apart. I moved my fingers, trying to reach him, grasp his hand. They only twitched in response.

Wind began to whip through the chamber, and Mae's delighted laugh made my skin crawl. "Ah, I knew you'd come if I gave it a little tweak," she said gaily. "Surprised to see me, dark one?"

Nitocris's gaze flicked through the maze before landing on me, and I realized she couldn't see the demon that held me pinned down. "Show yourself."

I realized that the queen was having the same trouble that Zane had—she couldn't see Mae while she had the halo. As a neutral party between both races, I wasn't affected by the 'blocking' power it had, though I wished I was.

"Why should I show myself?" Mae stepped over me, moving right into my line of sight. "I have you right where I want you."

The queen's lips curled back in a snarl, displaying the same shark-like teeth that Mae had. "You have nothing, demon."

"That's right," Mae said thoughtfully. "I *am* a demon. And I seem to recall someone stealing the essence of one of my sister demons for her own foul games." She drummed a finger on her chin, pretending to think. "Now who could that be?"

The queen's mouth thinned. She flicked a hand at one of the vampires hovering nearby, ordering him behind her.

"Oh, that's right," Mae cooed. "It's *you*, isn't it? And it's been far too long that we've let you have the run of the house, you foul old bitch. I do believe it's time I evened the odds, don't you think?"

The queen took a step backward, her eyes widening.

On the floor, across from me, Zane struggled to get to one elbow. When that failed, he reached a broken hand toward me. "Jackie, run."

I whimpered. I couldn't even make a fist, much less get out of here. "I'm not leaving you."

"I love you," he whispered. As I watched, a black feather fell from his wing and landed in a smear of his blood. "Never forget that."

"I failed," I told him, the words catching in my throat. "I've ruined everything."

A hard pulse of the halo's power throbbed through the room suddenly. The air got heavy, thick. Ominous.

"Do not do this," Nitocris warned, taking a step back.

Mae simply smiled, raising her hands into the air. I felt the halo's power surge again, as if she was gathering it. Then the demon extended her palms toward the queen and blasted her. Golden light shot from the demon's hands, and the sudden power surge in the room was so strong and thick that it felt like I'd been blasted with an inferno. My hair lashed around my head. Heat shot through the cavern like a nuclear blast.

The queen screamed.

Mae laughed, and continued to blast her with the power. As I watched, Queen Nitocris's skin blackened, then charred. Her body melted away before my eyes, devoured by the intense pulse of light.

And then she was nothing but a cloud of ash.

Zane's eyes met mine. One last tender look...

And then he was nothing but ash as well.

PART II

WITHOUT

CHAPTER TWELVE

"Everybody cries, sooner or later. Just do yourself a favor: save all the crying for when the dressing room door is shut."—*It's a Hard Cock Life*, by Remy Summore

~*~

I stared at the pile of ash, unable to believe what I was seeing. His clothing lay crumpled on the ground, shoes discarded. That lone feather still lay in a pool of blood. Behind him, clothing crumpled to the ground as the wearers disintegrated. A puff of ash filled the air.

A hot, tearing sensation ripped through my body, waves of agony engulfing me. It was like I was being ripped in half. I gave a choked cry at the sensation, only to feel that horrible tearing feeling ebb, leaving me... half. Empty. Aching. As if I were missing something.

My link with one of my masters had been broken.

Hollow, I stared at the feather. It was the only thing left of Zane. *"No."*

Mae's boot lifted from my back. "Collateral damage, little one. Now, I'm off to wreak havoc and have a little fun. Don't wait up." With a smoky chuckle, she walked away, pushing the doors of the tomb open and strolling out.

The heavy weight lifted from my back and I was free to move once more.

I crawled over to the feather and grasped it in shaking hands.

This didn't happen. It didn't. Didn't. He was just around the corner. He'd come back out and see me and smile that roguish smile that made my stomach flip, and I'd feel silly for imagining such a thing, and the hollow ache inside me would ease…

I stared at the ash. My fingers touched it. It felt smooth, silky. A trick. Mae had made them disappear somehow. That must have been it.

Yet I went back to his jeans, lying there, crumpled. His shoes. Something was in one of the pockets of the jeans, and I tugged it free. A half-empty pack of his favorite brand of cigarettes. My fingers brushed over the crinkling packaging and a hint of Zane's scent wafted through the air.

A sob tore from my throat. I held the feather close, cradling it to my chest.

I love you. Never forget that.

A hard sob ripped out of my throat, and then another, and then I couldn't stop. My body began to shake with the force of it, but I didn't care. I picked up his lighter and held it with the blood-spattered feather, tears streaming down my face.

Zane was… gone.

Just like that, gone. I'd never see him again, never kiss his mouth, never feel his fingers grab a lock of my hair. Never wake him up at night and see that slow, loving smile as his gaze fixed on me. Never feel his body over mine as we made love. Never feel his fangs dip into my throat for a taste. Never hear his laugh. His smile.

Oh God, his smile.

I love you. Never forget that.

"I love you, Zane," I sobbed. My world was ending. I'd lost the man who made life worth living.

And now I had eternity…

And it was *without* him. I was still here, because I had two masters. I was still tied to Noah.

Please no. Please. I'll give up everything. Just give me back Zane. I don't care if we have forever—I just want more than three months with him. Please. Please.

But no one heard my cries. And Zane didn't come back.

And I was left with nothing but ashes.

~*~

Remy found me some time later. She stumbled through the doors, wincing and clutching her head. "Someone get the number of the Mack truck that hit me?" Her grumbling stopped at the sight of my weeping. She paled and went to my side, dropping to her knees. "Jackie? You okay, hon?"

"Zane," I sobbed, unable to stop crying. I showed her the bloody feather instead. "He... he... I saw it. Mae killed the queen. They all... died. Just turned to ash."

Remy went pale. "No fucking way. Mae has the halo?"

I didn't give a shit about Mae or the halo. "Zane is dead," I cried. "I loved him and he's *gone*."

Remy tugged me close, stroking my bandage as if to soothe me. "Shh, sweetheart. I know. It's okay. I'm here for you."

I just wept harder. I felt numb. No, worse than numb. Sick. Dead inside.

Zane was gone. He was really, really gone.

I was going to have to endure eternity without him.

"They're all dead?" Remy asked weakly. "All the vampires? That means Sophie's gone too. And probably Ashara and Yue. They only had a vampire master left. Holy shit."

"I don't care about Ashara and Yue," I said between sobs. "Phryne did this. She called the demon on me. She wanted to slow me down."

Instead, she'd ripped out my soul.

Remy continued to stroke my shoulders and hair, and I felt her shake her head. "I don't understand. Why would Phryne do something so stupid?"

I said nothing. I just cried harder.

Remy continued to rock me, and I kept crying. I just couldn't stop crying. All I could think of was Zane. I didn't even have his body to mourn. A body I could fix. We could get the right spells, bribe a warlock...

All I had was a feather. A single goddamn feather.

Footsteps shuffled somewhere in the maze. Hope shot through me, hard and pure. "Zane?"

But the man that came around the corner wasn't Zane.

Noah turned the corner, gun in hand, his hair tousled with sleep. My heart crashed all over again.

Noah stared at me and Remy, then at the piles of clothing that marked all that was left of the vampires. "The halo... I don't feel it.

It's gone?"

"The vampires are gone, Noah," Remy said softly. "All of them. The queen was here. I think... I think the demon Jackie owed a favor to called it in, and then she destroyed the queen. The vampires are all gone."

Footsteps to my side. Then, Noah knelt next to me—standing in Zane's ashes. How *dare* he. I pushed at him, weakly, my lips curling in a snarl. "Move. You can't stand there."

He knelt, ignoring my wishes. His hands cupped my cheek, and I struggled to pull away, but I was feeling too weak, too shattered.

"Oh, Jackie, I'm so sorry," Noah said softly, and there was pain and understanding and pity in his voice. "Phryne must have found out about the demon. No one else would do such a thing. I'm so sorry."

His soft, understanding apology broke me all over again. I fell into his arms, weeping. "I loved him, Noah. I loved him and he's gone."

He held me close. "I know, Jackie. I know."

~*~

Ethan appeared at the entrance of the tomb a short time later, and the men helped us out of the cave. Noah carried me, all earlier traces of angry, bitter Noah gone. He only held me tight as I continued to silently weep, bitter tears sliding from my eyes as if they'd never end. He'd carried me up the endless steps and eventually out into the light again, with Remy filling him in on all the details of what had happened.

As we moved into the sunlight and I saw the sky again, my heart was a dull black ache in my chest. I stared up at the delicate golden-pink skies, the exact color of Phryne's sunrise hair.

Phryne. That *bitch*. She was somewhere around here. I struggled in Noah's arms and he gently set me down.

"Jackie?" He asked in a low, questioning voice. "You okay?"

"I want to find Phryne," I said. "Where is she?"

"That tramp shot me in the back of the head," Remy grumbled. "I wouldn't mind finding her either and giving her a piece of my mind. What little she hasn't shot away, anyhow."

"I don't want to give her a piece of my mind," I said blackly. I reached for the gun at Noah's belt. "She called a demon on me. She threw paint on me so it would know just where to find me. I want to fucking *destroy* her."

As my hands closed on Noah's gun, he stepped aside. "Don't," he warned me.

A freaking command. I glared at him.

"You can't go brandishing a gun back at camp," he said calmly. "The demon might still be down there. And if she is, she's going to be extremely powerful. We need to be careful."

"My mother's down there, the man I love is dead, and the woman responsible for this is getting away scot-free," I snapped, pushing him aside. "So you'll forgive me if I skip rational right now and move straight to pissed-the-fuck off."

To my relief, they let me go, and I stormed down the ladders in a fury, making it down the cliff wall in record time. My stomach rumbled, but I ignored it—food didn't matter anymore. Nothing mattered except destroying Phryne.

She was going to pay, and I was going to make it *hurt*.

By the time I got to the ground, I could see the camp in the distance. I raced for it, alarm shooting through me. I could see no one. I charged through the tents, shoving through them and lifting flaps hurriedly. "Mom? Mom?"

"Over here, honey," a familiar voice called, and relief flooded through me. I raced out to the camp and realized that she was at a nearby dig, squatting in the sun with a floppy hat on, her assistants at her side. They all looked at me as if I'd gone insane.

"Where's Phryne?" I asked.

"Who?" Mom looked at my appearance and wrinkled her nose. "Did you trip and fall, Jackie? Your bandage is soaked with blood and you've got dirt all over your face." She climbed the ladder as I stood there, and squinted at me. Then, she licked her thumb and began to wipe at my face, frowning. "You're a mess, honey."

I touched a hand to my cheek. I was covered in Zane's ashes. At the thought, tears welled up again but I forced them back. "I'm fine, Mom. Go back to your dig."

"Is that a bandage on your head? And what's with all this paint?" She froze. "Did you spill that paint at the ruins?"

Count on Mom to think about the ruins. "Nope. They're fine. I promise."

"I'm going to have to check for myself. If you dripped paint on anything, Jackie, I'm going to be furious at you." She shook her head at me, disappointed. "I thought you'd be more careful with these sorts of things."

"Guess not," I said, feeling dead inside. "Did you see another woman around here? Light red hair? Kind of pretty?" *Kind of dead the moment I lay my hands on her?*

Mom gave me a puzzled little nod and patted my back. "I don't know who you're looking for, honey. Maybe your little friend with the tattoos and the knives? We were having a nice conversation and then she wandered away. Dropped all her things over there on the ground and disappeared. Very odd girl."

Sophie. I closed my eyes, imagining her belt of weapons lying in a pile of ash. I wanted those knives. She'd have something to carve a buttload of misery and pain into Phryne. "I'll take them," I said softly. "We're leaving now."

"Call me when you get home," she said in a surprisingly motherly tone, and then returned to her dig. "We're in the middle of photographing everything before it gets disturbed by the wind, so don't mind me if I don't get out and hug you."

"I don't mind," I said softly. I wasn't surprised. Why would I have expected her to change? To see my agony? All she saw were artifacts. All she ever saw were artifacts. "Bye, Mom."

~*~

Sure enough, Sophie's things were in a neat pile at camp, also covered in that same awful, gritty ash. I fastened her gun belts around my waist, picked up her daggers and strapped them on. By the time Noah and the others found me, I was covered in her weaponry.

To my surprise, Noah had a stricken look on his face at the sight of the weapons. "Not... Sophie?"

"Zane was her master," I said flatly. "He dies, she dies."

"I didn't know," he said in a low voice. He closed his eyes, shook his head as if shaking off the loss. "I... liked her. She had a fierce spirit."

I was sure that wasn't all he'd liked, but I said nothing. "I want to leave here," I said in a desperate voice. "Please, can we go?"

"Go where?" Remy asked. "That demon is out there with the halo. If she's moving around, that means she's not constrained by hallowed ground anymore. She could be anywhere. Doing anything."

"We can't stop her. Not if she has the halo. The most we can do is warn the others to steer clear and hope that she manages to amuse herself in quiet ways before we can figure out a way to contain her," Noah said in a grave voice. "With that power, she's going to be close to unstoppable."

"I don't care about the demon," I said. "I'm going after Phryne."

A flash of annoyance crossed Noah's face. "Jackie, I realize you're hurting right now, but that isn't rational."

"I am *not* rational," I said to him, my fists clenching hard enough to draw blood. "I know that, and I don't care. I want to *hurt* her."

"We're going home and we're going to talk about this first," he said. "My hotel back in the city. We'll go there."

~*~

There'd been no conversation on the way to Noah's hotel. We were a shell-shocked group, no one in the mood for talking. Instead, my mind replayed the scene over and over again.

Zane's fingers reaching for me.

I love you. Never forget that.

Then dust.

Everything was dust. My heart, my soul, all dust.

The hotel was, of course, a Holiday Inn, since everything else didn't seem remotely close to Noah's posh standards of travel. Even this seemed a bit out of his element. He'd made up for it by renting an entire half of the top floor, it seemed. If there wasn't a penthouse available, Noah would make his own. Typical.

He'd suggested purchasing rooms for Remy and me, but that idea was quickly shot down, and even Noah didn't seem to mind. No one wanted to separate. Not while we were feeling vulnerable and in shock.

Noah's assistants had followed us into the hotel, and Noah sent them off with tasks to keep them busy (and out of our hair) before shutting the door. I sat down at the table in the kitchenette of the hotel room, staring at nothing. My shirt was still splattered in paint, but worse was the ash and blood staining it. I felt the insane urge to rip it off.

"How is your head?" Ethan murmured to Remy. I looked over to see him carefully brushing her hair off her forehead, then tenderly pressing a kiss there.

Remy's lower lip trembled. "Hurts."

His fingers were gentle as he brushed a knuckle along her jaw, caressing her, comforting her with aching tenderness. "What can I do to ease your pain, Remiza?"

She leaned into his caress, but shook her head. "I'll be fine. I—"

"She needs healing," I said. We all knew what that meant.

To my surprise, Remy hesitated. She moved to the table and sat next to me, her face drawn with pain. She hadn't had the healing that I had earlier, thanks to Zane.

Ah, Zane. That black agony in my heart flared again.

Remy clasped my hand. "I'm not going to leave you just when you need me, Jacks. I'm here for you. We both are."

"I'm okay," I said softly, and squeezed her hand. "Noah's here. You need to take care of yourself." My voice wobbled a little. "I can't lose anyone else."

Remy's eyes filled in sympathy. "Oh, Jacks, I know. I cried for weeks when I lost my master, and I didn't even like the bastard. I can't imagine what you're going through right now."

I nodded, the knot in my throat huge. I couldn't talk about this anymore. Didn't want to. I looked over at Ethan, where the big warrior hovered protectively behind Remy's chair, waiting to help her. "Remy needs healing right now, Ethan. Please."

The Enforcer's eyes flashed silver and he nodded, pulling Remy's chair out. She protested, but not much, I noticed, and when he scooped her into his arms, she put hers around his neck and laid her head against his chest wearily.

"We will return later, Jackie Brighton," Ethan said to me, his face grave. "And if you should require my assistance, I shall . . ." He swallowed. ". . .assist you."

My mouth twisted in a wry smile despite the ache in my breast. "I don't need healing, Ethan, but thank you for offering to make the sacrifice."

Ethan worshipped the ground Remy walked upon, but I was barely tolerated. I knew his offer had been an extension of friendship, nothing more. He wanted sex with me about as much as he wanted to hit himself in the nuts with a hammer, but he'd offered because he knew I was hurting.

He looked incredibly relieved when I declined, and I was too numb to be insulted.

I made a shooing motion at the two of them. "I'm fine," I stated again. "I'm alive. And Noah's here."

Noah. A fine piece of irony that he was the master I would be spending eternity with. My entire being ached with sadness at the thought.

Ethan carried Remy out of the room, whispering sweet nothings in her ears, and I watched as he kicked the door to the bedroom shut.

Good for Remy. After so many centuries of being alone, she had someone who was completely and utterly devoted to her. I was happy that Ethan hadn't been permanently obliterated with the queen's death like Sophie had. His sleep-hold had been removed the moment Ashara had turned into so much dust. At least there was one bright spot in things. Remy wouldn't have to suffer like I was suffering.

Noah approached the table, a pair of shot glasses in hand and a bottle of Glenlivet. He set the two glasses down, opened the bottle, and poured. Then, he nudged one toward me. "Drink."

Another command. I picked up the shot and raised it to my lips, then tilted my head back and downed the entire thing. The whisky burned in my throat, and I coughed in surprise.

"It's strong," he warned me, too late. Then he pushed the second glass in front of me and refilled the first.

I took the other shot and downed it as well. I hadn't eaten in I didn't know how long, and my head was buzzing after the two shots. My mouth was full of the syrupy, smoky flavor of the Scotch, and my stomach was burning with heat. Good, but not enough to make me forget. Not nearly enough.

Noah sat in the chair next to me and poured himself a shot, downing it quickly. He refilled his glass. "Another?"

"I don't want to get drunk, Noah," I said quietly. "That's not going to fix anything."

"No, it won't. But it takes the edge off for a little, at least." And he nudged the new shot toward me. "Drink."

"I hate it when you do this," I said, grabbing the shot glass and tossing it back. "If you're trying to make me despise you, mission accomplished."

He looked surprised at my words. "Jackie, I'm trying to help you."

I clenched my jaw. This wasn't helping anything, but Noah was trying to comfort me. I crossed my arms over my chest and sat back in the chair. "Sorry."

"You'll be okay," he said. "I'm here for you. I know I'm not Zane, but we've been friends for a while, Jackie. You know you can count on me. I want you to count on me."

I said nothing. He was probably secretly gloating that Zane was gone. Quietly delighted that I would have no choice but to turn back to him to serve the Itch.

In that moment, I *hated* myself. I hated this body that needed sex to survive. I hated that I'd have to have sex and worse, that I'd end up enjoying it. I hated that I couldn't turn the Itch off. I hated that I couldn't close my eyes and dream of Zane, because succubi didn't dream. I hated immortality. I hated all of it. What good was all this if I couldn't have Zane?

Noah must have noticed my bleak expression, because he began to pour again.

To stave him off, I spoke up. "Thank you," I said. Even though I wasn't feeling particularly grateful at the moment, I knew Noah was helping me. He was always there to pick up the pieces. Strange how that grated right now.

He reached across the table and put his hand over mine. "I'm sorry about Zane."

I said nothing, swallowing hard.

He gave me an awkward pat on the hand, as if sensing that I didn't want to be touched, no matter his good intentions. "Your friend Sophie too," he said after a moment, staring thoughtfully at the Glenlivet. "She was... unusual."

I looked over at Noah in surprise. Was I not the only one in mourning, then? Was he masking his own disappointment? When he took another shot, I asked, "Did you like her?"

He gave me a twisted smile. "I am a four-thousand-year-old fallen angel, Jackie. There is no creature on earth more jaded than I." He looked thoughtful for a moment, then added in a gruff voice, "But she was unusual. Untamed. I... appreciated that."

A strong, self-assured succubus who refused to be constrained by the boundaries put upon her? I could see how she would be fascinating to a man like Noah who valued control so much. "She was someone you couldn't control," I pointed out. "You liked that."

"I barely knew her." He looked at the empty glass in front of him, and for a moment, he looked just as sad as I did. "But what I saw, I liked."

He liked her enough to have sex with her twice, I wanted to point out, but did not. Noah never had sex for pleasure, only duty. "Well then, for your sake, I am sorry she's gone."

He gave me an appraising look. "Were you not friends?"

"She was Zane's creation," I pointed out.

"Ah," he said, and that seemed to answer everything.

And then I felt like a petty asshole for still disliking Sophie when the woman was dead. It didn't matter if I liked her or not. I'd gladly live with her at my side for the rest of eternity if that meant I had Zane back.

My thoughts growing too dark and despairing, I shook my head to clear it. "So… what will you do now that the halo is gone?"

He poured and nudged the drink toward me. "My plans haven't changed."

There was no command to drink the shot, so I ignored it. Instead, I frowned at him, my head feeling woozy from exhaustion, weeping, and Scotch. "What do you mean?"

Noah drank a shot of his own, then stared thoughtfully at the bottle. "I've been tasked to retrieve the halo as one of my burdens. That hasn't changed. It's still out there."

"A demon has it," I said dully. A vicious, murdering demon.

"Yes, and if I stop her, I'll have it."

I shook my head, staring at the dark amber liquid of the shot in front of me. My stomach was roiling from the alcohol burning in the pit of my belly. "And how exactly are you going to stop her? She vaporized the queen with a thought."

"There are ways," Noah said thoughtfully. He looked over at me, the tattoos stark against his golden skin. "There is still another halo on the playing field, after all."

I stilled in my chair.

There was another halo. I could get it—somehow—and defeat Mae. Somehow. And then I could turn both over to the Archangel Gabriel.

And Gabriel had promised to give me anything I wanted.
Anything.

And I wanted Zane back. I wanted him so badly that I could

taste it. I clenched my hands to keep my body from trembling in excitement. "You're going after the second halo?"

He looked at me and nodded. "I have no choice."

"Phryne will be after it," I told him. "I want revenge against her. Take me with you."

He shook his head. "Jackie, I don't even know where to begin for the second halo—"

"I do," I said quickly. "Phryne stole my manuscript page. I didn't understand why my page seemed to have all the information for the tomb and hers had nothing. But then I realized that there were two haloes and her page probably leads straight to the other if she can just decipher what it says. Of course, she doesn't have a vampire to read it to her now. She'd have to get Serim help."

"She won't approach the Serim," Noah said. "Her master is Ariel and she hates him fiercely."

Boy, Ariel had a string of unhappy succubi, didn't he? First Luc, now Phryne. That explained who'd given such deadly information to Phryne, then. The bastard. Of course, Phryne was even worse—she'd turned around and given away my position to the queen. I blamed her for Zane's death. "If she won't approach the Serim, it'll take her that much longer to decipher what she's got. In the meantime, we can hunt her down and I can make her pay for what she's done."

He eyed me, his pale eyes unhappy. "Jackie, revenge is not the answer."

"I don't give a shit," I said flatly. "Nothing matters anymore. Making Phryne hurt half as much as I'm hurting is the only thing that's driving me right now. It's either that, or I'm going to *lose* it, Noah." My entire body began to tremble, and the tears began to spill forth again. "So let me focus on getting revenge, because that's all I've got to go on right now. Okay?"

He sighed, ran a hand down his face. "All right, Jackie. All right. I'll take you with me."

"Thank you," I said quietly, and reached over and squeezed his hand impulsively. "I can always count on you."

Too bad he wasn't going to be able to count on me. I was going to have to double-cross him as soon as we found the second halo. It'd hurt and Noah would be furious, but I was going to get Zane back, and I was going to do it even if I died trying.

I had nothing to live for if he was gone.

He patted my hand, the understanding and sympathy in his gaze making my throat ache. "I know you're hurting, Jackie. I understand that this isn't easy, but you need to keep your strength up if we're going to do this. I know you don't want to think about it, but we can help each other out. I'm here for you." He patted my hand one more time and then poured another shot.

But my stomach did a sick little flip at the thought. Here for me? Like back when we'd been living together before? He'd proposed to me once, and I'd turned him down. And then we'd continued to have sex until I told him I was choosing Zane. And now that Zane was out of the picture, I'd just fall back into his arms again?

I swallowed the shot in front of me, sick at the thought. The nature of a succubus was that I had to have sex every two days or I'd die slowly of starvation. We were hedonistic creatures with strong appetites—we ate a lot, drank a lot, loved even more—but the only thing that we truly required to continue on was a steady diet of sex.

I looked at Noah, at his big, bronzed hands, tattoos looping his wrists. Thought of him putting those hands on me.

It didn't fill me with the instant lust it had before, back when I was torn between him and Zane. All I felt was sadness. The only hand I pictured was Zane's, outstretched as if to touch me one last time.

My hands trembled and I set the shot glass down. "Noah, before we go any further, I want to set expectations."

He arched an eyebrow at me. "Oh?"

"I want to be your friend and your partner in finding this halo. Nothing more."

The look on his face became dark. "Jackie, I'm not enough of an asshole to move on you while you're grieving. I was merely reassuring you. I know as well as anyone that you can't avoid your succubus curse, even if your heart is broken."

"I know," I said, and reached across the table to squeeze his hand in reassurance. "But I'm letting you know that I just want us to be friends. Nothing more. I can't... I can't handle more right now. You understand."

"Jackie, this won't be overnight. Phryne can blend in to her surroundings. She won't leave us a noticeable trail. I won't allow you to starve yourself because you're pining for the vampire." His hand caressed mine. "I've lost someone too, you know."

Rachael. My look-alike. The woman he missed so much that he carried an oil painting of her with him. I hadn't forgotten. And now he'd lost Sophie, the only other woman, apart from me, who had intrigued him in a very long time. No, Noah was no stranger to loss.

"I know," I said, my voice firm. But I hadn't changed my mind. I would rather starve than cheat on Zane. We were together, I thought fiercely. And I was going to get that halo and bring him back, and that meant waiting for his return.

I refused to accept any other options.

"You can't circumvent your succubus needs, Jackie," Noah said. "It's impossible."

His words made an idea flash into my mind. An idea… and a face. "No, actually, it's *not* impossible…"

CHAPTER THIRTEEN

"There are a lot of dicks in this business. And I don't mean their junk."—*Reality Through the Eyes of a Porn Goddess*, by Remy Summore

~*~

Las Vegas, Nevada

He was waiting for me by a row of slot machines in the Bellagio. Tall, dark, with long, sweeping hair that brushed against his collar and pale silvery eyes that caressed me as I approached. Luc Stone leaned against one of the machines, his beautiful mouth curling with sulky amusement at the sight of me.

He still unnerved me. Incredibly gorgeous, unbelievably selfish, and a creature just like me. The only incubus I knew, and a man with whom I had a rather unfortunate history.

I stopped in front of him, crossing my arms over my chest briskly. I watched his gaze move over the casual jeans I wore, the plain black T-shirt, and the no-nonsense ponytail I'd pulled my hair back into.

"Thank you for meeting me," I said stiffly to him.

"My master commands and I obey," he said in that lazy voice that held just a hint of a Cajun accent. But he tilted his head, regarding me. "Someone's destroyed your innocence, ma belle. Your eyes are like flint. Shame."

"Can we go someplace private to talk?" I asked him.

He gave me a languid smile. "Now why would I do that? You

assume I trust you, ma belle. Or that I want to help you."

"You want to help me because it's in your best interests to help me," I told him bluntly. "And I know you're all about your best interests."

He gave me a cool smile. "Well, now I am listening. Shall we go to my room?" He extended his elbow at me, clearly meaning for me to tuck my hand into his arm.

Close enough for him to reach out and touch me, to use his powers on me and knock me unconscious.

Of course, I'd be close enough to stab him with the knife I had at my belt.

Toss-up.

Still, this was going to require some trust on my part. I needed Luc's help, and I suspected he'd be interested in the information I had. So, grudgingly, I put my hand in his arm. "Not your room," I told him. "The bar."

"I am wounded, ma belle," he said with a laugh in his voice, but steered me to the nearest restaurant.

The lighting was soft and neutral, the floors and bar a beautiful pale wood that made the entire room look clean and luminous. It was also almost empty at this time of day, with a long row of deserted square barstools lined up against the bar. We headed for the far end of the bar, smiling as if we were on a date and this was a normal sort of thing. As we walked, people stared. Waiters turned, the few patrons scattered in the restaurant paused in conversation, and the bartender immediately began to head in our direction. Of course. Luc was beautiful. I was sexy. Together, we were stunning. Someone was probably racking their brains, trying to figure out if we were just blessed with good looks or if we were celebrities.

Once, it might have been fun to see that reaction. But not now, not when I felt like one of the walking dead.

I wanted Zane back. Nothing more. This was a means to an end.

I ignored the audience we were gathering and sat on the barstool. Luc sat next to me and clasped his hands, lacing his fingers as he leaned over the bar, all casualness. "To what do I owe this pleasure?"

I gave him a tight smile. "Oh, I was just thinking about the good old days. You know how it goes. Hey," I snapped my fingers and gestured at him, feigning wide-eyed enthusiasm. "Remember that time when you kidnapped me and chained me to your wall? And you put that choker on me to stop my curse? Wasn't that fun?"

He raised an eyebrow at my words. "As I recall, one of us came out on top of that situation and it was not me. Are you still taking these things personally, ma belle?"

"No," I said, though it was a little grudging. "I wanted to see you because I need another one of those chokers. I want something to block the curse again."

"And how long do you intend upon wearing it?"

"As long as it takes," I said grimly. "A week, a year… ten years. Doesn't matter."

He arched an eyebrow, intrigued by my hard words. "You are courting death. Should someone remove the necklace from you, you could die within a matter of seconds."

"Then make it something less easy to grab. A ring, maybe." My heart seized at the thought. The halo had been a ring, and I'd lost it. Maybe a ring was a bad idea.

Luc's mouth tugged up in a smile. "Very well then, a ring. What is it that I get out of this deal?"

The bartender came by, and I ordered a drink just so he'd go away. Luc ordered one as well, and we waited in silence as the bartender poured our drinks, then moved away again.

When he was gone, I put my hand on my glass and tugged it closer. Time to skip all the bullshit. "Your vampire master is dead, isn't he?"

Luc's expression didn't change. He was too good at hiding his emotions for that sort of thing. But he hesitated, then knocked back his drink. "And were you his assassin, ma belle?"

Not grief, not anger. Just mild curiosity. Good. That was the reaction I could handle easiest.

"Not his assassin," I told him. "I witnessed the queen's death."

Luc stilled. His gaze searched mine, as if seeking the truth. "All the vampires?"

"All of them," I said softly. I explained what had happened, while glossing over my deal with Gabriel. I told him about Phryne, the halo Mae had absorbed, and the queen's death.

He looked grim at my words. "I hate that demon."

"Me too," I said, and when he gave me a sneering look, I raised a hand. "I've learned my lesson by harming you. I'm suffering the consequences." My voice hitched on the words. "I wanted to let you know that if I get another halo, the angel Gabriel has promised me a boon. And if I get that boon, I'm going to bring the vampires back."

He laughed, the sound low and smooth. "And how does that help me?"

I turned my drink, not even sipping it, just letting the ice clink against the edges of the glass. "I think you want your vampire master alive."

"And why would I want that?"

"Because now that he's gone, you can't kill Ariel. If he's back…" I shrugged. "You have one disposable master, do you not?"

His eyes gleamed at my suggestion, and he laughed. "You play a dangerous game, little sister. You've learned much since I saw you last. I almost like this side of you."

I hated this side of me. But it was necessary. "So you'll help me?"

"I will make you a ring," he said slowly. "If nothing else, so you can ensure that the demon is put in her place."

"That is agenda item number one," I assured him. "She's going to pay for what she's done."

"I feel I must warn you, though," he said slowly. "Which succubus did you say you were chasing for the second halo?"

"Phryne."

"Ah, Phryne. My sister in servitude to Ariel." His mouth twisted. "He is not a good man to serve."

I knew he wasn't. "Phryne has… information that I need."

And a head I wanted to chop off her shoulders.

"She is dangerous. You would be best avoiding her entirely. Take that as a friendly warning from a brother."

Some brother. He'd tried to rape me and then kill me, once upon a time. Of course, I'd given him to a demon, so fair was fair. "You told her about my promise to the demon, didn't you? You sold me out."

"I did not sell you out," he said, his smile all white dazzling teeth. "You and I have never been on the same side… until now."

"And what makes it different now?" I had to ask. I'd been the one to approach him, but I had to know I could trust what he offered.

"Because, ma belle, Phryne and I may share a master, but we do not work together. That one has not sought to include me in her plans. In making her choices, she has eliminated mine." That smile took on a more feral cast. "I do not like being left with no options. And so because she has made a selfish choice, I shall make a selfish choice of my own."

"Then tell me where I can find her," I said. "She has a document that she stole from me that is critical to this plan."

The plan that I had that was basically looking like: 1) Find halo. 2) Kill all the sons of bitches standing in my way. 3) Get Zane back. I'd fill in the details later.

"She cannot be found if she does not want to be found. I imagine her house is empty right about now, and will be until she is satisfied that you are either neutralized, dead, or simply do not matter any longer. If she knows you are on her trail, she will try to lead you on a merry chase. Phryne is several thousand years old," Luc said, leaning an elbow on the bar and smiling at me. "And she values her own skin above all things. If you meet her, the element of surprise is your only hope."

"I'll keep that in mind," I said. "Thank you."

He inclined his head at me, acknowledging my polite response. "And you think you have a chance at getting this second halo and defeating the demon?"

"If it takes me a hundred years to find that halo, I'll do it. I have nothing but time. And once I get it, I'll be able to stand toe-to-toe with her."

Luc shook his head at me. "While it is true that you will be able to stand toe-to-toe with her, I think you are underestimating things, little sister."

I remained calm, toyed with my still-full glass. "Oh? How so?"

He gave me a roguish smile. "I do not think the current owner of the halo is all that interested in giving it up."

My heart pounded in my chest. "Current owner?"

Someone had gotten there before me? Already?

Luc reached over and plucked my drink off my napkin, drank half, and then set it back down on his side of the bar, not even bothering to ask permission. A little proprietary, but if he got me the ring, I'd forgive him for it. "Do you know whose halo it is you seek, ma belle?"

"No," I said bluntly. "Do you?"

"His name is Camael," Luc said, and his mouth twisted in a

grimace. "An old friend of Ariel's. And he is very much alive."

The archangel lived? That definitely put a kink into the plans. "Where is he?"

"Missing. Gone. Has not been seen in centuries," Luc said, lifting my drink and downing the rest of it. After he swallowed, he looked over at me and grinned. "Still feeling your bravado, little sister?"

"My plans haven't changed," I said stubbornly.

"And what will you do if Camael does not wish to give his halo to a stone-eyed little succubus? Will you cut him into a hundred pieces and burn his corpse so you can drag his halo from the ashes?"

I thought of Zane. His hand reaching out to me. The bloody feather I carried in my pocket still. "If I have to," I said, setting my jaw. "If he stands in my way."

CHAPTER FOURTEEN

"You need to have an exit plan for this line of work, or you're going to end up with a vagina like a pothole. No one wants that."— *"Hard" Truths*, by Remy Summore

~*~

Somewhere in the Upper Xingu, the Amazon, Brazil
Eighteen Months Later

Night.

I felt a surge of success when our small rowboat pushed past the thick jungle on the right bank and in the distance, the smooth sides of a chartered boat came into view. The *White Queen* was anchored near the bank a short distance away, the thick canopy hanging overhead. Calm. Unaware.

Good.

"It's there," Remy said a bit too loudly. "You were right, I was wrong. Can we go back now?"

"Shhh," I told her and dug my paddle into the water. "I just want to get closer so we can investigate things."

"Jackie, that's not the plan," Remy said. "We've found the boat. That's awesome. Now we need to make sure that we don't lose her again. As soon as she goes to shore, we can follow her then."

"I just want to see what things look like on deck," I said stubbornly and paddled a bit more.

Remy sighed hugely and dug hers into the water too.

When we pulled up next to the larger boat, I laid my paddle down and stood carefully. I reached for the iron ladder rungs that crawled up the side of the boat and pulled out my knife. Remy and Ethan sat in the back of the small boat, clutching paddles and watching me with dubious gazes.

"Wait here," I whispered. "I won't be long."

"Jackie, I'm not so sure this is a good idea," Remy began, but I was already climbing up the ladder, knife held in my teeth. I heard her sigh of annoyance as I disappeared onto the deck.

The *White Queen* was much like our own boat, the *Angel of the Amazon*. The deck was silent as it was the dead of night, but one of the cabins had a light on. I carefully took my shoes off and headed toward it, my bare feet quiet on the decking. There was no sound but the creaking of wood, the slap of water against the sides of the boat, and the faint hum of music coming from one of the rooms.

Well now, that'd make things easier.

I approached the lit cabin on the far side of the deck. There was a window that allowed the passenger to look out, but the blinds were pulled tight. Light leaked from behind them, and music pulsed in the air, the heavy beat of a dance song drowning out the snores of the crew.

I put my hand on the handle of the door. Locked. Undeterred, I pulled out the credit card I'd brought for such an issue and slipped it between the doorjamb and door, sliding it down. The lock was cheap, and I jiggled the handle until the tumbler snicked into place, and then the door was mine.

I eased it open a hair as the music swelled, peering in through the crack.

There she was. Golden-peach hair falling down her perfect back in a cascade, wearing nothing but a T-shirt and panties as she bent over a table, swaying her hips to the beat of the music. Nearby, a man's broad, tanned back was evident in bed, but he remained still, his back rising and falling in the rhythm of sleep.

There she was. Phryne. The bitch I hated more than I thought I could ever hate someone. The black hole that was my heart grew a little darker at the sight of her, books and maps spread open. She turned the page of another book, her back to the door, and appeared to be making notes. For eighteen months I'd chased after her, over continents and cities and oceans. I'd come so close over and over again, only to have her disappear on me.

For eighteen months, I'd been forced to live without Zane, and it was because of her. I glared at her back, filled with a cold, black anger. So arrogant. So careless. Too bad for her. I let the door fall open and stepped in, tiptoeing in behind her. My shadow fell over the table and she stiffened.

Before she could turn, I reached out, put my hands on the sides of her head, and twisted hard. There was a brutal snap and then she fell to the ground, lifeless, the thump of her body masked by the music.

I waited a moment.

She lay still at my feet, eyes closed, a string of drool forming on one side of her perfect mouth. Good. She was out for at least a few days, then. I kicked her aside, stepping to the table.

The man in bed stirred, rolling over and mumbling something in Portuguese. I moved quickly to his side and brushed my fingertips over his temples, putting him into a deeper sleep. His thoughts were entirely of Phryne, and I picked through a few of their sex memories with distaste, looking for bits of information I could use, but she hadn't shared her plans with him. He just knew that whatever she wanted, he'd give to her. Like a devoted dog.

I tied him up with the bedsheets, gagged him, and then tugged the pillowcase over his head so he couldn't see me. Then I released my sleep hold and let him wake up. He could only wake up again from my touch, so it was either now or never. And I was ice to my core, but even I hesitated at letting a man wither away in his sleep.

He struggled on the bed, clearly alarmed, but I left him there. "If you get up, I'm afraid I'm going to have to shoot you," I told him, not an ounce of pity in my voice.

He stopped struggling.

"That's better." I moved to the table, eyeing the stack of marked books, post-its flagged in multiple locations of each one. I couldn't take the library with me. So I scooped up the map that Phryne had been scribbling on, the laminated copy of the page—*my* page—and her journal. I paused over one stack. It looked like newspaper clippings. I pulled the first one out, curious.

Gunman tormented by inner demons kills twenty before turning gun on self. I flipped to the next one. *Man commits murder-suicide while on family vacation.* The next in the stack was a school shooting. Then a hostage situation that had ended badly. Then, a doctor who had poisoned thirteen babies in a nursery ward...

I dropped the stack, repulsed. The articles were arranged by date, and I noticed that at the back of the stack, there was a map that had been carefully marked. Was she… tracking the demon? I examined the stack of articles again, but the last one dated from several months ago. Damn.

Folding it all tightly, I tucked it into the inner pocket of my long, leather duster and examined the room one more time.

There were guns in the corner. Automatic rifles. That might make things tricky if they came after us. I grabbed them and tucked them under my arm, then left the room, relocking the door behind me. I paused at the side of the boat and dropped the guns into the moonlit waters of the Amazon, then rejoined Remy and Ethan in the rowboat.

Remy was clutching her paddle close, her eyes wide as she stared at me. "Can we get out of here? I'm pretty sure I just saw the world's biggest crocodile swim past."

"Let's go," I said, picking up my paddle as well. "Mission accomplished."

"That didn't take long," Remy said. "What'd you do? Tranquilize her?"

"I snuck up behind her, broke her neck, and tied up her boyfriend," I said calmly. "And then I stole her research. By the time she recovers, we'll have the halo in hand."

Ethan and Remy exchanged a glance, but said nothing. That was fine—they didn't have to like this. As long as it got me from Point A to Point B, I didn't care who approved or not.

I dug my oar into the water, waiting to feel it. The triumph that I'd pulled one over on Phryne. The rush of pleasure I'd been anticipating after eighteen long months of chase. I'd snapped her neck in cold blood. Killed her ass. She'd come back in a few days—unless her lover knew to heal her with sex—and she'd be spitting mad. It'd be too late for her, though. We'd be long gone, the halo mine. She'd led us on a merry chase but I finally had her right where I wanted her.

Zane was that much closer to me. I should have felt satisfied. Instead, all I felt was even more lonely. The leather duster he'd given me that day was my constant companion, and I tugged it closer to my body. It no longer smelled of him. It just smelled like me. My heart still ached with his loss.

They say time heals everything, but when you're immortal, even time is your enemy. More than five hundred days had passed and I still missed Zane like my heart had been ripped out of my chest.

I put my paddle on the bench in front of me and reached into one of the pockets of Zane's coat. It was too big and bulky on me, and the night was humid, but I couldn't stand to go a moment without it. I brushed my fingers over the feather in my pocket, and then pulled out a cigarette and lit it. I only puffed once, just enough to get the taste—the flavor of him—on my lips again. Didn't inhale, just let it burn down as I held it between my lips, staring into the star-filled jungle night.

I had defeated my enemy. Where was my satisfaction?

"Do you have to smoke right now?" Remy said crossly from behind me.

I touched my tongue to the filter of the cigarette, inhaling the smoke and then letting it out. I needed to anchor myself to him. Remind myself what I was fighting for, because some nights, the darkness seemed like it was going to overwhelm me. "I guess not," I said softly, and flicked the cigarette into the black waters of the river. "Sorry."

"Jackie," Remy said behind me. "We need to talk, girl. I'm worried about you."

"I'm fine," I said flatly. I picked up my oar again and began to paddle. "We can talk when we're back on the boat and I've looked over these documents."

Remy didn't protest, and we made it back to the *Angel of the Amazon* after a short time, mooring our little boat beside it. A deckhand was waiting and I thanked him in Portuguese, asking him to haul the small rowboat back up on board. The maps in my pocket burned my mind. I couldn't wait to be alone and take a look at them. I twisted the ring on my finger anxiously. So close to that second halo. So close.

Remy stepped in front of me, her hands on her hips. "You. Me. Talk. Now."

"Can't it wait?"

"No," she said, grabbing my arm and dragging me toward the cabin she shared with Ethan.

I rolled my eyes but allowed her to drag me off. If this would get it out of her system, might as well let her say her piece.

She hauled me into her room and turned to Ethan, looking at him expectantly. The big warrior bent down and she gave him a quick, affectionate kiss, then patted him on the arm. "Stay in front of this door, baby, and don't let anyone come in until I give the word."

"Of course, my beautiful heart."

I rolled my eyes again. At least Ethan had given up on the slang. Now he just showered Remy with ridiculous, flowery nicknames.

It would have been cute if my own heart weren't so dead.

She pinched his cheek, slapped his ass lightly, and then turned back to me. She shut the door to the cabin behind her, and leaned against it, blocking my way. "Sit, Jacks. This talk has been a while coming, but I think it's necessary."

I shook my head at her. "Remy, I know what you're thinking—"

"Pretty sure you don't," she said tartly, and pointed at the lone chair in the small cabin. "Sit."

I sat, eyeing the cabin. My own cabin was tiny and sparse. Noah's was the same. Remy and Ethan's was a mess of rumpled sheets, empty candy wrappers and chip bags, laptop cords, and a stack of DVDs in the corner. Remy's now-fat journal lay off to one side, the pen hanging out of it.

"Jackie, I'm worried about you," Remy said.

I twisted the ring on my finger. "I know you are."

"No, I mean, I'm *really* worried about you." She came toward me and knelt in front of me, putting her hands over mine. "When I look at you, I don't see my friend anymore. I look at you and all I see are the burned edges of my friend. I see someone who is too hard. And I worry that you're going to cross a line that you won't be able to recross."

I tried to tug my hands from hers. "Remy—"

"No, listen to me," she said, her hands digging into mine. "No one starts out as one of the bad guys. Road to hell, good intentions, and all that. I just look at you and I see someone who has no boundaries anymore. I can't believe you went and snapped Phryne's neck."

"Why not? Sophie did it."

"Sophie was an assassin," Remy pointed out. "It was her job to kill people. Not yours."

"Phryne shot us both in the back of the head, remember? She called a demon on me."

"And so instead of sticking with our original plan to follow her when she went on land, we boarded her ship in the middle of the night, snapped her neck, stole her documents, and tied her lover up?" She paused, her eyes widening. "You just tied him up, right?

You're not just saying that?"

"I didn't kill him, Remy."

She looked unsure.

"I didn't. Jesus, I'm not that much of a monster."

"Not yet," she said. Her hands squeezed mine again and she looked up at me with solemn gray eyes. "But you wear Sophie's weapons at your waist, Jackie. You have more knives strapped to your thighs than they have over in the mess hall. You carry a gun with you at all times."

I did. After Sophie's death, I'd confiscated her weapons. They reminded me of my new goal, and more than that, I practiced with them. I wasn't so great with the knives, but my aim had improved with the gun. If it came down to killing, I'd be ready for it. "That doesn't make me an assassin, Remy."

"But where do you draw the line, Jackie? If I were standing between you and the halo, would you call a demon on me? Shoot me in the head to get what you want?"

My mouth went dry. Because I knew the answer to both of those questions, and it wasn't pretty.

"That's what I'm worried about," she said. "I look at you, and I see Phryne. I see that same ice she has in her eyes. I look at you and I see someone who's willing to use and abuse others to get what she wants."

"I just want Zane back," I said softly and licked my lips so I could taste the cigarettes once more.

"I know, girl," she said. "But I want you to stop and think. Let's say you get him back. Let's say this all works and we can go back to how we were before. Are you even going to be the same person? Will he recognize who you've become? Because he didn't fall in love with Phryne, and he didn't fall in love with Sophie. He fell in love with *you* because you have a good heart. Because you're smart and funny and optimistic. Not because you're a brutal, single-minded destroyer."

I said nothing.

She moved in to hug me. "I just want you to stop and think, is all. Don't cross a line that will change who and what you are."

"Thanks, Remy," I said softly. "I'm going to go to my cabin now and take a look at Phryne's papers."

She patted my shoulder and stood, then began to clean empty chip bags off her table, shutting the laptop and tossing it onto the bed. "We can look at them here if you want."

I hesitated. I'd wanted to look over the information privately, to obsess over Phryne's notes, but I forced myself to pull everything out of my pocket and hand the stack to Remy.

She turned to the table and began to spread it out, and I watched her, my blackened heart aching all over again. Because I knew the answer to her questions, and I had no doubt in my mind that I would have cut down my own best friend to get him back.

And I wasn't proud of it.

~*~

The next morning we packed our gear and met on the deck of the *Angel*. Noah rolled his eyes at my bulging backpack, Zane's long leather duster stuffed into it. I'd almost worn it, but the oppressive daytime heat of the jungle was too sticky for leather. I wasn't about to leave it behind and trust that it would be here waiting for me, though. Instead, I was dressed in a plain white tank top, short cargo shorts, and sturdy hiking boots. My knives were strapped to my waist, my belt, and one was strapped to my lower arm. A gun was holstered under my arm. My hair was pulled into a tight braided crown and I wore a bandana over it to protect my head and keep the sweat out of my eyes. I was ready.

At my side, Remy straightened her clothing. She wore Daisy Duke shorts and cowboy boots with a matching red cowboy hat that glittered with rhinestones. Her red tank top proclaimed *I'm with a stallion* and had an arrow pointing to the side. Ethan, I noticed, was wearing a matching shirt that pointed in the opposite direction and said *I'm with a goddess*. Ethan's bo was held in his hand like a walking stick rather than strapped to his back as it normally was. I noticed he had hitched Remy's pack over his own.

Noah had a wide-brimmed hat and wore jungle khaki as well, his tattoos stark on his lower arms and across his neck. I knew that under his shirt, they covered his chest. The last year and a half hadn't given him much time to work off his servitude. His pack was smaller than mine, and he looked rather cross with me, since he'd found out this morning about my midnight escapade and hadn't approved.

It didn't matter if he approved, though. I had the map and I knew exactly where to go.

The rest didn't matter.

The last eighteen months with Noah had been a bit rocky. Truth was, he was slowing me down. Every time I would get close to Phryne, she would throw something in our path to delay us. I had no idea how she did it, but she always managed to arrange situations that would make Noah stop in his tracks, determined to do the right thing. We'd almost caught up to her in Australia a few months ago when we'd found a man on the side of the road, a shot to the groin causing him to bleed out. Noah had insisted on helping him, as we were the only people around for miles. I'd wanted to leave him and catch Phryne. The man was obviously a decoy.

And it had worked. That galled me. We are immortals, Noah had told me. It doesn't matter if it takes ten years or a hundred to find her.

But it mattered to me. Every day without Zane was like a knife in my heart. Every day, I felt a little less connected to everything around me. All that mattered was getting that halo. And if it made me cold and hard like Phryne, then I'd unthaw when I had my vampire in my arms again.

A wooden plank ladder was lowered to the shore, and the guide we'd hired frowned at us. "You need more clothing," he said in thickly accented English. He wore long sleeves and almost every inch of him was covered. "The bugs will attack you. Malaria. Disease. Very bad."

As I watched, he slapped his skin, brushing a bug away.

I glanced down at my pale, bare arms. Nothing was biting me. Nor Remy, Noah, or Ethan. How to explain to the man that we were immortal and not affected by things like disease? Even the bugs avoided us.

"This is as far as you take us, my friend," Noah said to the man. "We can handle it from here." He pressed a wad of money into the man's hand.

To our guide's credit, he tried to hand the money back, shaking his head. "If you go into the jungle alone, it will mean your death. Please be sensible about this."

Noah shook his head, pressing the money on the guide again. It would be damn hard to try and go treasure hunting with a guide along, but we hadn't been able to charter a boat without one. The man was genuinely concerned for our well-being, refusing Noah's money again and again. Eventually, he and Noah switched to

Portuguese and continued to argue. Despite Noah's commanding Serim presence, he couldn't convince the man that us walking into the jungle was not a mistake.

And damn it all if they weren't going to sit there and argue the entire morning. I looked over to Remy and Ethan, but they were lost in their own little lovey-dovey world. Remy had her fingers looped into Ethan's belt and was grinning up at him, her pose suggestive. They wouldn't be much help. The crew stood around, watching our guide argue and gesture at the jungle while Noah crossed his arms grimly and shook his head.

I looked at the watch on my wrist. While they stood here chatting, Phryne would be healing from her broken neck. Even now her crew could be turning their boat and coming after us. We didn't have the time to spare.

I calmly walked up behind the guide, unsheathed my knife, and slammed the butt of it against his head.

He went out like a light.

The crew began to yell at me. Noah gave me a look of disbelief. "Jackie!"

I sheathed the knife and picked up the wad of cash Noah had been trying to give the man. I turned and slapped it into the hand of the closest crew member. "We're going into that jungle alone. You keep this boat here for us until we come back and we'll give you a bonus. You keep him," I said, gesturing at the guide, "from following us and I'll double this when we get back."

I turned to Noah. "Come on. We haven't got all day."

He stared at me as if he didn't know me. Then he shook his head as I passed him and headed down the plank ladder into the Amazon.

~*~

The Amazon sucked. While I'd initially been fascinated by the lush greenery, after a day of hiking through the jungle, I hated it. There were vines and trees everywhere. The undergrowth crawled with insects the size of my hand, as well as snakes. Jaguars roamed the area. It was hot and humid and there was not a bit of a breeze. Nor was there a path. Within a few hours of hiking, Ethan had strapped the packs to his front and was carrying a complaining Remy in his back.

We'd been forced to stop at nightfall, and though the mosquitos and bugs weren't biting us, they crawled over everything. We'd managed to find a fallen tree that wasn't completely covered with ants and built a small fire next to it so Noah could rest for his sleep. He slept encased in netting while the rest of us huddled around the fire and tried to keep our spirits up. At least, Ethan tried to keep Remy's spirits up. I just studied the map by firelight, obsessed.

We were so close to the halo. I glanced over at Noah's sleeping form. He didn't know the Serim was still alive—though how anyone could live in this hot mess, I didn't know. Noah thought we were going in to retrieve the halo and just walk right back out. He didn't know that the halo might not want to go with us.

That was okay, I thought as I touched my backpack. I had a plan B. Before we'd left for Brazil, I'd purchased a few vials of unholy water and some implements Luc had sold me with the assurance that they would harm an angel. If I had to destroy the current holder of the halo to take it from him, that was what I'd have to do.

I noticed Remy watching me from across the fire. Her gaze was uncertain, and she glanced down at the backpack I was caressing. "You okay, Jackie?"

I picked up the map again. "Just thinking about tomorrow."

I could still feel her gaze on me for a while longer. I forced myself to relax, to be calm. Nothing was going to keep me from getting that halo.

Not Noah, not Remy, and not a four-thousand-year-old archangel.

CHAPTER FIFTEEN

"If you can travel the world on someone else's dime, do it. I'd say 'just don't sleep with the director to do it,' but let's be realistic. Everyone sleeps with the director."—*Big Trouble in Little Panties: A Memoir*, by Remy Summore

~*~

"How much farther did you say it was, Jackie?" Remy panted.

I pulled out the page from the Melledin manuscript and compared it to the map that Phryne had drawn on. "Should be right around here."

At my side, Noah hacked at a thick growth of jungle vine with a machete and paused to wipe his brow. "There's nothing around here. Exactly how close?"

"Within a couple of square miles," I said with a grimace, folding up the maps and pulling out my own machete again. "Sorry. This thing isn't exactly pinpoint accurate."

Remy groaned in protest.

"I will carry you again, Remiza," Ethan said, dodging a low-hanging vine.

"You're going to have to carry all of us soon if it gets any hotter," Noah said, swinging the machete into the thick underbrush. "It's like trying to hack aside the entire jungle. I'm not entirely sure we're not going in circles."

Complainers, all of them. "You can go back to the boat."

Ethan snorted. "Jackie Brighton, I do not think we could find the boat."

He had a point. I paused to stare up at the sky, but it was

impossible to see the sun overhead. The canopy of green was so thick and high that no direct light penetrated—it was impossible to tell if it was midday or late afternoon. The jungle itself was a sauna of dirt, bugs, and hooting monkeys. Birds flew through the branches high overhead, their calls overloud to my frayed nerves. It was noisy, hot, breezeless, and utterly miserable.

Noah stopped and extended his hand. "Are you sure you're going the right way? Let me see that map."

The compulsion ripped through me and I glared blackly at him, sheathing my machete to jerk out the map again. "Thanks for the command, Noah. You're a real pal."

He gave me a flash of a grin, but ignored my protests. With the months that passed, Noah and I had gone from awkward ex-lovers into friendship. Now that sex wasn't an issue, we were friendly, but it was more like sibling bickering than anything else. He seemed to finally accept that I carried a torch for Zane and always would, and he hadn't approached me about the relationship—or heaven forbid, marriage—again. I knew now that when we'd parted last time, he'd been furious because I'd hurt his pride. Noah Gideon had a great deal of pride, but the tattoos of servitude were teaching him humility and patience, slowly but surely.

That, and his booty call to Delilah once a month, back in New Orleans.

Well, he was learning humility unless it came to me, that is. Then he was free to command with abandon. "You're a dick," I told him, slapping the papers into his hand and turning back to glare at the bushes in front of us.

"Yes, but we all know how much you like dick, Jackie," Remy said cheerfully.

I twisted the ring on my finger and scowled at her. "You're not helping."

She simply gave a sunny smile from her perch atop Ethan's large back, and it only irritated me more. I was tired, hungry, and wanted someone to carry me too. But we were so close, and Noah kept stopping us. What if Phryne got the drop on us? I gestured at the bushes ahead. "I'm sure it's just right over there…"

My words trailed off as the bushes ahead of me parted, and a spearhead emerged, aimed right at my heart.

I stilled.

"Um, guys?" Remy said with a note of alarm as the bushes

began to rustle.

The spear pushed forward even more and I found myself staring at a man in a loincloth, his black hair flat and plastered around his head in a perfect circle, his body painted a bright ochre. He held the spear at my breast, while other men began to emerge from the bush. My fingers twitched over the knife at my belt.

"Do not fear, my beautiful lotus," Ethan said, standing taller to hide Remy's smaller form behind him. "I will protect you."

"Remain calm, all of you," Noah said. I glanced over at him and he was tucking the map into his shirt. "And Jackie, don't do anything reckless."

"I like how I'm the one that gets the warning," I murmured, taking a step backward as more brightly colored men poured out of the bushes, pointing bows and spears at us.

"He knows you very well," Ethan said unhelpfully.

"Who are these guys?" Remy asked. "I'm guessing they don't know that spears are more of a nuisance than a setback?"

"I wouldn't be so sure," I told her, eyeing the spear closest to me. "Some of the uncontacted tribes are rumored to be cannibals. I'm not sure you can regrow your body if they eat it."

"Oh," she said weakly.

We all raised our hands in the air and surrendered.

~*~

The tribe led us through the thick growth of jungle, and to my surprise, within a few minutes we were on a narrow path. I looked over at Noah, uneasy. The tribe urged us forward, speaking in a language we didn't understand, but it was obvious they wanted us to go down the trail. And since it beat using the machetes to move a foot at a time—and they had spears at our backs—I was happy to comply.

A few minutes down the trail, the canopy opened up and my breath caught in my throat.

A great stone ruin lay before us, half-swallowed by vines. Enormous flowered vines grew up the sides of the broken rock, the shape clearly a gate of some kind. More crumbling stone buildings were beyond the gate, each building heavily covered with vegetation. I saw people duck into the houses, and my breath caught in my throat. A lost city. How amazing. My mother would have been so excited to see this.

And then I felt a little stab of guilt that I hadn't kept in contact with her since I'd lost Zane. I'd call her when I got back, I vowed. As soon as my life got back on track. It wasn't her fault that my life had gone upside down since I'd been turned into a succubus. I made myself a promise that if I got back from this—and got Zane back—that I'd contact her again, invite her to stay with me.

After I got Zane back.

As we walked into the city, people stopped to stare at us. I stared back, studying the architecture that was clearly centuries old, the paintings and murals on the buildings that were still fresh. It was like we'd stepped through time into a pre-Columbian civilization. My stomach fluttered.

As we walked forward, I realized it wasn't my stomach that was fluttering. My internal tuning fork was going haywire. A halo was here. I could feel its power pulse around me. Excitement mingled with anticipation. I was *so* close to success.

The tribesfolk led us down a dirt path that had been cleared of undergrowth. Suddenly we turned and faced the largest building. A gigantic, tiered pyramid rose from the jungle floor, the sides of it covered in greenery. At the base of the pyramid, a scatter of half-crumbled stone buildings lay lined up in rows. Behind the pyramid, I could see glimpses of cleared fields. The pyramid drew my attention once more. My archaeologist's eye thought it to be a temple, except that there was a throne in the front, about halfway up the steps. Just high enough so the occupant could peer down at everyone below.

And that throne was currently occupied.

Power pulsed toward us as the man on the throne slowly stood. He was beautiful, ethereal. His long hair was as pale as moonlight, his skin as milky as the rest of him, and his eyes were light gray. He looked like a ghost. A length of red fabric draped over him, much like a toga, and as he stepped forward, his power whipped over us.

Ethan sank to one knee and bowed.

"Camael," Noah said, stepping forward with his hand extended. "Brother."

The one called Camael moved toward us, regal and proud. When he reached our small group, he gave Noah a nod of greeting and took the hand offered, though there was no warmth in him. There was no warmth in him anywhere. His gaze moved over

Remy and Ethan, and then landed on me. His eyes searched mine, and then he looked back to Noah.

"Yours?" he inquired mildly.

"I created her, but she answers to no one." He looked over at me and raised an eyebrow, as if daring me to challenge it.

Like I'd sass mouth to this icicle. His power was pulsing like a nuclear bomb. Even I knew when to keep my mouth shut.

Camael's cool eyes turned to Noah, and I noticed that his face was exquisitely made. I'd thought Noah and Zane pretty, but this man was unearthly. "Why do you seek me out after all these years?"

I looked at Noah to see how he'd respond to that. To my surprise, he chose honesty. "I have been tasked by the Serim Council to seek your halo. I had no idea you still lived. The Council will be pleased to hear of it."

Camael waved a hand. "I do not care if they are pleased or not. They are a pack of power-hungry fools."

"I like this guy," Remy whispered behind me.

I turned to give her a shushing look when I noticed that Camael had moved to stand directly in front of me. I gave him a tight smile, but he only studied me. "You are not surprised to see me alive," he said in a low voice pitched so the others could not overhear. "I can see it in your eyes."

Taken aback, I shook my head quickly. "You're mistaken."

"I'm never mistaken."

That wave of power emanating from him blasted through me, making my stomach churn. "I just have a great poker face," I lied. "Win at cards all the time." When he continued to study me, I decided to change the subject. "So how come you're out here at the edge of civilization?"

"Because I wish to be left alone," he said flatly.

Remy kicked me in the back of the leg. As if it were all my fault somehow.

"Well, we won't stay long," I lied. "Now that we see that you're up and kicking, I'm sure we'll be on our way. It's obvious that this is a bad time—"

Noah grasped my arm. "Jackie, hush," he said in a low voice.

I fell silent. No choice.

"Nonsense," Camael said slowly, his cool voice a breeze in the humid jungle. His gaze lingered on me for a moment longer and then he looked to Noah. "You must all be my guests tonight. We shall have a feast."

"Sounds good to me," Remy said. "I'm friggin' starving."

~*~

As part of the celebration, we were offered new clothing (loincloths, which we declined), body paint (which we also declined) and flowers for our hair. The feast was held at sunset, and the entire village showed up, serving delicacies that I didn't recognize in the slightest. Every time I tried to refuse something, someone frowned at me—Noah included—so I took a bite of everything that was offered.

"I'm pretty sure you just ate roasted fire ants," Remy pointed out after one particularly crispy bite of something unrecognizable.

"I hate you for pointing that out," I told her, grabbing my canteen and drinking heavily.

She grinned and chewed on a leafy green roll stuffed with what looked like nuts. At her side, Ethan seemed to be a big hit with the tribe. They couldn't understand a word he said, but he ate with great gusto and seemed appreciative of everything. Brave man.

"So what do you make of all this?" Remy asked me, leaning over. "I kept thinking that it reminded me of a movie a friend of mine was in. It's very *Bro-Mancing the Bone,* except you're not gay, I'm not gay, and the orgy hasn't started yet."

"There's no orgy, Remy." At least I sure hoped not.

"Yeah, so why the party? The Great White Dope over there didn't exactly look thrilled to see Noah."

The two men sat next to each other near the front of the small gathering, talking in low voices. I wouldn't have called it friendly. I'd have called it strained on Noah's part and bored on Camael's.

Camael had known that I'd come after him, known he was alive. Surely he was wondering why I was here to collect his halo, then?

"I don't know, Remy," I said quietly, and managed to not grimace when someone passed me another helping of food. I took a bite of the white, shredded meat that had been handed to me on a wooden plate. Tasted like chicken. Oh God. It could be anything. Across from me, a woman wearing only a loincloth smiled and nodded, speaking her native tongue. I made a face of appreciation and nodded back at her. Mmm mmm mystery meat.

Remy giggled at my expression. "At least that one doesn't have discernible legs or wings."

"Still hate you," I said.

At the front of the feast, Noah and Camael stood. Camael spoke in the native tongue for a moment, and then he turned, his pale gaze focusing on our small trio. "It is time for the Serim to retire. We shall all speak in the morning."

I felt a stirring of excitement at that. The Serim were retiring. That meant Noah was going to be out of commission for the rest of the evening, and Camael would be unconscious.

Helpless.

And I could take that halo from him. I thought of the knives strapped to my waist, and hated the little surge of excitement that pushed through me.

I was going to murder an immortal to steal his power. And I was looking forward to it. How sick was that?

~*~

I sat in the darkness, waiting, fully dressed.

Feeling the pulse of the halo so close nearby, my skin prickled constantly, my senses alert. My thoughts were entirely of Zane, and I pictured his face over and over again. If I closed my eyes, I could almost imagine the brush of his wing feathers over my skin, his fingertips grazing my lower lip, as if parting my lips for a kiss. The empty, dull ache of his loss gnawed at me, and I embraced it.

I would have him back soon. All I needed was that halo.

But I waited, because I would only get the one chance. All around me, it was silent. The night air was heavy in the stone house I'd been given, a jaguar hide tossed over the doorframe. Outside, I heard the shuffle of a few stragglers going to bed, then nothing but the noise of the jungle itself.

And still I waited.

When I could wait no longer, I carefully pulled my belt around my hips, checked the knives that I strapped to my thigh, my wrists. The one on the inside of my boot. I discarded my gun—too noisy for what I wanted. Then I stood and peeked out the door of my small stone hut.

Everyone was asleep. The large central fire that had blazed so merrily earlier was nothing but a heap of coals. The flaps were drawn over the village's stone huts and everything was silent. At the far end of the camp, two men with spears guarded the base of the pyramid. Halfway up the side of the monument, there was a small door covered in leopard skin, the rock around it completely covered in vines. Bingo. That'd be where Camael was. Nice and secure and just a little bit pompous.

I slunk out of my stone hut and moved to the next one, keeping in the shadows. The guards occasionally glanced in my direction, but they didn't spot me clinging to a shadowy wall. I used the shadows to creep closer, moving through the camp quietly. This was it. My chance.

Not much longer, Zane, baby.

Camael's sleeping spot was high up the pyramid, and I circled around to the back, ignoring the cry of a monkey in the distance. At least, I hoped it was a monkey. Lord only knew what was out here lurking in the jungle.

There were no guards along the back of the pyramid, so I grasped the rocks and began to climb, supporting myself on the vines and hauling myself up. It was slow, difficult work—some of the footholds were spaced far apart, and I wasn't much of a climber. I took my time, making sure each rock that I grabbed was solid. Not because I was afraid of falling, but because I was afraid of giving away my position.

When I finally pulled myself up to the top, I was panting and flushed with sweat. I bit back my gasping breaths and flattened myself against the side of the rough pyramid, moving toward the front.

The two men with spears were still there. I listened to them converse quietly. One laughed and then they fell silent again. I tensed as one shifted, glancing around the corner to where I stood in the shadows. He said something to his companion, then stepped toward me.

This was it.

I threw myself at him, brushing my fingers over his bare arm before he could raise his spear, and used my succubus powers to knock him unconscious. He went down, his memories flashing through my mind.

The other came around the corner a moment later, and I turned to face him, trying to put my back to him. Too late. He thrust his weapon. A stabbing pain shot through me and he jerked his spear out of my stomach. Blood welled in my mouth and I hunched over, hugging my stomach protectively. He raised the spear again, and I collapsed to the ground next to his friend, my eyes closed.

Silence.

After a moment, he prodded me with the spear again. I didn't move.

He edged closer.

Victory. I reached out and grabbed his ankle, sending him to dreamland as I did so. He fell with a heavy thump, and I pushed his fallen body aside, dragging myself up.

I spat blood on the concrete, my mind hazy with pain. Damn it. I hadn't expected one of them to really *stab* me. Luckily, it was just a belly wound. Those only hurt like hell, but it wouldn't knock me out, at least. I pressed my hands to the freely bleeding gash, grimacing. I took my shirt off and bound the wound as best I could. I'd fix it later.

I hauled myself to my feet, feeling weak and dizzy with pain. Sticky blood was all over everything and shone like ink against my pale skin in the moonlight.

But I was so damn close. I moved to the front of the house and pushed aside the jaguar hide, stepping in to see my prey.

Camael lay there atop a nest of animal skins in the low bed, utterly still. His long, white hair lay smooth around his beautiful face, and his features were composed and noble even in sleep. His hands were clasped over his heart, his body perfectly straight. He looked as if he was dead. But the pulse of power that throbbed and swelled in this room told me he was very much alive. It was that power that dragged my feet forward, and I knelt at Camael's bedside, reaching for my knife, ignoring the pain in my gut.

The halo's power throbbed inside me, intermingling with my longing. My need.

My hands felt slippery with my own blood as I pulled my knife out of the sheath and readied myself. I stared down at Camael's beautiful, sleeping form, so very peaceful. Angelic. And I forced myself to look at him dispassionately. I'd need to sever the head from the neck. Chop his arms off, next go after the torso, and once he was in bite-size chunks, scatter the pieces into the woods and hope the animals would scavenge him. I couldn't be sure that would work, given that mosquitos were avoiding our bodies. I studied the sleeping man dispassionately, thinking hard. Maybe I could dump the smaller pieces into the river for the piranhas. Or maybe I could soak his body parts in the unholy water and hope it acted like acid and dissolved them—

I squeezed my eyes shut, gagging at the thought. What was I doing? Calculating the best way to dispose of a body? That was sick. Revolting.

Think of Zane, I told myself again. *Zane needs you. This depends on you getting that halo. You didn't come this far—suffer through this much—to give up because you're a little squeamish.*

I took a few deep breaths, ignoring how much that hurt, and raised the knife again, laying it at Camael's marble throat. He was beautiful in the low light, pale and flawless. My knife didn't seem large enough and I looked at his throat, then at my knife again. I'd have to saw through him, shove through tendon and bone, hacking at this beautiful man.

Not a man. An angel.

Like Zane had been. And here I was going to murder him in cold blood, hack him to pieces, and feed him to the jaguars, all so I could have my lover back.

It was a total dick move. I knew it. I'd dreamed of this dick move for months on end. And now that it was here...

I stared at his angelic face. Raised the knife again, then lowered it.

I couldn't do it.

This wasn't me. I couldn't murder a man in cold blood and hack his body to pieces.

I look at you and I see Phryne. I see that same ice she has in her eyes. I look at you and I see someone who's willing to use and abuse others to get what she wants.

I lowered the knife and stared at Camael, hating the tears that rose to my eyes. Weak, stupid tears because I was pathetic and couldn't kill a man to save another. I'd come so close. The halo sang to me, setting my nerve endings on fire. I wanted it so badly. I *needed* it.

And yet I couldn't kill a man who had done nothing wrong. I couldn't kill in cold blood. Angry at myself, I swiped at the tears on my cheeks, feeling utterly defeated.

"I was wondering if you would be able to do it," a calm, low voice said.

I looked up into Camael's colorless eyes, shocked.

He stared back at me, unmoving. Power crashed, making the

hairs on the back of my neck stand up.

I lowered the knife, hesitant. A Serim should not be awake in the middle of the night, staring at me. Yet the power was his. I could feel it all around us, so thick that it felt like a mist clinging to the air. "I don't understand. How…"

He sat up, watching me, and rested one arm across his lap. On his wrist was a thick golden cuff. A power inhibitor—just like the ring I wore. He must have had it made to override the Serim sleep, somehow. Tricky of him. Camael gave me a small smile but didn't move, as if daring me to reach out and pluck that bracer from him to see what happened.

"I—I'm sorry," I blurted. It seemed like both the right and wrong thing to say.

"You are here to kill me," he said thoughtfully, studying me. "I could see it in your eyes the moment we met. Noah accepted defeat as soon as he realized I lived." The long, gossamer hair spilled over his shoulder and bare chest, exactly the same color as his ghost-pale skin. "I expected to see defeat in your face, but you had a fire of determination instead. I knew then that you would come for me."

"Was I that obvious?"

"Perhaps not to the others. But I recognize when someone has lost everything."

I looked into his eyes and saw that hard, despairing ache I saw in the mirror every morning. This man had loved and lost and had been centuries without the one he loved more than anyone else. An ache formed in my throat. I knew what that was like; but to be centuries—millennia—without that one, I couldn't bear to imagine. "I need your halo," I told him. "The Archangel Gabriel promised me that I could have a boon if I returned the two missing archangel haloes to him."

A wry smile touched that cool mouth. "Did he, now? He should not ask for things that do not belong to him." He leaned forward, moving closer to the edge of the bed of furs, where I hovered, crouched on my knees, bleeding on his floor. "And the other halo, have you found it?"

I noticed the note of emotion in his voice and felt a pang of alarm. Oh no. Did he want the halo too?

"I had it and lost it," I admitted. "I owed a promise to a demon and the moment I grabbed it, she showed up to collect."

He recoiled, almost seeming to wither a little. His eyes

narrowed, as if trying to digest extreme pain. "Azazel's halo?" He breathed. "A... demon has it?"

At his agony, I realized the truth. "Azazel—he was the one you fell for?"

Two archangels in love—that must not have gone over well upstairs. I thought back to the murals in the tomb. Someone had targeted Azazel and destroyed him deliberately. I suspected it was because of the love he shared with Zephraim. I thought back to Noah and Zane, and the other angels that had fallen. The women they'd loved had all been murdered by jealous archangels who wanted them to suffer. Had Azazel suffered the same fate?

Best loved of all the archangels. I imagine someone built this for him to show how much they loved him. An homage to him even in death. I stared at Camael's melancholy face and knew I was looking at the creator of that tomb.

"My love has been gone for twelve hundred years," he said slowly, his gaze fixed somewhere beyond me. "Thousands of sunrises without him. Endless lovers who were not him, who did not have his wondrous touch. I miss everything about him. Life is agony without him. Immortal life without him... it is unendurable." Camael's eyes focused on me again, their depths glimmering with a hint of tears. He tilted his head, studying me, my eyes. "But then, you know this."

"I do," I said softly. "I don't want to live a thousand years without the one I love. Please, help me."

Camael's hands went to his chest, covering his heart. "To think that my love's essence has been taken by a demon. His soul swallowed as he waited for his return to heaven, stolen from the tomb I built him." He shook his head. "You have done this to my love in your ignorance, but I cannot punish you."

I stiffened in my seat. Punish... me?

His gaze grew cold, hard, the smile curving his mouth unwelcoming. "Yes, punish. You think I would allow you to destroy my lover's soul and not feel the sting of my wrath? But I see you, and I see in your eyes that whatever I did to you would not matter. You have already been punished more than a mind can bear. It has driven you to the brink of madness. Your humanity is almost gone. I was not sure that you would not kill me. Part of me wishes you had."

"Part of me wishes I had too," I said, then shook my head,

dropping my gaze to the ground. "Would you have let me?"

His gaze was unwavering. Then, after a long moment, he said, "Perhaps."

I shook my head. "I couldn't do it. The loss of my Zane isn't your fault."

"And you would bring him back?" Camael asked. "With the wish you are given, you would wish for his return? I wandered for many centuries, seeking answers that would bring my love back. When I realized it was hopeless, I retreated from the world."

"It's not hopeless," I said, and meant it with every fiber of my being. "I'll do whatever it takes to get him back. Will you give me the halo?"

He reached out to brush my cheek with his fingers. They burned with power against my skin, but I remained in place, waiting. "I cannot."

I was shattered at his refusal. "Why not? You don't want to live anymore."

"I do not," he agreed. "But you cannot defeat the demon if she has stolen Azazel's power. It will take another archangel." At my inquiring look, he straightened on the bed and stared at the golden cuff on his arm. "I will destroy the demon for you and then give you my halo. You shall have your love back so one of us may have an eternity that is not full of torment."

Tears burned my eyes. "You'd do that for me?"

"No," he said gently. "But I would do it for *my* love. How can I not make the same sacrifice for yours?" His gaze went distant again, and he stared beyond me. "This immortal life crawls on through dirt and rock and mud and unimaginable loneliness. I have spent a thousand years without him and felt the ache of every moment. If Gabriel chooses to destroy me upon my return, I would welcome it as an end to my suffering."

"Thank you," I said, and placed my hand over his in his lap.

His eyes gleamed in the darkness, and I was not sure if it was tears or something else. "Does your master know that you planned to destroy me?"

I grimaced. "If he'd known my plan, he'd have never come with me."

"And you would have left him here? Crept away with my power like a hungry mongrel with a bone?" He knew I could not have left with Noah at my side, not with Noah's ability to command everything I did.

"I would have," I said. "He would have never forgiven me, but I would have accepted the loss. Collateral damage," I said, then wished I could bite the words back in to my mouth.

The demon had said that to me.

"I do not know if you are determined or merely foolhardy," Camael told me.

I figured I was both.

CHAPTER SIXTEEN

"You need to have two personalities to win at this sort of thing. When I get on stage and the cameras start rolling, everyone wants to see the cock-gobbling, horny she-beast who wants to be used by everyone in all kinds of dirty ways. But leave that girl on stage. Well, if you can. And if that's how you really are, give your stage persona a sexy lisp or something."—*Life, Love, and the Pursuit of Porn*, by Remy Summore

~*~

Several weeks later

I had never been so glad to be back on American soil. I looked out the window of Noah's private jet at the landing strip and sighed, feeling weary. Soon. Very soon.

We disembarked, grabbed our luggage, and headed for customs. Remy gave Camael a pair of sunglasses and we paused for him to put them on. I pressed a hand to my wounded side out of habit, but I was getting used to the dull, throbbing ache.

"Now, I've done this sort of thing before," Remy said to him, moving to his side. "It's a little game we like to play called Two People, One Passport. You're going to pretend to be blind, and when he reaches for your passport, you slip him mine. I'll touch his hand and implant some memories that make him think he's already checked us both in, and then off we go. It'll be easy."

"Lead on, then," Camael said quietly, holding out his arm for her to take.

We breezed through customs and moved out to the taxi stand. I paused in front of a newsstand, frowning at the headline.

CULT KILLS 30 IN MASS SUICIDE. A smaller byline read *Churchgoers believed that demons walked among them.*

My stomach gave a sick little clench. I knew of one demon who walked freely. I stopped to buy the paper and then tucked it under my arm, moving to rejoin the others.

Noah stood there, waiting for me. His hair brushed the white collar of his shirt, a light gray jacket covering his shoulders. He looked like something out of a men's magazine—tall and strong and powerful. The dozens of tattoos were carefully hidden by the clothing.

"We ready to go for the final battle?" I asked him, moving to his side and pulling out the newspaper I'd just purchased. "I have an idea of where our demon might be."

He didn't glance down at my paper. Instead, he regarded my face. "Jackie, I'm afraid this is good-bye."

"Good-bye?" I stared up at him, uncomprehending. Then I waved my newspaper at where Remy, Ethan, and Camael stood waiting for the taxi. "But we're so close. In just a few hours, we could have that halo away from her—"

"Jackie," he said, grabbing my hand and clasping it in his. The paper fell to the ground. "We both know that I'm not going to get that halo."

I bit my lip and said nothing.

He smiled down at me, his blue-eyed gaze fond, and he took my other hand in his, then clasped them both to his chest. Noah studied me for a minute and then shook his head, as if regretting how things had turned out. "You want Zane back so badly that you'll move heaven and earth to save him. I lost Rachael. How can I possibly stand in the way?"

My throat went dry, and I gave him a sad smile. "You're ruining my master plan, Noah Gideon. Here I was going to have to be all badass and somehow you before you turned it over to the Serim Council."

"The Serim will only use that halo for their own purposes. They are immortals with too much time on their hands, and the games they play are beneficial to no one. They don't need the halo. Not like you do. And you don't need me there. My presence will only cause more problems. You only need Camael."

I looked at his open collar, where I could just see the hint of one of the words written on his skin peeking out. "But what about… you? Your promises?"

"It's not compulsion for me," he said gently. "They are debts of honor, no more." His hand went to his shirt and he unbuttoned the first button, then pulled the shirt aside to expose one tattooed word written directly over his heart. He tapped it. "I'll wear this one for you."

I stared at the name emblazoned on his chest, unable to read it. It was a promise written in the angelic language. A promise that Noah had made, and was going to break. For me. For Zane.

Shit. I was not going to cry again. My lower lip wobbled a bit but I managed a soft smile and rebuttoned his shirt for him. "You're a good man, Noah. I wish I could have loved you like I love Zane."

"It wouldn't have been fair to either of us," he said, and a slow smile curved his mouth. "Zane and I have never been good at sharing. You would have had to pick sooner or later. I'm only sad that you have such poor taste in men."

I laughed softly and smacked his chest with my hand. "I have excellent taste, thank you."

He grinned at me, so easy. We were so comfortable now that we were just friends. Why couldn't it have always been like this? "I just ask one thing, if you can."

"Name it," I told him and meant it.

"If you can somehow find a way… bring Sophie back, too."

I gave him a surprised look.

He shook his head, waving a hand. "Nothing like that. I just think…" he shook his head. "She was so determined to be unbroken, despite her succubus nature. I liked that. I admired her." His gaze grew distant. "She deserved more."

"I'll bring her back too," I said. "And I'll tell her to look you up."

He smiled. "You do that."

We stood there for a moment more, merely facing each other. Good-bye was so… final. I knew Noah would never be more than a phone call away, and yet… Sadness filled me. "You've been good to me, Noah. Thank you. For everything."

He reached over and pulled me into his arms. I stiffened, expecting a kiss, but he only hugged me, tucking me under his chin and holding me close. My wounded side flared, but I ignored it. "I will always be there if you need me. All you have to do is ask."

I nodded against his chest. "I will."

He released me and stepped away, smiling. "Now go and save the day."

I scooped up my newspaper, smiled at him, and raced for the waiting taxi.

Soon, Zane.

~*~

Last I'd checked, we were somewhere in Pennsylvania. I'd stopped paying attention. My thoughts were on nothing but Zane.

"Here," Camael said as Remy drove down a narrow one-lane road.

I looked out the window and noticed that there was nothing but rolling green fields around us. In the distance, cows grazed. "Here?" I asked.

"This is empty of people. It is a good place."

Encouraging. I nodded at Remy, indicating she should pull over. The car edged into the grassy ditch and I slid out, putting my hands on my hips as I looked around. Very distantly, up a hill, I could see a small farmhouse. The road we drove on was deserted despite it being midday.

"Okay," Remy said cheerfully. "This is where we set up?"

I looked over at Camael, but he was staring off into the sky, as if deep in thought. I stepped around him and shook my head at Remy. "I want you and Ethan away from here."

Ever at her side, Ethan scowled at me. "I do not approve of this."

"Me either," Remy protested. "You need us—"

"No," I interrupted, and moved forward to hug Remy. "This is going to be a one-shot sort of thing. Either Cam can destroy Mae, or we're accidentally handing her a second halo." I patted my belt, as I'd come prepared for anything and everything. Holy and unholy water. A rosary, a crucifix, and a pentagram locket. I also had my phone strapped there, and I gestured at it. "I'll call you. If I don't call in a few hours, just keep on driving and try to get some distance between you and her. Understand?"

Remy looked at Ethan, eyes wide. Then she shook her head at

me again. "No, Jackie. We're here with you."

I smiled at that and turned to Ethan. "Ethan, can you protect Remy by making her do what I say? Please?"

His eyes flashed bright with the power of the boon. "I will."

"Oooh, you tricksy bastard," Remy said with a scowl, then grabbed me in a fierce hug. "If you die, I'm totally burning all your shitty clothes."

"Deal," I said, hugging my best friend in the entire world. "But I'll be back for them."

This would not fail. Would not.

Remy looked rather misty-eyed, but she gave me a bright smile and then turned to Ethan. "Okay, love dumpling. Let's hit the road. My cell's on, Jackie. Call me. And I mean that." She wagged a finger at me and then pulled her keys out again. And hesitated. She looked back to me.

Ethan plucked the keys from her hand and strode to the car door. "Come, my beautiful sugared rose petal. We must go."

She sighed, gave me one last look, and then followed him.

The rental car started and then moved down the empty road slowly. I watched them go, feeling a twinge of sadness. Would that be the last time I ever saw my friend? When they had disappeared and several minutes had passed, I turned to Camael. "Are they far enough away? Can you feel them?" My tuning fork had been drowned out by the constant presence of the fallen archangel.

He tilted his head, as if sensing their presence. "They have parked the vehicle a short distance away."

I swore and pulled out my phone. I dialed Remy, and as soon as she picked up, I barked, "I'm serious, Remy. *Move* it. I will call you when it's safe."

"Hater," she muttered, then said, "Love you girl. Give 'em hell," and hung up.

"I will," I said to the dial tone, and then clicked the phone off and replaced it in my utility belt.

Camael looked over at me. "Come."

"Lead the way," I said and gestured for him to move ahead of me.

He did, maneuvering easily over the low barbed-wire fence. I had a bit more trouble with it, settling for squeezing in between the wires. The quick movement aggravated my wound. Even though I'd been stabbed well over several weeks ago, it hadn't healed. I wasn't having sex, and my body was stuck in an unnatural state. Instead, I simply bled, and bled, and lived with the aching, stabbing pain in my gut.

I'd come this far, gotten this close to getting Zane back, and a little wound wasn't going to make me seek out another man when I was so close to success.

Or total failure, my brain reminded me, but I ignored it. Failure was not something I was even considering. There would be no failure, because I couldn't contemplate a life without Zane. The last eighteen-plus months had been pure hell every minute of every day. I still felt that ache reminding me that one of my masters was gone. Remy had said hers had faded after a few weeks, but mine seemed to grow stronger every day. Perhaps because I wouldn't let his memory go.

I reached into the pocket of the leather duster and pulled out a cigarette as I followed Camael into the field. I needed the taste of Zane on my lips. It bolstered me. I took a quick drag, grimaced at the smoke, and then dropped and stepped on it. The taste lingered on my lips and I resisted the urge to lick them out of longing.

Camael walked to the center of the field and nodded at me. "This is the place."

"And this will work?"

"It will. She will not be able to resist the lure we will set out for her." His clear eyes focused on me. "Do you have it?"

I pulled out the gold necklace and dangled it in front of him. "It really doesn't look much like a halo to me. Sorry to be a party pooper."

He took it from my hand and pinched the links between his fingers. I felt a pulse of power and watched as he carefully stiffened the links, shaping it until it was a thin, gleaming circle. His power pulsed again and it began to glow from within.

"How'd you do that?"

He shrugged carelessly. "It is a simple trick."

For an archangel, maybe. When he held the halo out to me, I took it with careful fingers. It felt cool to the touch and still felt like the golden chain it was. But to my eyes, it was a softly glowing halo, a perfect circle of power. I looked to Camael. "And she'll buy that I have this?"

"Demons are not clever," he said. "And Azazel dwells inside her. He will wish to seek out the source of my power. He knows me. He will want to touch me again in some way."

"Well, call away," I said, gesturing with the halo. "I'll stand here and be your decoy—"

Before I could even finish the sentence, I was knocked backward by a pulse of power so strong that it sent me sprawling to the ground. Wave after wave of the power rushed over me, the grass around me whipping like knives into my skin. I shut my eyes and hid my face to protect it from the angelic supernova.

Then, just as quickly, it died away again.

I squeezed one eye open to look around. Distant trees swayed, and cows picked themselves up off the ground, struggling back to their feet. Camael was gone. Okay. That was weird. "Hello?"

Silence.

I got to my feet, brushing off my coat with my free hand, the other holding the chain-halo. "If you're still here, give me a sign that I haven't been abandoned?"

A caress brushed my cheek.

"Okay then," I said, sitting cross-legged and adjusting my clothing. "I don't see how archangels got to hog all the superpowers, but it's pretty handy for this, I have to admit."

I could have sworn I felt amusement in the air.

I stared at my surroundings, waiting. Every instinct in me told me to grab one of the blades I kept at my waist and hold it at the ready, but the demon needed to think that it was me giving off all this power so she would attack me and then Camael could get the drop on her. It was the world's most obvious decoy plan, but it was brilliant in its simplicity.

Except I was the only one in the equation who didn't have archangel superpowers. That seemed like a flaw in this grand plan, but I was in this too deep to think about backing out now. I rubbed the wet bandages in place over my wound as I waited, letting the pain keep me alert.

Something twinged at the edge of my consciousness, like a gnat. It grew stronger, the buzz harsher as the seconds passed, and the air grew heavy and ominous.

She was coming. I felt Camael brush my cheek, but it was unnecessary. I already knew she was on her way. I could feel it in the air.

Down the small country road, a figure walked in an old-fashioned, plain black dress. I felt a bit of alarm for that woman—didn't she know? Couldn't she feel the threat in the air?

But she turned toward us, and I could see from my spot a safe distance away that her eyes were entirely red.

I swallowed hard and held my ground, my hand digging into that halo.

Her gaze focused on me, sitting in the field, and she paused.

I got to my feet and held the halo up and shook it like a tambourine. "Over here, demon."

She raised a hand and the rickety fence collapsed. Neat trick. Wish I could do that sort of thing. A smile touched her face and she strolled toward me. With every step, I could feel the malevolent power surging off her.

"You amaze me, girl," she said in a slow voice. "I don't know how you managed to acquire so much power twice. They must love you up above."

"I get around," I said lamely and hugged my halo to my chest. "You stole something from me. I want it back."

"Oh, child," she purred as she approached, slinking toward me with menace. "This is going to be like taking candy from a baby."

"So you say," I said bravely, my hands trembling just a little.

She cocked her head, coming to stand in front of me. Her senses were alert, and her red eyes skimmed my form, as if fascinated. Camael's power shimmered all over the meadow.

"You don't believe me?" she asked, surprised. "When I could simply slip that ring off your finger and end all this?"

I felt my hand jerk and I gasped, stumbling backward. My hand curled into a protective fist and I dropped the halo, wrapping my other hand around it. How had she known? If I lost that ring... I'd gone so long without sex that I'd die instantly. Mae knew that, damn it, and she was going to take me out. Fear pounded through me.

Mae leaned forward and casually scooped up the halo I'd dropped. She picked it up with a pleased smile... and then frowned as it melted back to a chain in her grasp. "How..."

Power slammed into her, a fury of white light that pushed her across the field and slapped her into a nearby tree. It cracked under the force and she dropped to the ground. Camael appeared beside me, his hand up, white-blond hair whipping about his head.

"You have Azazel trapped inside you," he said in a low, calm voice. "You cannot have him. He is *mine*."

Mae looked at me, then at Camael, struggling to her feet. Then to my surprise, she began to laugh, hard. "Oh, this is too perfect. Too, too perfect. You set a trap for me? That's so adorable. But here's a tip for you both," she purred. "I'm about to have two haloes, and this dumbass," she gestured at me with a sneer, "is the one responsible. What kind of idiot makes a deal with a demon anyhow?"

Before either of us could respond, she launched herself at Camael, power pulsing out of her like a thunderstorm. She raised her arms and I recognized that pose—she was gathering power, just like when she'd destroyed the queen.

I screamed a warning for Camael. "Look out!"

The Serim rocked on his feet and stepped to the side, and that bolt of power blasted through the field, missing him. In the distance, a cow gave a cry of pain and I heard the rest of the herd stampeding away.

I didn't blame them; I felt like running too. My hands went to my belt, feeling for the holy water there.

A chorus of snarls drew my gaze back to the demon. She held her arms outstretched, her body stiff as if she wanted to put her hands around Camael's throat. He stood a short distance away, his eyes flashing silver, hair whipping. I could feel the power surging between the two of them. First a dark pulse like Mae was surging to dominance, only to have Camael's silvery pulse of power take over.

They were evenly matched. But Mae was still smiling, her lips bared in concentration. Camael's face was strained—a reflection of my own. The power here was making my stomach flip with nausea, my skin itching at the sensations. I crept a few steps backward, getting away from the two of them, the holy water in hand.

The struggle went on for endless minutes, the two of them locked in place, neither moving. I grew anxious and then impatient. These two were immortals—they had all the time in the world. Exactly how long was this standstill going to continue?

Even as I thought it, Mae dropped to her knees. She fell into the grass, her breath gasping in her throat. Triumph flickered over Camael's face and he looked over at me before moving to place a hand on Mae's head.

He was winning!

The demon's eyes flashed white and to my surprise, her gasps turned into laughter. Choked, garbled laughter. Her power pulsed.

As I watched, the golden cuff on Camael's arm fell to the ground, broken neatly in half.

Camael choked. His hand fell away from Mae's head and he held it up, watching the skin wither. He looked over at me and his eyes grew hollow in his face, his cheekbones more pronounced.

His curse was kicking in. He was going to die.

Mae's laughter grew louder and she struggled to her feet. "You stupid idiots. Why not paint a target on your back that says kick me? You leave a demon an opening, and she's going to take it. Fools."

With that, she threw her arms around Camael's withering form and planted her mouth on his.

Power went haywire around us. The skies grew dark, lightning crackling from the ground. My hair thrashed around my face and the air felt heavy, as if a storm was coming, but there was nothing but Camael and Mae slowly draining his life force from him.

I was about to lose everything.

I quickly unscrewed the cap of the holy water and tossed a bit of it on her, trying to distract her away from Camael. Her skin sizzled at the contact, but she ignored it, continuing her draining kiss. As I watched, Camael seemed to bend at the knees, collapsing in on himself, and Mae went with him, her skin gleaming with power, her eyes glowing like beacons. She was absorbing the other archangel, sucking away his life force and pulling it into her own body.

"No," I cried, pulling out my knife and pushing forward, only to slam into some sort of force-wall. The air was so thick around them that I couldn't get closer than a few feet. I had to do something.

I needed another archangel—a strong one.

With a gasp, I pulled out the holy water again and began to shake it in the grass. I had to do something. This would either work or just piss the demon off, but I didn't care. I was about to lose everything. I forced myself to concentrate on the task at hand even as Camael's power grew weaker all around me and Mae's malevolence grew stronger.

One could call demons by consecrating ground to them and calling their names—I hoped that it'd work for an archangel as well. I'd done it in the past to call Mae... but there was no reason why I couldn't turn the tables on her now.

I poured the holy water in a circle around the two locked in the awful embrace, and then to make sure that I'd completed my circle, went around them again. The Serim had always prayed before calling the angels. I babbled off a hasty prayer and then touched the word etched in my wrist.

"Gabriel," I shouted to the heavens. "I've got your two haloes. Come and get them."

Power surged all around me, knocking me flat once more as the Heavens opened up.

CHAPTER SEVENTEEN

"Have an end game. What's your goal in this career? Is it to make the Guinness World Record for the most dicks in your vagina in a twenty-four-hour period? Is it to be a millionaire? Is it fame and fortune? Have a plan and don't deviate from the plan."—*Porn and the Art of Business*, by Remy Summore

~*~

Birds chirped somewhere overhead. My entire body ached, but that didn't register as much as the awareness that the field was supremely, supremely quiet. The heavy, oppressive air was gone.

I opened my eyes and sat up, grimacing. My head throbbed like I was on the south side of a drinking binge, and my muscles ached. Camael was nowhere to be seen. Neither was Mae. I squinted at the late afternoon sky, then at the cows in the distance. They'd returned.

A shadow fell over me, quickly followed by the familiar scent of sunlight and vanilla. Angels—true angels—were always accompanied by soft, comforting scents. This particular scent was as clean and crisp and sweet as anything I'd ever smelled.

My stomach clenched and I turned to stare into the hard, beautiful face of the Archangel Gabriel. Naked bronze skin covered the biggest, smoothest, most muscled torso I'd ever seen, topped by a pair of fluffy white, oversized wings. In contrast, the face adorning that perfect body was cold and severe in its perfection.

I scrambled to my feet. "Oh, crap. Hi." I brushed off my clothes and glanced around, but the field was utterly quiet. "Uh. Where's Camael? And the demon?"

He watched me with fathomless eyes, his expression neutral. "They have been returned from whence they came."

That was good, right? "So… Azazel and Camael are back in Heaven? That means Mae has gone back to Hell?"

He inclined his head.

"Is… Camael okay with that?" Because judging from Gabriel's expression, the other archangel was not coming back.

A hint of arrogance curved Gabriel's hard mouth. "Camael has been reunited with the Host. He is quite content. For him, living in dirt and squalor amongst humans became wearying quite some time ago."

Gee. "Well, that's good, I guess."

Gabriel then turned his back as if to walk away.

"Wait," I said sharply. "What about our deal?"

He turned to look at me, his face hard. "Our deal?"

I raised my wrist and showed him the word etched on my skin. "You promised me. Two haloes for a boon. You can't take that back. You gave me your word, remember?"

He turned back toward me, his eyes narrow and ice cold. He moved so quickly that I thought I'd imagined it and then he was looming over me again, the power blasting off him making my hair ruffle in a nonexistent breeze. "Your thoughtless pursuit of my 'favor' caused the destruction of half of the fallen, and you nearly let a demon take not one halo but *both* of the remaining ones. And you feel you should be rewarded?"

He was furious with me. Utterly, coldly furious as only an angel could be.

"That's right," I said, getting pissed off myself. "I fucked up and I fixed it. You didn't say how I had to get the haloes back to you, just that they had to come back. Well guess what? They're back."

"And in the meantime, you let a demon kill countless humans—"

"I didn't let her do anything," I yelled. "She did that of her own free will. And I stopped her."

"And yet you did not stop her before she wiped out the vampires." A dangerous muscle clenched in his jaw.

Realization dawned on me. "You… You're upset that they're gone? Not at me?"

"Of course I am *upset*." He sneered the word at me, his gaze blasting fury as he stared down at me. "Even if my brethren have chosen the wrong path, they are still part of the Host. Each of them is still one of mine. While they lived, there was a chance for redemption. There was hope. Now they are all destroyed, thanks to your ineptitude."

Hope began to flare through me and I clamped my hands together tightly. "You may not want to give me my boon, but you should hear me out."

A sneer cut his face, cold and marvelous in its beauty. "And what shall you ask for, little one? Freedom? Riches? You already have immortality and beauty."

Yeah, I'm so damn lucky aren't I? I had immortality without the man I loved. "I want them back. The vampires, the succubi who were destroyed when the vampires were killed—I want them *all* back. I want them restored. Here, on earth. Just like things were before I got involved and messed everything up."

He regarded me with what might have been a hint of surprise, if Gabriel allowed himself to show human things like emotion. "You would wish back the fallen?"

"I would," I said, my throat aching with the need of that. "Oh, I would. Please. Please give them back." Give Zane back.

He was silent for a long moment. "What you ask for is impossible."

Anguish rocked through me. "You said I could ask for anything. That's what I want."

The archangel's jaw clenched. "The queen has been destroyed. She cannot be restored. What she was cannot be re-created—she was a perversion, an unholy union of a demon's power and dark magic. I cannot bring that back, nor do I wish to."

I refused to budge. "You promised." I held my wrist up, practically shoving it under his nose. "You promised me I could have whatever I wanted if I got this for you. Well, I got it. Now bring back my vampire and skip that queen business."

"You do not understand. As long as the queen lived, they lived. If she cannot come back, then neither can the vampires. They were tied, their haloes bound to her."

No, no, no. I pressed my fists to my temples, thinking. It was either that, or start screaming. I didn't go through all of this for nothing. Zane was the goal. I forced myself to remain calm. "There has to be something," I said, my voice wobbling. "Please. I don't want to live forever if I can't live with Zane. I don't want to live another *day* if I can't have him back."

A hesitation. Then, the archangel spoke. "Their lives are

tethered to an anchor. When the queen existed, she was their anchor. There must be another anchor for their souls to be connected to. Another queen. Do you understand what it is I am saying?"

I did. I stared up into his blazing eyes, hope flaring. "You need an anchor. Let me do it."

"What you ask is not an easy task," he said, his tone contemplative. "The weight of their sins will weigh upon you. My brethren have not lived chaste lives since they fell. Some struggle for their humanity, and as they do so, it will affect your own."

"I don't care," I said quickly, lest he change his mind. "I can handle it."

"The tether would have to be… adjusted. I cannot replace the demonic bond they had with the queen, but I can construct one given by me. And I will expect you, little sister, to bring them back."

"Bring them back?"

"Bring them back to the Host. To the light. So many are lost in darkness. They cannot continue as they are, not without losing all that they have been. They are my brothers. I do not want them to be damned eternally—not when there is still a chance for them to return."

"I can lead them," I said. "At least, I can try. It might take a while to bring anyone back from the dark side."

"They are immortals," he said, and I could have sworn I saw a hint of pleasure in his cold eyes. "You have time. This is what you want?"

"It is," I told him. "I want them back—the vampires, the succubi, everyone who was destroyed. I'll handle any repercussions."

He grasped my wrist and turned it toward him. As I watched, the word written on my skin flared and burned bright, then disappeared.

Gabriel leaned in, cupped my chin, and kissed me.

My brain exploded. Lights swam through my head, and my thoughts became… a swirling cacophony of minds, a spider web of thoughts. A morass of blood, need, darkness, wings, and pain. Loss. I felt a hundred tethers hooking into my mind, felt a hundred souls suddenly tied to my own. My head felt like it weighed a thousand pounds.

The weight of it made me stagger.

"Good luck, little anchor," Gabriel said in a kind voice.

When I opened my eyes, the Archangel was gone.

I was alone.

I was the anchor. I'd... won?

I sat for a minute, trying to compose my wild thoughts, but they were too crowded, too turbulent. Zane, I thought, but I couldn't make him out from the chatter in my mind. Surely Gabriel wouldn't have tethered the vampires to me and not returned the one I truly wanted?

Surely...?

I closed my eyes and searched through my mind, but it was like looking for a needle in a haystack of thoughts, thoughts that I was too untutored to sift through.

My phone rang and I blinked back to the present. While I'd been sitting in the field, the sun had set behind the horizon and night had arrived, the skies purple with twilight. Nearby, a cow chewed grass and looked at me placidly.

I took a wobbling step forward. How long had I been standing there? I didn't even remember standing. My phone rang again, and I pulled it out of my coat, hissing at the graze of my hand over the holy water. The stakes, the crosses, the rosaries strapped to my waist... they made my head feel... wrong, even though they weren't hurting me. It was my connection to the vampires. I dropped the weapons belt where I stood and stepped out of it. As I flipped open my phone, I caught sight of my reflection. My eyes were glowing red.

Well... holy crap. That one was going to be hard to explain. I picked up the phone.

"Jacks! Are you there?"

"I'm here," I said weakly. "Come and get me."

"You're alive?"

"I am," I said. "We did it."

PART III

QUEEN

CHAPTER EIGHTEEN

"Once you've hit that pinnacle, it's time to reevaluate your goals. Fame isn't everything. An endless supply of sex isn't everything. The money doesn't seem so great over time (though don't get me wrong, it's pretty great to get paid for having sex). After a while, it becomes just a lot of meat dangling in your face and too many expectations."—*Sometimes It's Not Just About the Fucking*, by Remy Summore

~*~

We caught a red-eye flight back to New City, Wyoming and then drove out of the city. We headed to a destination that I'd only been to once before, but it was engrained in my mind. No one had to tell me where to go to find the vampires. I knew. I knew it deep within my core, and as if to prove me right, the closer we got to that destination, the louder the voices in my head became.

By the time we made it back to Wyoming, the low murmur of confusing thoughts had become a muted roar, and it took everything I had to sit still and be patient.

I was almost with Zane again. Only distance separated us this time.

"Jackie, honey, I'm not sure this is wise," Remy said for the hundredth time. Her gaze kept flicking to my newly-red eyes. "I worry about you."

"I'll be fine," I told her and forced a light smile to my face. And it was true. Once I saw Zane again, I'd be great. My fingers itched to touch him. To see his beautiful wings, feel his body against mine.

I could deal with a little bit of crazy in my head if it brought him back to me.

Remy pulled up to a long, circular driveway, the grounds achingly familiar. To my right, a stately pale mansion loomed before us. I knew that high, gabled roof. I knew those artful white columns that dotted the oversized porch. I knew the dozens of windows and even more than that, I knew what that enormous house contained.

She put the car in park and then turned to me. "You sure you don't want us to go in with you?"

"I'm sure," I said and then reached out and squeezed her hand. "This is where I belong now. You and Ethan need to have your life. Turn in that book. Go on tour."

She frowned at me. "Are you ditching us? Is this good-bye?"

"It's not," I told her, and that was the truth. "It means we meet for cocktails and girl talk instead of being roomies."

She beamed at me. "Now *that* sounds like a good idea to me. You sure they're going to want you in this house?"

"I'm sure," I said and knew it with every fiber of my being. It was mine now.

I got out of the car. To my surprise, Remy and Ethan got out as well, and Remy grabbed me in a hug, patting my back. Ethan wrapped his arms around both of us.

Tears pricked my eyes. Through thick and thin, they'd been at my side. I didn't deserve friends as good as these two. "You guys are amazing. You know that, right?"

Remy was weeping, too. "I love you, Jacks. I know the last while has been hard on you, but you never once gave up. I hope you find everything you want in that house."

I hugged her again. "I'll call you. I promise."

"You'd better," she said, wagging a finger at me, her eyes wet. Then she turned and smiled up at Ethan. "Come on, babycakes. Let's go see our kitty cat. I bet Angelbait misses us."

"Of course, my divine flower of beauty."

"If you're good, I'll even let you massage my feet before you start transcribing my memoirs into the computer," she said as they shut the doors to the rental car. As it pulled down the driveway, Remy turned and waved back to me, then made a "call me" motion with her thumb and pinky.

I repeated the motion, indicating that I would definitely call her. I waited until they drove away, then turned to the house. I stood outside of it, staring at the front door. I hesitated a moment longer, almost terrified of what I'd find inside. What if it... wasn't what I'd wanted? What if Gabriel was playing a cruel joke on me and I'd find the house abandoned, the thoughts in my head only the lingering aspects of the vampires?

What if I was crazy and this was just a psychotic break and Zane wasn't coming back? I wanted it so badly I didn't even trust myself anymore.

I put my hand on the doorknob, took a deep breath, and stepped inside.

I was in the foyer. It was clean and spare as I remembered it. A small end table near the door was covered in a wealth of dust, and my throat knotted at the sight. I looked around as I walked in. *Everything* was covered in dust, cobwebs dotting the fixtures overhead. It was as silent and unlived-in as a mausoleum. My heart tripped painfully in my chest.

Had the Archangel made a mistake?

My pulse began to pound at the thought, anxiety clenching my jaw tight. *Please don't be a mistake.* The murmurs in my head continued, as wild and loud as ever. *Don't be a mistake,* I repeated, and the voices in my head seemed to respond to my panic, muting and turning soothing. Encouraging me.

The sunken staircase lay ahead. I put a trembling hand on the railing and walked forward, down the steps. Once upon a time, I'd descended these steps and they'd led to a ballroom filled with excited women and handsome, dangerous vampires. I closed my eyes and took a step down, hand clenched on the railing. I was almost afraid to look. After a few slow, careful steps, I squeezed one eye open, scarcely daring to breathe.

Afraid of what I'd find.

Someone was standing at the foot of the stairs. I looked into the red eyes of a vampire I didn't recognize, dressed in a tuxedo, the back of the jacket modified to let his wings hang freely. His gaze met mine, and as I took another wobbling step forward, he knelt in deference, bowing his head.

My queen, he said, and I heard it in my mind.

Hope. A wonderful burst of hope bloomed in my chest, and I nearly wept with exquisite, sweet emotion. A vampire. They were not all gone.

I took another step forward, and then more vampires came into sight, emerging from the shadows of the room. Dozens of them. All men. Beautiful, gorgeous men with red eyes and dark wings. And I could feel each of them in my mind, a shining thread of thought that would drive me crazy if I listened in. And I felt hope and joy at the sight of each face.

As one, they went to one knee and bowed in deference. *My queen.*

A hint of a smile before bowing. *My queen.*

Stiff anger and resentment. *My queen.*

The cacophony of thoughts threatened to overwhelm, and I forced my mind to absorb them—all their emotions overlapping. Hate, anger, distrust, amusement, and even affection whirled in my brain as they continued to approach and bow. Their salutes echoed in my mind as I stepped forward, wobbling. They were back. All of them were back, their minds linked to my own. There was Caleb, with the wicked tattoo around his eye. I felt his thoughts in my mind.

Well well, lovely. You are unexpected.

When my gaze focused on him, he bowed, a smile edging his hard mouth. *Welcome, but unexpected... my queen.*

I turned, staring at the men in the room, clutching my worn leather duster to my body. Where was he? Where was the one I wanted more than anyone else?

Where was Zane?

Princess.

A pure bolt of thought soared through the jumble of my mind. *Yes! I'm here,* I replied, a sob catching in my throat. I pushed my fist to my mouth, biting down on my knuckle to keep from breaking down into tears. *I'm here.*

My thoughts crashed through the others. I saw a few flinch away and I quieted my own mind, seeking that one soft word. Had it been my imagination? I needed to see. Needed to touch. Needed to know.

Princess, came the thought again, stronger. I pushed past two of the vampires who were straightening, their darker, mixed thoughts cluttering my mind. They weren't sure what to make of a new queen. They'd never served anyone but Nitocris, but angels had been created to serve, and—

I put my hands to my forehead, unable to shut out the thoughts that began to crowd me. I wanted them to leave me alone. I wanted them out of my head.

But I had asked for this. Had known the consequences. I dropped my hands and dug my fingers into my palms, determined to ignore the rumbling in my mind. I willed my gaze to focus. I stepped forward in the room, and suddenly the vampires were parting before me, stepping back to clear the room, as if realizing that I needed space.

One man stood alone at the far end of the floor in front of the vacant throne.

I started forward, then stumbled at the sight of him, a sob breaking in my throat. "Zane."

For months, I'd dreamed of seeing him again. Wanted to hold him in my arms so badly that my soul had ached. He moved forward as if in a dream, his steps slow and sure. He wore a duster identical to my own, one of his favorite black T-shirts on his chest. His wings swept the floor behind him, glorious in their inky depths. His eyes were bright red, his hair rakish over his brow. And he was smiling, a hint of fang gleaming.

I rushed forward, pushing into his arms. "Zane!"

"Princess," he said, and I heard it echoed in my mind.

If this was a dream, I never wanted to wake up ever again. My gaze caressed him. He looked whole, uninjured. His wings were beautiful and sleek, unlike the trashed feather that I still carried in my pocket. My hands trembled, went to his cheeks. I felt the barest hint of unshaven scruff on his jaw. My fingers brushed his lips, warm and soft.

Tears spilled down my face. "You're real. You're here."

"I'm here, Princess," he said softly, grinning at me. "Or should I call you 'my queen'?" He took my hand, pressed a kiss to the palm, and then as I stared, he knelt before me and bowed his head. "I am yours to command."

He was here. His hand was warm in mine. He was back.

I burst into tears and tugged at his hand, pulling him back to standing. "Zane. You were dead. You were all dead."

"But you fixed it. Somehow. I don't know what you did." His hands pressed to my chin, and then he was cupping my jaw and his eyes looked into mine. "Your eyes—"

"Who cares about my eyes?" I said with delight. I didn't give a crap if they fell out and rolled across the floor. I had Zane back. "Just kiss me!"

His arm wrapped around me. A thumb went to my chin and he tilted my head, then pulled me in for a kiss. It was long, exquisite, and slow. His tongue swept into my mouth, and he tasted like Zane, warm and sweet and just a hint of his favorite cigarettes. I twined my arms around his neck, deepening the kiss, even when his fangs scratched at my tongue and drew blood.

I felt his mental hesitation, felt him pull back at the decadent taste of my blood. He wanted to drink me, so much, but he didn't want to put me to sleep, not yet—

When the kiss broke, I sobbed again, kissing him frantically one last time.

Why so sad? Zane asked.

To my surprise, his thoughts were a strong bolt of light in my mind, drowning out all the others like a comforting blanket. The echo of his emotion was so strong in my head that it muffled the noise of the others, made it bearable. His arms went around me and I curled up against his chest, pressing my cheek there.

So long, I wept, the knot in my throat preventing me from speaking. *It's been so long.*

What has happened? How much time has passed? Zane's mental voice sounded puzzled. *We woke up here—all of us. The cavern was gone. The queen was gone. The time we lost has been nothing but a black hole in our minds, and we knew we had to wait here for our queen. Somehow. I just didn't realize it'd be you.* His fingers stroked my cheek, brushing away the tears. *Princess, what have you done?*

What I had to do, I told him. *And I regret nothing.*

"Then sit, and tell us what happened," he said, tugging me from his arms and gesturing at the empty throne nearby.

I swallowed hard, giving him an uncertain look. But this was the path I'd chosen, and his hand gripped mine with warmth and strength. I nodded and stepped forward, moving toward that throne. And then I sat and looked out at the crowd of vampires.

The chaos of their minds was still muted thanks to Zane's possessive, blanketing thoughts, but I could feel them in my head. Some were nearly shrouded with darkness. Some still had a lot of light in them. And all of them were mine.

I was their queen.

I looked at Zane. He stood a step below the throne, deferring to me.

I held my hand out for his. We would do this together.

A faint smile touched his mouth and he moved forward, placing his hand in mine. Our fingers linking, I looked out on the crowd of vampires who watched me. Waiting. I was their queen, but I was an unknown ruler to them.

And I would be kind. And I would bring them back to the light.

I could do anything with Zane at my side.

"I should start at the beginning," I said slowly. "And this begins over a year and a half ago, when the queen was destroyed..."

CHAPTER NINETEEN

"And finally, get out of this business if you fall in love. Because at the end of the day, sometimes you'd like to have only one dick in your face. And it's there because you want it there, not because the director thinks you need a pair of balls hanging over your nose as another guy hammers into your pink. Bottom line is—if you find a guy that's worth it, give up the porn and keep him. Some men are worth a career-change. Mine is."—*Porn Is Not Reality*, by Remy Summore

~*~

When my story was finished, the vampires introduced themselves to me, one by one. Some faces I recognized—and not in a good way. Some were new to me. Each one felt like a familiar twinge in my mind and I knew that given time, I'd be able to sort through the myriad cobwebs inside my head and touch upon each one's mind individually. I could listen in on private conversations, or even take over their thoughts, pressing my will against theirs. And I knew that because of the tether, I would win any mental battle.

The latter thought made me shudder. I didn't want to become like the old queen, treating them as puppets for my own amusement.

When the introductions were finished, I stood... and immediately wobbled. My body was exhausted.

Zane rushed to my side, sweeping me up before I could fall to the ground, and I was surprised to see the concern of several vampires as they hovered close by, ready to assist. The thought made me laugh, just a little.

I was the queen to the biggest set of immortal bad boys ever. They had to protect me with their lives, because it meant theirs. The laugh bubbled up in my throat, and continued even though I tried to stifle it. Immortal bad boys... with a mother-hen side to them. I continued to giggle.

"She's tired," Zane said to the others, gesturing that they should give me space. "I will see to her."

Still they hesitated, and I knew what they were looking for. I waved a hand. "Go. Feed. Play nice."

One by one, they scattered from the room. I could feel the muddled confusion of their thoughts, their grudging concern for me—and for themselves. This would be a new world order and they were unsure how to approach things.

It'd take some time for all of us to adjust. I knew that. Even so, there were some things that hadn't changed. I leaned heavily against Zane, inhaling the delicious scent of him. His thoughts were a white light in my mind, a delicious teasing melody of affection that soothed my senses.

I didn't protest when he carried me out of the throne room and back up the stairs of the mansion. Instead, I burrowed closer, my eyes closed in bliss. My Zane. Oh God, he was back. He was really, really back. Everything hadn't been in vain. I could touch him again. Taste him. Feel his warm body against mine, his skin—

"Princess," Zane said softly as he carried me. "Don't cry."

I wiped at my cheeks. I hadn't realized I was crying again. I was just so emotional. For months and months I'd been dead, a walking zombie with no heart and no soul. Now everything was back.

And I was overwhelmed with joy. With love. With wonder.

I wrapped my arms around Zane's neck and buried my face against his skin, inhaling deeply. I barely noticed when he kicked open a pair of double doors and laid me on an immense, opulent bed. My thoughts were full of him.

Until I slid over to the side on the satin sheets, that is. I sat up, frowning at the feel of the slick sheets against my skin. They were blood red, and I looked around. Everything in the room was *red*—from the walls to the enormous four-poster bed to the carpet. Ugh. It was like I'd been dropped into a giant bloody tomato. "The queen's room?" I asked, sitting up in the bed and regarding the surroundings as Zane moved to close the double doors and give us some privacy.

"Guest room," he said. "The queen took no room for herself. Nothing we had was off-limits to her. It was all hers."

"Oh," I said, frowning. Well, that would change. The vampires were individuals, not my toys to play with. "If I'm the new queen, does that mean I can redecorate?"

He nodded, moving back to the bedside and sitting on the edge next to me. "There's enough money in the bank accounts to redecorate a dozen houses."

Well, that'd be good. I'd call Remy after I'd settled in and see if she wanted to come play interior decorator for me.

Zane's eyes flared with need as he stared down at me.

Oh, I wanted him *so* badly.

"I heard that," he murmured with a smile, getting back to his feet. He dragged his duster off his shoulders and tossed it to the floor, then pulled off his shirt, exposing his chest, and letting his wings flare out behind him. My mind went blank. Entranced, I slid off the side of the bed and went to his side, running my hands along those chiseled abs, that delicious body. "God, I missed you," I said in a voice gone hoarse with need.

His hands moved back to my face and he was cupping my jaw, angling my mouth toward his. His lips brushed against mine, his tongue flicking against my lips, and I moaned in desire.

"You're going to have to stop crying at some point," he said softly, and I felt his fingers brush away the wetness on my cheeks again.

"It's been so long," I whispered, aching with love for him. "I've missed you so much. You don't know how much."

"I'm so sorry, Princess," he said, pressing light kisses to my damp cheeks. "I wish I could have been at your side to help you."

"Getting you back was the only thing that made me keep going," I said, my words a half sob. "I wasn't about to spend the next four thousand years without you."

He grinned and leaned in to kiss me again, his teeth grazing my lip. I could feel his hunger, his desire for me—and a cord of love that pulsed stronger with every heartbeat.

I had Zane back, and I was linked to him forevermore. As I pressed my forehead to his and drank him in, I sighed with pleasure and just let his thoughts roll through my mind like a dark wine.

His hands moved to my coat and he grinned. "This looks familiar."

"I wore it every day so I'd remember you," I said quietly. I didn't mention the cigarettes. That seemed a little too needy.

He leaned in and gave me a light kiss. "My poor, sad princess." His hand slid around my waist and I hissed as his hand came into contact with my spear wound. He stilled, and I felt the flash of alarm in his thoughts a moment before he spoke. "Jackie, what the hell is this?"

"Flesh wound?"

"Don't quote Monty Python at me," he said, and I felt the flash of anger in his mind. "Why are you hurt?" His hands skimmed over my shirt, then he pulled it up carefully, exposing the bandages. "You're bleeding everywhere."

"And it totally turns you on, right?" I teased, not caring that my wound hurt or that I was going to bleed all over this red, red room. I had Zane back.

I had him back! I was giddy with the thought, my hands looping around his neck and tugging him down for another kiss, bouncing with excitement against him.

"No wonder you're so weak," he said, detangling himself from my hands and going to pull the bandages off the wound carefully. "I'm going to kill Noah for letting you walk around with this kind of damage."

My laughter died in my throat, and I put a hand over the bandages. "Noah didn't help me."

"That's obvious," Zane snarled, his concern for me a shot of lightning sparking through his mind. I could feel his worry and his anger at Noah… and a surge of jealousy.

He thought I'd been with Noah while he'd been gone, and he was furious that the Serim hadn't taken care of me. I could feel it in his mind with absolute clarity—rage, bitter frustration, and a tinge of envy.

Suddenly everything made sense. I brushed my fingers over Zane's cheek as he knelt in front of me, examining my wound. "Zane," I said softly. "Noah didn't help me. He didn't touch me at all. No one did."

He looked up at me, confusion etched in his dark gaze, his brows angry slashes. "What do you mean?"

I showed him the ring on my finger, the one I'd worn where most women wore their wedding bands. "I got a little help from an old friend."

He took my hand, clasped it in his own. Stared at the ring. *Stayed true... to me? You didn't have to...*

"I didn't want anyone else but you," I said softly. "The thought of touching someone else made me sick. I wanted to wait for you. I didn't care how long it took."

"Jackie," he said softly, a wealth of emotion in his voice.

"Of course, the downside is that I haven't been healing," I said with a small shaky laugh. "No sex and all. The machine here feels a little run down at the moment."

He pressed his mouth to my hand, shaking his head. "Jackie, I am... humbled." I could feel it in his mind. Shock that I'd gone to such extremes and put myself at risk. If that ring had ever left my hand, I'd have died. Humility that I'd gone through so much to get him back. Anger at himself for being jealous of Noah. And a surge of fierce exultation that I'd stayed true to him.

I brushed my fingers over his cheek and then touched that floppy lock of black hair that fell across his forehead in a way that made me melt. "I love you," I said simply. "Now and forever. When I said I loved you, I meant it with every fiber of my being. I'd wait for you until the end of time."

He simply pressed a kiss to my hand again, and when he looked up at me, I saw the gleam of tears in his own eyes. "You are everything to me, Princess."

"Then come and love me," I said softly to him. "I've waited forever for you to touch me again."

His fingers ripped the shorts from my legs, and I shivered at his strength. My panties followed in a flurry of fabric, and I barely noticed as his hands slid down my legs and removed my boots, kissing the cuts and bruises dotting my now bare legs. They didn't matter. All that mattered was that we were together again.

He finished divesting me of my clothing, straightened the bandages on my waist, and then gently lifted me back onto the bed. I lay there, stretching with sensuous need, waiting for my lover.

Zane shucked his jeans, and I watched as they hit the wall opposite us, admired his beautiful, lean body, the jut of his cock. His thoughts were a balm over my own turbulent ones, his own singular need to have me drowning out all the others that clamored in the back of my mind.

I'd have to keep Zane at my side at all times to drown out the others, I decided, and liked that thought very much. Eternity together? I could *so* handle that.

To my surprise, Zane moved to the far side of the bed and slid in on the opposite side of me. He rolled me gently to my side, mindful of my wound, and spooned my body against his own. I felt the heat of his body against my own and my skin prickled with pleasure. One wing extended over the two of us, and as Zane began to lightly kiss my neck, I curled against him, feeling his skin press to my own. His erection was insistent against the cleft of my ass, but he wasn't pressing me. He wanted to love me, first. Kiss me, hold me close.

He moved his arm to tuck me closer to him and eased it under my neck, his hand going to my breasts. His fingers grazed one of my nipples even as his mouth moved to nip at my earlobe.

I gasped in pleasure at the sensation, my hand covering his over my breast. "Zane," I breathed, my voice catching in my throat. "Oh, Zane."

"Don't start crying again, Princess," he warned with a nip at my neck. "You'll kill my erection."

I gave a small laugh at that, closing my eyes and enjoying the feel of him spooned up against me. His fingers teased my nipple to an aching peak, his mouth moving over my neck from behind me, teasing at my shoulder. He hadn't bitten down—he was drawing out the pleasure. His other hand slid down my hip, brushing over my thigh. His cock dug into my side and I shifted, rubbing my skin against it in a way that made him groan with need.

I flexed a little at the stroke of his hands, shivering. My knees nudged apart, welcoming him to touch me where he pleased, and his knee pressed in between them, parting my legs from behind.

I gasped as his warm hand stroked over my sex. He stilled and I felt the flash of his concern in my mind. Was I hurting?

"I'm fine," I assured him, and placed my hand there, over his, pushing his fingers through my slick folds. "Touch me."

He growled low against my throat, his teeth nipping at my skin. I moaned and shivered against him, and when his fingers slid into my slick sex, I cried out his name.

He raised his knee, lifting my leg a bit higher, and I felt his fingers brush over my clit, sending tremors through my body even as he continued to tease the round globe of my breast, caressing and petting the tip as he did my clit. I rocked my hips gently in response.

"Shh," he said, the words a whisper against my neck. "Let me touch you. Heal you. Love you."

I pressed my mouth to the arm crossed over my breasts, the arm that pinned my back to him.

He brushed against my clit again, and I sucked in a breath in response. His fingers slid lower, and I felt one dip at the well of my sex, sliding in to stretch and tease. A second finger followed, and he thrust. "So wet for me, Princess," he said against my neck, and I felt his tongue flick against the hollow of my shoulder.

"Bite me, Zane," I said, lost in desire.

"Not yet, love," he said, raising my leg a little higher. His hand gripped my thigh and I felt the head of his cock nudge against my core. "Not until I'm seated deep inside you."

I moaned, pressing my mouth against his arm in response.

He slid into me, hot, hard and oh so thick, and I nearly wept again at how good it felt. Zane. I was in Zane's arms again, his body deep within mine. It felt... perfect. Exquisite.

It felt right.

He thrust lightly, and the sensation rocketing through my body in response was incredible. I whimpered, scoring my teeth over his arm. Zane hissed and thrust harder, the feeling of him so deep inside me, so full.

So wonderful.

"Bite me, Zane. Take all of me," I told him.

Not yet, I heard his whisper in his mind, even as he thrust again, rocking back into me with a hard thrust that left me breathless.

But I wanted it all, and I wanted it now. I'd waited too long for anything else. I sank my teeth into his arm, biting him with my own blunted teeth. I felt the desire rock through him, hard and sharp. He loved biting. Nothing was more erotic to a vampire. I realized that, now that I could feel his thoughts, and vowed then and there to bite him every night from now on.

Princess, his thoughts wrapped around me. *Mine.*

He thrust deep inside me again, at the very moment that his fangs sank into my neck.

And I came apart.

~*~

We made love throughout the night, wrapped in each other's arms. For some reason, his bite didn't put me to sleep any longer. I supposed that was one aspect of being the queen—my connection to him now overrode any side effects.

Of course, once Zane had found that out, his need to take and sip from me had gone through the roof, and he'd drunk from me everywhere, gently licking the blood from each graze of his teeth, savoring me. It was something his mind told me that he'd dreamed about forever, and the sensation was so exquisite—both the pleasure I felt in his mind and the feel of his tongue against my skin—that I was screaming with need. Then he'd lay me back down on the bed and throw my legs up in the air, fucking me until I couldn't see straight. I came dozens of times, and each time, I felt my strength coming back. The wound in my side had long been forgotten, and by the time the sun rose and Zane lay in my arms, his head pillowed against my breasts, I was both exhausted and feeling better than I had in a long, long time.

I looked down at my breasts, covered in bite marks, and had never felt such joy. My fingers played with his dark hair, and I listened to his mind drift, sinking into the day-sleep of vampires. One by one, I could feel the other vampires quietly dozing off, having returned home. Their thoughts turned into a low hum that I felt in the back of my mind, like a sleeping cat's purr. The man in my arms purred the loudest, and I touched his mind, expecting to see it filled with the dark dreams of vampires.

But they were only thoughts of me. And that filled me with contentment.

I lay in bed for a bit longer, savoring the feel of Zane in my arms and then slipped away to wash up. I felt good. More than good. I felt amazing.

I showered and put on a silky red robe that I found in one of the closets, eyeing all the unrelenting red with distaste. Bad enough that my eyes now matched my hair. I stared into the mirror, grimacing at the red irises. Maybe I could get contacts or something like that. Maybe I should invest in sunglasses. Lots and lots of sunglasses. It was superficial, and in the long scheme of things, it didn't matter a whit.

I'd take the red eyes as long as I had Zane back.

Smiling, I padded around the big house, eyeing the rooms that were now mine. Each one was swathed in Goth queen décor, and I wrinkled my nose with distaste. The upper floors seemed to be for guests, and I suspected the vampires used them when seducing human prey to feed upon. The thought made me a little uncomfortable, but I could change that. There was no TV room, no library, nothing to entertain. I did find a single room and old computer at the back of the house that looked to be used for financial purposes, and I wondered who here amongst the queen's entourage did the books. Something to find out.

I wandered back to check on Zane, but he continued to sleep peacefully. I touched him again, straightening that lock of messy hair on his brow, happy at the small pleasure of simply being able to touch him once more. As I reached out to caress his cheek, I noticed the ring on my finger. That old thing.

I pulled my hand back, studied the ring for a moment, and then ripped it off, tossing it against the nearest wall. I braced myself for any adverse effects.

Nothing. Absolutely nothing happened. I gave another happy laugh—I was full of laughter now, wasn't I? —and left the room again. My stomach was growling.

The kitchen proved to be a waste, as there was nothing in it. Well, that'd have to change. I found myself drawn back to the big sweep of stairs that led to the basement and traveled down it, looking around. The big marble floor was empty, the room dark. I felt the vampires sleeping here, and as I stepped through the room, I saw the marble slabs they slept upon, lined up in rows. Like toy soldiers, waiting to be brought out for amusement. That seemed wrong to me. They were men. Individuals. I made a mental note to get them their own rooms. If I was going to change things, the first thing would be to start treating them like individuals with their own needs and wants, not as my slaves. I passed through the ranks of the vampires, looking at them as they slept. As a whole they were beautiful, though some seemed more entrenched in darkness than others.

I wouldn't be like the old queen. I'd remember my vow to Gabriel.

Something tickled at my mind, and I found myself drawn to the back of the large underground ballroom, my internal tuning fork vibrating with a peculiar need. I found a small, narrow passageway built entirely of stone, with a dead end. A single flat platform lay against the wall, with an ancient protection symbol etched into it. Instinctively, I pressed my hand to the symbol.

The wall slid open, revealing a secret passage. Naturally. Immortals loved their hidden rooms. I strolled forward, curious what was stashed back here. A double door lay at the end of the hall and I pushed it open.

And gasped.

I stepped forward, staring. In this room, a hundred haloes hung in the air, suspended by magic. Each one burned with power, shimmering in reaction to my presence, responding only to me. I felt them in the tether of my mind, a delicate burden. I knew that the vampires wouldn't be able to sense these, just as I'd known how to open the door. It would only respond to *me*.

When they'd fallen, one by one, the vampires had handed over their most precious gift to the queen—their halo. Each one was an individual who now responded to me, and I was responsible for their safekeeping.

These were my haloes now.

I moved forward, stepping toward one of the haloes, reaching out my fingers to touch the spinning light. It shone red, blood red, and as I moved closer, I noticed the halo was made up of drops of blood, a circlet of pure crimson liquid.

The haloes of the vampires. I looked at them a moment longer, then turned and left the room, shutting the doors behind me. I left the hall and pressed my hand on the symbol keyed to the queen of the vampires only.

I would tell no one about that room, ever. It was mine to protect.

Just like my vampires.

~*~

I wandered back through the house, snagged the cordless phone, and then crawled back into bed with Zane. He was sleeping soundly, his body heavy, but I pulled his arm over my waist and snuggled close, not caring.

Then I called Remy.

She picked up on the third ring. "Either this is a total prank call or your ass is bored of the vampires already."

"They're asleep," I said softly, playing with Zane's hair. "And there's not a lick of food in the house."

"And now you want me to haul my gorgeous man out of bed and bring a pizza?"

"You got it," I told her. "That's what friends are for, right?"

"All right, all right. Baby doll," she said to Ethan on the other end of the phone. "Would you do the honors of calling in the order while I chat with Jackie?"

"Of course, my shimmering flower." I heard a loud, noisy, slurping kiss, grimaced, and waited for Remy's attention to wander back to the phone.

"Soooo," Remy said after a minute. "Everything okay in Vampire Funland? I'm guessing so, since you sound bored and not, I don't know, scared out of your mind."

"We're okay," I said softly, rubbing my fingers against Zane's sleeping cheek. I couldn't stop touching him. I didn't have to, and the thought filled me with intense pleasure. "I'm their leader now, for better or for worse. They can't hurt me without hurting themselves. I don't think they know what to do with me yet, but Zane's at my side, and that's all that matters."

"Yeah, well make sure you tell them that your bestie Remy and her boytoy are off-limits."

"I will," I said with a smile. "Guess who's got a mansion that's in need of some serious redecorating?"

"Are you thinking what I'm thinking?" Remy said with excitement. "Purple zebra couches?"

I grimaced. "We'll see. Anyhow, come over and bring the pizza and we'll chat."

"Be there shortly," she said, and hung up. I hung up as well.

The phone rang again a moment later and I answered. "Hello?"

"Me again," Remy chirped. "I'm glad you're back, Jackie. Really glad."

My eyes welled. "Me too."

"Now don't get all sappy and shit. I'm bringing some catalogs and pizza and nail polish, since you have some time to burn until sundown. You can get emotional over pepperoni, okay?"

I laughed. "Deal."

We hung up and I stared at the room, sighing with contentment.

Queen of the vampires. Who would have thought that was ever possible? I'd hated the queen. Never wanted to be her in a million years. But… this felt good. This felt like purpose. The Serim would be off my back because they weren't about to come after me—not if it meant stirring up the ire of every single vampire out there. And the vampires? They answered to me now.

As for Zane—nothing could keep us apart ever again.

I had everything I'd ever wanted. Life would never be the same, but I didn't care. Somewhere out there, Sophie was back, and I'd find a way to drop her a line and let her know that Noah wanted to see her. I hoped for Noah's sake he'd cross her path again. But that was his move to make. I'd fulfill my promise, no more, no less. It was up to Noah to find his own happiness.

I buried my face against Zane's sleeping chest and snuggled close.

The world was perfect.

EPILOGUE

Weeks Later… Somewhere Else

Noah Gideon crouched next to one of the double doors, gun in hand, waiting. Any moment now, the intruder would come through that door, and Noah would put a bullet through his brain.

The intruder had slipped into the sanctuary by climbing over the roof and then lowering himself down into the nearest window. He didn't know if the man had arrived to destroy the Enforcer boys that were even now being shepherded to another monastery, but the Serim were taking no chances. They'd evacuated the premises, with only a command to Noah to take care of the vampire as best he could.

Noah Gideon, the expendable Serim. It rankled, but he told himself he didn't care. Another task down. Eighty-two to go. Finish one and then move on to the next.

Something thumped just on the other side of the door. Noah calmly removed the safety on his gun and hefted it, aiming. The door handle turned. Opened a crack.

A figure stepped through.

It… wasn't a man.

It was a woman. A familiar woman who moved like a dancer, her tall body toned and strong. A woman with bronzed skin swirling with hennaed designs over every exposed inch. Thick dreadlocks pulled into a high ponytail. Arching cheekbones. Eyes that were incredibly blue.

Noah paused, just long enough for Sophie to raise her own gun and point it at his head.

"Why, Noah Gideon," Sophie said in a slow, purring voice throaty with an ancient accent. "We meet again."

And she smiled at him.

AUTHOR'S NOTE

I always had a plan for Jackie Brighton. As soon as she set foot on the page (or woke up in that dumpster), I knew she was going to be the queen of the vampires. Someday. She just had to put on her big-girl panties and gear up for it.

In the meantime, I had to write it, of course. You cannot imagine how crushed I was when I found out from my publisher that they couldn't buy more books in the series. My editor has been a huge supporter of the books and my writing. I think she was just as disappointed as I was that they weren't a hit. Unfortunately, just because I want something to succeed doesn't mean that it will, and the sales numbers weren't what they needed to be for my publisher to buy more of the series.

I was still determined to finish the story. Even if no one else wanted it, *I* needed to see Jackie sit on that throne and get some closure in my brain. That was the impetus for what you've just read. This book took a darker turn than the previous stories, but I felt like Jackie needed to experience love and loss before she could truly appreciate what she has with Zane. I hope you enjoyed *SUCCUBI ARE FOREVER* and feel a bit of completion. I know I do!

Of course, now that closure is here, there's still more to be told. I could go on and on with stories in this world. There's so much that there's never enough time to cover. I've barely tapped into the vampires and succubi. And of course, there's a little piece of me that wants to follow the sparks that fly now that Noah's met up with Sophie again...

But Jackie's tale is done. For better or for worse. I hope you've enjoyed it. I'm positive she and Zane will show up in more stories in the future, but it's smooth sailing for them from here on out.

If you're interested in reading more of my books, check out my

Jessica Sims shapeshifter books, and if you're looking for something a little sexier, I've also got a new series starting as Jessica Clare. They're erotic romances set in a small town and I think they're a lot of fun.

Lastly, if you've read this far, I just want to say **thank you.** Fan support for this series means a lot to me. I'd love it if you left a review and let me know what you think (good or bad) and if you'd be interested in more stories in this world.

ABOUT THE AUTHOR

Jill Myles writes under three pseudonyms. She writes hot paranormal shifters as Jessica Sims, erotic contemporary romance as Jessica Clare, and everything else under Jill Myles. She lives in Texas with her husband, two cats, some dustbunnies, and far too many video games. She has a weakness for k-cups and embarrassingly loud knitted hats. You can find out more about Jill on her website at www.jillmyles.com.

www.ingramcontent.com/pod-product-compliance
Lightning Source LLC
Chambersburg PA
CBHW032119170626
46808CB00006B/2010